Murder in the Glen

Murder in the Glen

A Tale of Death and Rescue on the Scottish Mountains

Set in the West Highlands of Scotland

HAMISH MACINNES

Glencoe Productions Ltd.
Glencoe, Argyll,
Scotland PH49 4HX

With thanks to editor Margaret Body
and all the other experts who cast their eyes
over the manuscript and gave advice.

First published in 2008 by
Glencoe Productions Ltd.,
Glencoe, Argyll,
Scotland

ISBN (10): 0-9514380-1-8
ISBN (13): 978-0-951438-01-5

Printed in Scotland by
Bell & Bain Ltd., Glasgow

Typeset in 11 point Sabon
by 3btype.com
0131 658 1763

Principal Characters

At Grey Corries Lodge

Captain Horatio 'Horror' Dewar
The Hon. Mrs Victoria Dewar
Deirdre Dewar
Kenneth Dewar

Penelope Almen, guest
Clem Fular, guest
Karl von Spielman, guest

The Rescue Team

Willie 'Watery' Fyffe, publican
Watty Gilchrist, estate gamekeeper
Duncan 'Toń' MacGillvery, poacher
Rev Isaac McMillan, minister
Basil Thorndyke, engineer
Douglas Stewart, smelter worker
Chris Watkins, geologist, team leader

The Police

Chief Constable John Templeton
Procurator Fiscal Peter Frew
Superintendent Donald MacDonald
Detective Inspector Angus 'Thumper' Wilson
Sergeant Archie Campbell
Constable James 'Bookam' Munro

Chapter 1

An icy wind was deflected by the damp wall of rock above the laird. He thrust his hands deeper into the pockets of his plus-fours and stole an anxious look at the sky.

'Aye,' he said to himself. 'Watty was right, we'll have snow later this afternoon.' Presently, he lifted his binoculars and looked, from his high position by the bealach, across the floor of the strath. Vole-sized human figures, well camouflaged in tweeds, moved in the heather. He let the glasses hang from their strap again, then returned his hands to his pockets. Over his lined brow his fore and aft was pulled well down. A heavy frost crisped the deer grass and the ground had that dull resonance like the deck of a cruiser, though Captain Horatio Dewar hadn't felt a deck beneath his feet for over a decade.

'Horror', as he was known to his minions, still had a sailor's long-sea eye and a petulant sea-dog bark. He would have fitted to perfection Coleridge's famous character. A .270 magnum rifle was lying cocked on a high heather tussock in front of him and he moved his position slightly, so that he merged, chameleon-like, against the porphyry background. He had spied several deer, a fine herd of hinds, fat and sleek after the good summer. Despite his arthritis, he dropped smoothly down into the deep heather, lying flat in the white hoarfrost. But the cold didn't bother him as he felt the surge of his hunting blood run through his veins and fussily adjusted his rifle so that it rested bolt uppermost, with the safety catch on. One knarled finger cleared a fragment of heather from the rear lens of the sight. There was a tense look on his face. Fleetingly, he had a guilty thought of Kenneth and his abhorrence of stalking.

'Young idiot,' he consoled himself, 'blowing his top over hind shooting. He doesn't seem to realise that it's imperative to cull, and he doesn't refuse venison for dinner!'

'Just my bloody luck!' The Toń spat vehemently as he put his glass down. However, he didn't put the telescope away in one of his many capacious pockets, but placed it in front of him with just as much precision as the laird had placed his rifle. The poacher had scanned the glen with the thoroughness of a peregrine.

'Bloody Horrible himself,' he spat again.

Duncan MacGillvery, like many a Highlander, was a crofter by profession and a poacher by inclination. 'Toń' – the Gaelic for backside – was a nickname earned by his prowess in moving through heather at high speed in an almost prone position, offering only sporadic glimpses of a tweed-clad bottom. His larder was regularly replenished by the products of his backyard, as he liked to call the hills behind his croft. Duncan was also a bit of an athlete in the heavy events, and was the only man alive to toss the notorious Lochgelly caber. The caber had defeated all comers since Murdo James tossed it in the summer of 1903. But he wasn't thinking cabers just then, but of 'cabarach' – the pursuit of deer – as they say in the Gaelic.

He had come over Horrible's march to get a beast, not knowing a stalk was in progress.

'What next?' he pondered. 'Is nothing sacred? The ploddy chentry stalking hinds. Times are hard!'

He put his glass to his right eye again and focussed on Watty Gilchrist, the keeper of Grey Corries Lodge. The keeper also had his telescope up, resting it professionally on his cromag, his stick. Duncan saw he was spying up the glen towards the bealach, to the right of where the laird was lying. The poacher swung his glass round to see what Watty was looking at, but could see nothing. There was a lot of blind ground there so he concluded that Watty must have seen a beast.

'Ah, there they are ...' he observed. Several hinds emerged from a gully below the laird and picked their way with precision over a small boulder field.

'Well, well, it's certainly a busy day in Grey Corries,' Duncan mused. 'Watty and the chentry there. I bet the laird is waiting for a shot when the deer move up towards him. Getting a bit lazy in his old age – fly old bastard; and those stupid Sassenachs no doubt paying a fortune for the privilege!' He put his glass in a pocket and turned away with a disgusted shrug. 'I'll try Laith Coire Bheag; the bastards can't be everywhere at once!'

The still air was shattered by several shots.

'Two ... three?' Duncan asked himself. He hadn't been expecting the shots quite so soon but turned in time to see a hind fall. It dropped as if forced into the heather by an invisible weight. Quickly, he took out his telescope again. Horrible became encircled in the lens. There was something wrong ... He was doubled up on his side; Duncan saw that right away. Then the laird started to roll down the slope, clutching his rifle. Toń knew that he couldn't have shot the hind because, as they moved up they had gone beneath a slight brow and were hidden from where Dewar had been lying. His keen eye followed the figure as it gathered speed. The rifle dropped and was immediately arrested in the heather. The arms were flailing and his fore and aft dropped off. After 50 feet or so he stopped, face upwards. There was blood pouring from his neck. With an ease gained from years of practice, Duncan held the telescope rock steady. He could see the gory mess that had once been the side of Horatio Dewar's neck. He knew that only an exiting bullet could have ripped away the flesh like that. The telescope began to shake perceptibly and, without realising the pertinence of his remark, Duncan muttered, 'Horrible!'

Chapter 2

P C 'Bookam' Munro made hard work of the climb to the bealach. His size 14 wellingtons left gargantuan prints in the fresh snow. He turned up the collar of his regulation police raincoat and cursed, sandwiching his vast vocabulary between gulps of air. His normally florid face was crimson and his moustache was covered with rime. Like the good page, Bookam marked the footsteps of Walter Gilchrist, the keeper; Watty had the long, loping, easy-going stride of the hill man.

The snow had been falling steadily and heavily for several hours and a north-west wind was twitching its muscles, sending up columns of spindrift.

'Aye, it's going tae be a coorse night, James,' the keeper shouted, turning round to make sure the policeman was following. James Munro was his proper name; Watty only used the policeman's nickname when its subject was out of earshot. 'Book'm-all' had earned his title when still an eager beaver young constable. He had started his career with a record number of arrests; so zealous was he, in fact, that he had been hauled before his Chief Inspector at Kinlochsanda and told to lay off. A country policeman, he was informed, should enforce the law without having to bloody well book'm all. A police cadet, overhearing the conversation, spread the news and the name, albeit a shorter version, had stuck. PC Munro didn't feel inclined to answer Watty, even if he had had enough breath to do so. As far as he was concerned, it was a gae coorse afternoon as well!

'I put my cromag in at the spot, James,' the keeper pointed, his hand wet with melting snow, to where his crook bore lonely testimony to the laird's last lair on the hill.

'I dinna ken what possessed you to move him. You should have known better. To think that you were once in the Army Medical Corps, Watty Gilchrist.' Constable Munro was annoyed, partly at this own lack of fitness, as well as by the fact that Dewar's body had been shifted before he arrived.

'We couldna leave him oot and the snow just aboot tae come on,' the keeper replied defensively.

'It's no' as if he'd feel the cold, is it?' the constable barked. 'And how dae ye know that he wasn't shot on purpose?'

'Dinna be daft, man,' Watty said. 'Who'd want to do away wi' old Horrible? Naebody wad bother,' he added contemptuously. 'It was just an accident. I heard the ricochet myself.'

'Don't call me daft, Watty Gilchrist,' the policeman retorted tersely. 'You know well enough from rescue that bodies shouldn't be moved until we've had a look at them … Now, which way was he lying when you found him?' The law ground to a grateful halt.

'I'll show you.' As good as his word, Watty lay in the snow, face upwards, with his right hand outstretched above his head and the other doubled under the small of his back.

'It was just like this. I took special note for I kent you would be asking ...'

'You say he was waiting for the drive o' deer?'

'Aye, the gentry knew aboot it as well; he told them himsel' that he would be up here. His hip was bothering him, ye ken,' he added apologetically.

'This doesn't seem to me to be all that great a place to get a shot.' The Constable glanced around, considering with his shrewd eyes. 'Every deer from Kinlochsanda to Glasgow would see him.'

'It was up a bit, on that level place,' Watty pointed to where the slope eased above. 'He must have fell doon after he was hit.'

'Ah, well,' the policeman sighed, resigning himself to the prospect of climbing a few more knee-weary steps. 'I suppose I'd better inspect the locus ...Where was the rifle lying when you arrived?'

'Just there.' The keeper had risen and stood alongside the constable. He moved up a short distance. 'Here. I put this stone at the place.' He wiped several inches of fresh snow from a small boulder. 'The barrel was pointing down-hill,' he added.

'And you took it back to the Lodge?'

'Of course, man.'

'Had it been fired?'

'No.'

'Well,' the policeman's tone implied that he didn't trust the keeper. 'I'll have a look myself when we get back to the big house.'

As they moved up, snow got into PC Munro's wellies and he cursed anew. Grey clouds had descended to blot out the summits and the rising wind was causing drifting; all in all a dismal day.

'I think it was aboot here he must have been.' Watty inspected the flat area of snow-covered ground. 'I did spy him, ye ken, when he first came up, but it's a bit hard to say exactly where …'

'Aye.' The Constable studied the area approvingly. 'This gives a better lie o' the land, but it could have been any part o' half an acre about here.' He cleared the heather with the side of his boot. 'I can't see any sign; are you sure this is the place?'

'No,' Watty admitted slowly, wiping a drip from his nose. 'I was too busy with those Sassenachs to bother aboot Horrible.' He looked thoughtful for a moment and added, 'Chris Watkins may have seen him. He had aboot the best view since he was doon on the flank o' the glen.'

'Well, I'll be seeing him later.' Bookam spoke with finality, then added sharply, 'What time were the shots fired?'

'Ten past two. I looked at my watch just afterwards.'

'Well, now,' the PC suggested, 'let's get the hell out of here.'

'I wonder if Horatio's death was an accident?' Clem Fular's words dropped like a stone in the large room. All eyes swivelled towards him.

'What do you mean?' asked Penelope Almen, a long-faced woman wearing a superb pearl necklace. 'What on earth do you mean, Clem?' she repeated.

'I presume that if he wasn't shot accidentally – as I had assumed – he must have been shot on purpose. Three shots were fired?' Clem asked, swirling his drink round the cut-glass tumbler and gazing into the amber liquid without enthusiasm. 'First of all,' he continued, 'Chris fired a shot and killed the hind, right?'

'Nein, I shot the deer,' a large, fat German retorted possessively.

'Nonsense, you couldn't hit a deer holding it by the tail,' Chris stated flatly. Karl von Spielman glared at him.

'You English,' he retorted, 'think only you can shoot. The keeper, who saw me, will correct me.'

'Support you, dear,' Penelope suggested gently as she knocked back her Talisker.

'I must admit, though,' she carried on, 'that I, too, thought that Chris dropped the beast. He was on the heather and had fired before I'd even seen it. I suppose that's the advantage of being a local – your eyes get tuned to spotting them.'

Clem inspected the long ash on his cigar. He was dressed in what he thought were sporty tweeds: baggy plus-fours and homespun stockings. The fact that he wore a yellow bow tie with this outfit didn't perturb him.

Just then the door of the large panelled room opened and Kenneth Dewar entered. His face was pale under a tan. Penelope Almen studied him with renewed interest. She assumed he would be the new boss of Grey Corries Ltd. A young man, she decided, with a future, and wondered if he would remain so left-wing in his views. They had already commiserated with him over the loss of his father.

'A drink, Ken?' Without waiting for an answer, Chris poured a Highland-sized dram and handed it to him. 'I'm really sorry. He was an old bastard in many ways, but I liked him.'

'Thanks, Chris.'

'How's your mother?' Penelope asked, her face looking haggard in the light of the log fire.

'I don't think she's taken it in yet,' he replied as he took a sip of the Talisker. His sharp features gave him a clean-cut look and despite his old anorak and climbing breeches he had an air of distinction.

The housekeeper, the wife of Watty Gilchrist, opened

the door. She had a sexy suppleness which demanded attention.

'The police have arrived,' she announced in a lilting voice. Kirsty had, besides, an adequate surplus of what Penelope herself most lacked, an impish vivaciousness. Seeing Kirsty for the first time a few days before, she was reminded of a poem she had known as a child about a flower that blooms unseen …

'But Constable Munro arrived some time ago and went up the hill with Watty.' Kenneth looked surprised.

'I mean the proper police,' she retorted. 'Sergeant Archie Campbell and two big men from Kinlochsanda,' she added laconically.

There were three policemen in the hall: the Superintendent, Donald MacDonald, Sergeant Archie Campbell and Detective Inspector Angus Wilson (better known as 'Thumper') who had just entered. Kenneth knew them all well from the mountain rescue team.

'Hello, Superintendent,' he said and nodded to the Sergeant and Inspector. 'Good of you to come down.'

'Least I could do, Kenny.' Superintendent MacDonald put out his hand. 'Sad business.'

'Yes, it's been a blow,' the younger man said quietly.

'How's your mother?' The Superintendent lowered his right eyelid, an involuntary and, on occasions, an unfortunate affliction.

'I don't think she's taken it in yet.'

'Aye, it's a sad day for the Corries,' Sergeant Campbell echoed sententiously.

The front door swung open to reveal a snow-splattered PC Munro, looking as if he'd just been collecting King Penguin eggs. Loosening his chin strap, he took off his cap and stamped his feet vigorously on the mat, his bald head reflecting dancing lights from the chandelier. With him was Watty Gilchrist.

'Well, Constable,' the Superintendent greeted him.

'All in the course of duty, sir,' PC Munro returned with a certain amount of deference. Watty followed him in with sharp, deft movements, placing his stick by the door under the stuffed head of a royal stag. He took off his fore and aft and shook it.

'Aye, it's gae coorse.' He offered his habitual greeting which covered all weather conditions, from a smir to a blizzard.

'Hello, Watty.' The Superintendent acknowledged the keeper.

'I had a look at the locus, sir.' PC Munro now addressed the Superintendent, Donald MacDonald. 'But it's difficult to see anything with the snow.'

'Yes, it must be,' his superior agreed and, turning to the keeper, he added, 'I understand that for some reason you brought the body back here.'

'Aye, he's in the chapel at the back o' the hoose, we didn't want to leave him on the hill. The doc was looking at him when we left.'

'He died instantly,' Munro put in and added, 'he'd only half a neck left,' forgetting that the dead man's son was standing beside him. The Superintendent gave an embarrassed cough, then cleared his throat and said reprovingly, 'I think, Constable, you might spare us unnecessary details.'

'Sorry, sir,' Munro mumbled.

'When you say 'we', Watty, who exactly do you mean?' The deep voice of Inspector Wilson filled the large hall. He was a bear-like man with feet rivalling the Constable's and hands to match.

'Most of the guests, eventually,' Watty returned. 'It was Chris Watkins who spotted him first. I had the walkie-talkie with me – we use it for telling the gillie where the culled beasts are – it saves him a lot o' time.'

'We're quite aware of that, Watty, and also of the fact that the radios are not licensed,' the Inspector interrupted coldly.

'Ah, weel, I wouldn't know aboot that, sir. All I know is that they save us a lot o' miles.'

'What's this about a walkie-talkie?' the Superintendent intervened.

'Well, as I was trying to say,' Watty gave the big Inspector a withering glance, 'I contacted the gillie who had the garron, the pony, down here by the Lodge and sent him over to my cottage to bring up the old stretcher – the one that used to be at Queenshouse before the replacement arrived.'

'So you carried him back on the stretcher?' the Inspector asked.

'Aye, we did that.'

'We met Dr Khan on our way here,' the Superintendent cut in, 'and got a verbal medical report, but the doctor had a maternity case to attend to and had to get back to Faileadh.'

'Did you see the accident, Kenny?' Detective Inspector Wilson asked the dead man's son.

'No, but I heard the reports; I was out for a short walk. I assumed hinds were being shot – not my father. You're aware, Angus, that I'm not in favour of stalking?'

'So I gathered,' the Inspector responded. 'I seem to remember your saying that once before – when we were out on the hill. Wasn't it during that rescue of the gillie with the broken leg on Bheinn Bruhm? You said it would be a 'fairer sport if the deer had guns ...'

'Well, it was someone else who said that.' A fleeting smile played on Ken's lips. 'I was just quoting.'

The Superintendent now drew himself up to his full six feet two and spoke authoritatively.

'We'll take statements from everyone here, Inspector ... Is there a room we could use?' He looked enquiringly at Ken.

'Why, yes.' The young man paused for an instant. 'The breakfast room is empty – use it.' He led the way across the hall and opened a door, then stood aside for them to enter.

'Thanks,' the Superintendent said, then turned and spoke again. 'We'll have a word with the keeper first and then see the guests in turn afterwards. Can you tell them to remain available?'

'I'll do that,' Ken replied. 'And I'll ask someone to bring some tea.'

Ken moved across the hall with a heavier step than normal. He's taking it badly, the Inspector mused. He knew that Ken hadn't got on with his old man, but then he recalled vividly the friction there had been with his own father. Jacob Wilson had been an Elder in the Free Kirk and had wanted Angus to take up 'the Meenistry', as he had called Holy Orders. But Angus had other ideas and, after running away from home at 18, had acted as a chucker-out at a dance hall in a rough area of Glasgow where you had to be hard.

'Vell, have they gone?' It was Karl von Spielman who addressed Kenneth. Penelope felt the fine spray of his words on the back of her neck. She was sitting on a low-backed chair in front of the fire, with the German standing directly behind.

'Do you mind, Karl?' she spoke coldly as she ran her hand down her neck. 'You might put the fire out.'

'If you mean the police, Karl,' Ken replied, 'the answer is no. They want to interview everyone.'

'But I only shot the hind; my bullet did not shoot your fader.'

'I don't believe you've ever shot anything in your life,' Clem Fular retorted. 'At least, not intentionally.'

'What do you mean?' the German snapped.

'I mean it may have been a ricocheting bullet that hit Horatio Dewar but one thing is certain: you couldn't have done it if you'd tried!'

'Let's not have any bickering, children,' Penelope cooed. 'Naughty, naughty.'

'Oh, shut up,' Clem said. He downed the remains of his whisky in one gulp and glowered.

'I don't think this conversation is in good taste,' Ken said impatiently.

'It's just that Clem here has a theory that your father may not have been killed accidentally,' Chris explained. 'Both Karl and I claim to have shot the hind but Clem says there must have been three shots and, thinking back on it, I think he may be right despite the fact that he wasn't there.' Chris narrowed his eyes slightly as if trying to recall the event. 'You should be more careful, Clem,' Chris admonished, 'in voicing opinions on a such a serious incident.'

'We've been discussing it, Ken, and getting nowhere,' Penelope added. 'But it appears that the third shot didn't come from our party.'

'Blood sports should be banned.' Ken's eyes were hard.

'You made that patently obvious to your father last night,' Clem retorted, trying to regain his cool.

'I suppose it's typical of a man in your position,' Ken spat out. 'You feel you have a franchise to eavesdrop.'

'You would have needed a jet flying directly overhead not to have heard!'

'Very funny. Anyhow, as from now all stalking and grouse shooting ceases at Grey Corries Lodge and I want all guests out of this house as soon as possible.'

'What about my money?' von Spielman protested. 'Do you realise I spend ridiculous money to come to shoot; and the hinds, they are like, how do you say … like goats, skinny goats. We should be paid to do your fader's culling!'

'Why don't you go back to the Faderland, then?' Penelope suggested sweetly. 'You'll get practice there.'

Further altercation was prevented by the entrance of Kirsty.

'I came to ask about dinner, Mr Kenneth.' She looked directly at him, poised and cool.

'The usual time, Kirsty … but Mother may want hers in her room.'

'She's not having anything, sir.'

'Take her up some soup,' he ordered brusquely. 'And, Kirsty …'

'Yes?' she looked at him steadily, conscious that more than one pair of male eyes was studying her.

'The guests will be leaving as soon as the police complete their inquiries.'

She turned and, without a word, left the room.

'I don't mind pulling out, Ken,' Clem agreed. 'But von Spielman's right. We've paid a lot of money for this vacation and we've only been here a few days …' He raised his cigar to emphasise his remarks.

'Oh, don't worry,' Kenneth replied. 'You'll all get your pound of flesh – in sterling, not venison!'

Penelope had been following the exchange with interest. It didn't matter to her if she never saw another deer – it was just her way of spending three weeks in the Scottish Highlands in what she thought would be pleasant surroundings. But she had a suspicion that both Spielman and Clem Fular were not pleased with the prospect of premature departure. Her suspicions were confirmed by the American.

'Well, I guess I'll go along part way with your sentiments, Ken. I was against killing even ducks at one time – and we have some fine duck shooting in California – but there must be some control, you know. Why, over at my pad there wouldn't be any ducks if it weren't for hunters who re-stock and breed them. The same goes for other game … '

Before he could finish there was a quick knock on the door and Watty came in. There was a look of urgency on his face and his jacket was still wet from melted snow. He spoke to Chris.

'There's a couple stuck on Pinnacle Buttress. One's dead, I think.'

'Have you told the Inspector?' Chris was suddenly alert.

'Yes, he's coming with Bookam, er – Constable Munro. The rest of the Law is staying here.'

'What about you, Ken?' Chris looked at his friend with concern, uncertain whether to ask him.

'Of course, I'll go; better than moping here, talking useless ethics.'

'Aye, it's always on a day like this,' Watty muttered in disgust. 'Wouldn't it be nice to have a rescue on a fine day?'

'Has the rest of the team been called?' Chris asked the keeper who was already moving to the door.

'Aye, I've done that. It was me who got the call from Kinlochsanda Police Headquarters. The Superintendent is on the phone now …' The two men followed the keeper out into the hall.

Chapter 3

The estate Range Rover, with Watty behind the wheel, seemed as if it would take off. The twisty Glen Liath road was single-track with near vertical drops into the river. The fact that several inches of snow covered the road and some of the inclines were one in six didn't deter the keeper.

'We pay a fortune in rates,' Kenneth spoke loudly above the noise of the racing engine. 'Yet they never come down here with the snow plough until two days after they clear the main Glasgow road.'

'Aye, they'll be out on the main drag tonight,' Angus muttered. He had his feet braced on the bulkhead in front of him.

'Who gave the alarm?' asked Ken.

'It was a 999 call to the station, wasn't it?' Watty said.

'Yes,' confirmed the Inspector. 'But Willie Fyffe phoned later: one of the survivors came into Queenshouse and he got the full story.'

'Is he keeping him at the hotel?'

'Oh, aye, he'll do that. Willie is no daft!'

'Two climbers, you said?' Ken mused.

The Inspector answered, 'So it seems, on Pinnacle Buttress.'

'I bet it's that last pitch on the Greasy Slab,' Chris's voice was almost inaudible above the roar of the diesel which was in second gear. All four wheels attacking the snow, Watty drove with the verve he used to display as a younger man in the Six Day, the famous motor cycle trial. 'It was bound to be icy by three o'clock, don't you agree, Ken?'

'Could be – but it would have a fair covering of snow.'

'Have you climbing gear with you, Inspector?' Chris asked.

'Aye, some, but I'd better stay at base – I've no crampons.'

'Bloody snow-shoes we'll need tonight,' Watty moaned, pulling his fore and aft further down over his eyes to combat the glare from the headlights blanching the snow. 'But you won't need them Angus; you and Bookam have them permanently attached!'

'One of these days, Watty Gilchrist,' the Inspector replied good-humouredly, 'I'll let you savour my 'snow-shoe' on that place on which you spend too much of your time contemplating!' The others laughed.

'Isaac the Rev will have trouble coming from Faileadh tonight,' Chris chuckled at the thought of his cousin the minister fighting his way through the snow on his 1000 cc Laverda.

'Och, he'll get a lift surely,' the Inspector said. 'He wouldn't want to take his brand new bike out in this weather, wi' a' the salt on the road.'

'He's no' interested in taking it oot at a' if he canna dae the ton.' There was a trace of envy in Watty's voice. 'The man's a holy terror!'

'That's the reason he's in the team, I think,' Ken offered. 'So that he can exceed the speed limit on a call-out!'

'Aye,' Watty added sagaciously. 'He must be the best practised meenister on sudden deaths in Scotland; we have a fair pickle o' fatalities in these parts. But we'll be giving him his personal rites one o' these days, when he runs into a sheep or some dawdling towrist.'

'The extra height here makes quite a difference,' Angus observed, fingering his long nose absently. 'There must be all of eight inches of snow.'

'Lucky the big road's still open,' Chris replied, watching the lights of several vehicles approaching across the expanse of moor that formed the base of Eagal Mor, the peak on their left. By leaning down and looking out of the window, he could just see the summit. The cloud lifted slightly and some stars had come out of the blackness. Then he saw a lonely twinkle of light to the left, below the summit.

'There's a torch on Pinnacle Buttress.' Ken and Thumper also craned their necks to see but Watty didn't slow down; his eyes were focussed religiously on where he thought the road was.

'That's a help, anyhow,' he said. 'Mony a time we've had to go up only to find they were somewhere else! It's no' often a survivor gets the accident location right.'

'Well, the boys should be at the pub; we'll get the full story soon enough,' Chris remarked.

'Aye, it's gae coorse, Willie.' Watty spat thoughtfully before he passed through the doorway of the Queenshouse.

'That it is,' rejoined the publican, taking a reluctant glance outside. His prodigious frame was silhouetted against and almost blotted out the light from the open door. 'But I've a feeling it's passing.'

'I think you're right,' Chris commented, kicking snow off his shoes. He was carrying the rucksack which he always kept in the back of his car. 'I must change, Willie.'

'Help yersel',' the landlord responded. 'The front room's empty … Did ye see the light?' he added as he opened the door.

'Aye, the Fourth Pinnacle looks about right, I would say,' Chris responded.

'That's what Duncan and Basil thought …' Turning to the Inspector, he added, 'I just heard aboot the laird's accident. He'll be sadly missed …' Just then Ken entered, in the rear of the party. 'Oh, I didna think ye'd be oot, Kenneth. I was just saying to Angus that it's a tragic day.'

'Thanks, Willie,' Ken replied quietly. 'Are the others inside?'

'Aye, they're having a cuppa. Douglas is here as weel.'

Willie Fyffe, known to all as 'Watery' ever since he was prosecuted for diluting the whisky in his pub, was tall and stout and with a liking for both the hard and soft stuff, as he acknowledged – whisky and women! His latter pursuit was somewhat hampered by a formidable wife, a woman of stature and of proportions similar to those of her husband with the addition of a bosom vast and tremulous. She tackled those tasks too strenuous for her husband – Watery was not partial to work. At that moment he was worrying in case he might have to go up the hill. He broached the matter circumspectly as Chris went into the room leading off the foyer.

'I suppose you'll be wanting me to operate Base, Chris?'

'It's either you or Inspector Wilson; he hasn't brought his crampons.'

'Och, I'll soon fit him oot,' Willie brightened. 'He's aboot the same size as me.'

Chris smiled. 'Anyhow,' he said, 'Bookam Munro will be up shortly; he's at Grey Corries. You'd better sort that out with the Inspector, Willie. But I suppose as one of them is reported dead he had better be in attendance. They're getting concerned these days about the possibility of foul play.'

'They wouldn't know the difference between a murder and a gralloch,' the hotelier retorted, his balding head glistening. He ran a hand fondly over it and turned to go out.

'I'm afraid you're right, Willie.' Chris had taken his jacket off and was reaching in his rucksack for his boots, he was sitting on a ruptured, red upholstered chair. 'We'd spot something amiss, mind you, but I've often wondered if I'd bother to report it, as all hell could break loose. It would be like dropping hot shit on a fan and probably never be proven, anyway.'

'I've seen a few suspeecious deaths on the hill in my time here at the Queenshouse,' the proprietor mused. 'Remember that Iranian couple who were supposed to be walking up the Eagal the easy way?'

'Yes, I do. He pushed his wife over that cliff just east of the summit, or I'm a Dutchman,' Chris recalled.

'Talking aboot sudden death ...' Willie closed the door with a cunning expression on his face, as if he'd just gained access to a bonded warehouse. 'What happened to old Horrible? I heard he was shot.'

'Yes, that's right,' the other agreed, marvelling at the speed news travelled in this remote area. 'It was on a stalk – most likely a ricocheting bullet.'

'Puir man, puir man.' The publican had the lilting accent of the Mullach, a native of Mull. He shook his head sagely. 'He'll be missed, the old bugger, Chris. His bark was worse than his bite.'

'Ken will find it hard,' Chris remarked, zipping up his snow gaiters and standing up. He took a cagoule out of his pack and put it on.

'His sister, Deirdre, she'll take it badly too; she was awfu' fond o' the old boy.'

'Yes, Ken phoned her. She'll be up here in the morning.'

'A bonny lass is Deirdre,' the hotel owner reflected. 'I suppose she'll still be teaching?'

'As far as I know.' Chris didn't like the tone of the hotelier's voice. 'Randy old devil,' he muttered to himself. Willie must have sensed this passing coolness for he glanced at the retired geologist with a calculating eye.

'I hear,' he remarked warily, opening the door again, 'that the American who wears the funny clothes, the American Copper boss, was trying to get old Horrible to sell a bit o' the lower Liath, doon by the tailraces o' the dam.'

'Oh?' Chris replied casually.

'Something aboot mineral deposits. You would ken the possibilities o' that, being involved with geology.'

'Probably just rumours.' Chris followed Willie out and along the corridor. 'Of course, the old copper mine further down was worked out at the beginning of last century.'

'Ah, well,' Willie Fyffe commented. 'I just thought you would have been consulted, being a local now and wi' a' yer degrees.'

'First I've heard of it, but the way copper's rising, it could be a viable proposition.'

'Ah, the team leader and rock master himself.' This cheerful greeting came from a fit-looking man leaning against the bar. Chris had been kidded about his profession from the day he first set foot in Faileadh, ten years before. He had retired at the age of 42 when a New Zealand company he'd been working for was wound up. A legacy from his late father had allowed him to devote more time to mountaineering. He'd always been a keen climber and had become leader of the local rescue team five years before. His only family connections in the area were his aunt, Mrs McWhirter, a widow of means, who lived close to Faileadh and his cousin, the local minister, the Rev Isaac McMillan.

It was Basil Thorndyke who had addressed Chris. He was the Chief Engineer at the nearby Loch Gorm hydro-electric station.

'You know, Chris,' he continued with mock seriousness, 'we've been waiting here all of five minutes. We could have been halfway up the Eagal!'

'You just get going then, Bas,' Chris replied good-humouredly; he liked the skinny engineer. 'But don't forget to take the stretcher.'

'Whilst you go up carrying your thermos and sandwiches, courtesy of the management?' the other chuckled.

'Now you're speaking – a dram, who's for a dram?' Willie Fyffe enthused, looking about him. His offer was declined.

Chris noticed a small, tired-looking youth at the far end of the bar. He went over. Behind him a peat fire was flickering in its lazy way. 'Are you the one who came down for help?'

'Yes.' A rusty mop of hair was tossed back as its owner replied.

'The Fourth Pinnacle?'

'I think so.'

Chris noticed his eyes held a wild look and realised that he was suffering from shock. 'I'm the team leader – Chris Watkins. Can you go over it again for me?'

The climber gave a cold smile, revealing a gap where a

tooth was missing on his lower jaw. His eyes surveyed Chris
as if he was checking credentials.

'Claude – that's my friend who was killed – came off on a
smooth icy section and fell into a col between two towers.'

'To the right or left?'

'The right, looking up. He was hanging on the rope and
we had a hell of a job getting him up.'

'We?'

'Carol and me.'

'Is she a climber?'

'Yes.'

'Still up there?'

'Yes, at the Gap.'

'Has she any gear?'

'A down jacket and I left her a bivvy sack.'

'Why didn't you return with her?' Chris asked as the
Inspector came over and joined them, stuffing a spare battery
into his anorak pocket.

'Her fingers were burned by the rope when he came off
and, besides, she seems to be suffering from exposure. I
thought it safer to leave her and get help.'

'Umph,' the policeman interjected. 'You may be right at
that. At least we'll be able to locate her if her headlamp
doesn't give out.' The policeman looked at the young man
from under bushy eyebrows, then rubbed his left hand along
his nose. 'I'm Detective Inspector Wilson. I'll be wanting a
few details from you before we go ... What's the name of
the fallen man?'

'Claude Reynolds. He is – was – a doctor of medicine.'

'Address?' Angus Wilson had taken out a dog-eared notebook and jotted down the particulars with a stubby pencil.
From the other side of the bar Willie Fyffe produced a pair of
crampons and surreptitiously placed them beside the Inspector.

'You might be needing these tonight, Angus.'

By the time the Inspector had raised his eyes from his notebook to the crampons Willie had eased off to the other end of the bar and was now clutching a bottle of Grouse. Two more policemen came in, reinforcements from Kinlochsanda.

'Ciamar a tha,' Duncan MacGillvery greeted them.

'Well, if it isn't the poacher himsel',' returned Robert, the first constable. He was a large, ungainly man with a West Highland accent.

'Hello, lads,' the other – a smaller man – spoke. Chris, returning from the fire, gave them both a smile.

'Fine night for the hills, Robert.'

'Aye, that it is, Mr Watkins. I hear it's another fatal.'

'Seems like it; on the Pinnacle Buttress again.'

'That'll be the fourth this year on the Eagal,' the other constable stated soberly.

'You're right, Ian,' the team leader answered. 'Too damned many.'

'We've brought the Rev with us,' Robert remarked, jerking a thumb over his shoulder as the bar door opened and a small ferret-featured man entered, wearing a duvet jacket. He was dark with a bristling moustache which made his resemble an inquisitive rat. He wore a crash helmet with '1000 cc' emblazoned across it. He blinked, then glanced petulantly around the bar.

'I might have known ... drinking! Drinking when someone has just departed from our midst.' He pointed an outstretched arm dramatically towards Eagal Mor.

'Slainte, Isaac,' Duncan, who was the only one with a dram, held up his glass derisively. 'We know your whims, Rev ... The country needs more private homes, not public houses, etc ...'

'You're impossible, MacGillvery,' the minister retorted angrily. 'But you'll be judged ... You and your poaching!'

'Now, Isaac,' Duncan admonished. 'Get off that high horse o' yours – the pulpit or your hot rod; remember it was a namesake of yours who advocated such things – look up Genesis ... "Then Isaac spake to Esau, his son. And Esau went to the field to hunt for venison and to bring it ..." The poacher gave the minister a wide grin.

'Okay, children, let's go.' Chris's voice cut across the room which hung heavy with cigarette smoke. 'You know what gear to take ... Duncan, you carry the stretcher. You'll be quicker than Basil and it might even slow you down a bit.'

'Aye, I'll do that. Take the stretcher I mean – no' slow down!'

'There may be more o' the lads coming over from Kinlochsanda,' Robert commented, zipping his anorak.

'Well, if they do, will you send them up, Willie? They'll be appreciated for the carry out.'

'I'll see to that, Chris me lad. I'll see to that. Fine lads, the Kinlochsanda boys, fine lads.'

'One thing I like about you,' Basil remarked as he shouldered his rucksack, 'is that you never repeat yourself, Willie, never repeat yourself.' He chuckled as he went out.

'I think you'd be pullin' my leg now, Basil, m' lad,' the publican called after him.

'Very thoughtful of you to lend me your crampons, Mr Fyffe.' The Insperctor spoke with heavy sarcasm as he lumbered to the door. 'I'm sure you'd give away your last bit of climbing gear to a friend – if it meant you hadn't to go up the hill!'

'Now, Angus, that's not fair! Here at the hotel I can get things organised and I'm sure you'll not be averse to a bite to eat when you get back and maybe something stronger.'

'It'll do you the world of good, Angus,' Chris interrupted with a laugh. 'You may even be able to catch Toń one of these days, and him with a stag over his shoulder.'

'No hope.' Douglas Stewart, the most recent member of the team, gave a broad smile. 'Perhaps if Duncan was carrying a brace of stags.'

'Sin, I'm surrounded by sin,' Isaac moaned, taking out a pair of mitts from his pocket.

'If I poach anything, it's from the good Lord,' Duncan boomed grandly, his blue eyes twinkling. 'And he's no' a bad laird at that ... But come on, Robert, move yourself, or we'll be having a bloody sermon.' The poacher was a good two inches bigger than Robert, the larger policeman. They had competed together on several occasions at Highland Gatherings and were friendly rivals. 'Och, you're no' such a bad character, Isaac,' the poacher ventured, 'and if you ever get the money to start that orphanage of yours, I'll be there to give a hand and perhaps supply some protein!'

The wind had risen and flurries of snow spewed down the hillside like tracer bullets in the head lamp beams. Duncan was in front, carrying the folded stretcher and setting a hard pace, despite the fact that the snow was deep and as unstable as loose sand.

'He's a beast of a man is MacGillvery,' Angus Wilson gasped as he halted for a breather. 'He's not human!'

He's certainly fit, I'll grant you that, Angus,' Chris agreed, pulling his anorak hood up; there was a heavy coating of rime on it.

'I thought it was going to clear,' Isaac McMillan said, turning away from the wind. 'It's worse than ever.'

'Did you hear about the laird, Rev?' Chris asked.

'I did, and I should have gone down to see the Honourable Mrs Victoria, but this call came just then.'

'Two fatals in one day – and both on my beat,' the Inspector groaned. 'More work.' He passed a gloved hand over his face to remove melting snow.

'Do you think Ken will live permanently at the big house now, Chris?' Isaac inquired, the beam of his lamp swinging round to rest on Chris's face.

'I doubt it,' he replied. 'He's keen on photography and making quite a name for himself in the glossies, and the estate is under a partnership now and he may not have much say in the outcome.'

'He's not at Grey Corries that much, anyhow. It'll be another case of an absentee landlord, I suppose.' Angus spoke morosely.

'It'll be interesting to see what happens,' Isaac mused. 'I doubt if I'll see him more regularly amongst my flock. The Dewars are not ardent churchgoers. I was in seeing our aunt today, Chris. She's not at all well and appears to be failing.'

'I'm sorry, Isaac. I really must call, but she always seems curt. I don't really understand it.'

'I think you're both too strong-willed, Chris. I've told her that and I've told you before.'

'I wish it was as simple as that, but it isn't; she just doesn't like me.' His voice tailed off and he turned away from the small man.

The three rescuers moved on, following the trail broken by Duncan. To the rear, the rest of the party formed an illuminated crocodile with Basil in the lead. A portable searchlight stabbed the night from this group like a flashing broad sword. Between the swirls of spindrift they could see the faint, solitary light directly above.

Duncan moved into a steep, unstable snow gully. He kept to one side where the edge of the rock afforded some handholds.

'Watch it doesn't avalanche, MacGillvery,' Chris shouted. 'It looks unstable.'

'Aye, that's why I'm keeping to the wall.' The poacher's voice was muffled by the snow.

Duncan was on high-angled snow which led between the pinnacles to form a flat-topped col. Suddenly, he broke through the cornice which had formed to emerge on the top, shaking himself like a dog despite the stretcher on his back. The col was narrow – the width of a narrow wall. Suddenly, the snow beneath his feet gave way, exposing a glassy gleam of ice which his torch for an instant illuminated. The cornice on the farther edge of the narrow neck of snow had disintegrated leaving a clean cut edge of slab break away. As the poacher fell, the stretcher shot over his head and bounced silently down the gully on the other side of the pinnacles. The others didn't discover that he had fallen until they reached the gap.

'Hey, look at this, Inspector.' Chris swung round in alarm. 'Duncan's gone through the cornice!'

'What was that?' the policeman gasped as he floundered up the deep steps and stood on the small area of unbroken snow which had not gone down with the avalanche. His light illuminated the u-shaped hole in the cornice.

'Duncan, Duncan, are you all right?' Chris shouted.

'MacGillvery?' Angus's powerful voice cut in and reverberated from the gully below. 'Aye, I'm okay, but no thanks to that bloody cornice.' Duncan's voice was close at hand to their right. Both beams hinged round to reveal a white-covered figure minus a headlamp and with a great rent in his tweed jacket.

'What happened?' Angus shouted.

'I went through. The stretcher's gone.'

'Well, we can manage without it, seeing it's a dead body

we're recovering. But it's lucky we're not having to carry you back,' Chris remarked.

'Aye, I was fortunate, right enough,' the poacher admitted, brushing snow from his plus-fours. 'I hit a drift about 100 feet down. Otherwise I'd have reached the road! ... And my Maker,' he added as an afterthought.

When Isaac arrived, Chris told him what had happened.

'You have a charmed life, MacGillvery,' the minister observed as they reached the poacher. 'And it so happens I have a spare headlamp.'

'That'll be handy, Rev,' Duncan said thankfully. 'At least I've still got my ice axe.'

They all went up to the cornice. Fifteen minutes later they reached the girl. She was cold and shocked and obviously pleased to see them.

'Can you manage down?' Chris asked her.

'Yes, I think so, with some help,' she replied in a weak voice, attempting to overcome her stiffness and stand up. She was still inside the bivvy sack. Duncan steadied her.

'Take it easy, lass. We've got all night. Now let me see those hands of yours.'

'It seems as if I've been here all night.' She gave a faint smile as he helped her off with her gloves.

'Umph,' he murmured. 'We'd better put dressings on these. You've some nasty burns, my girl!'

The Inspector had been concerning himself with the body. He had traced it by following the rope; it was partly covered in snow. He came back in a few moments.

'He's dead, all right, Chris. Didn't have a chance, I would say; his helmet must have been knocked off in the fall. At least it's a blessing he didn't strangle on the rope.'

Directly below them the lights of the others were now close by.

'Have you got the cas bag, Rev?'

'Yes,' the small man replied, gasping for breath.

'We'll put the body in and slide it down. We can have a look for the stretcher tomorrow.' Duncan had put a short length of rope on the girl and, holding her on this leash, he told her to start moving. Far below, through a gap in the clouds, they could see the friendly lights of the Queenshouse.

Chapter 4

Clem Fular was the next to walk into the breakfast room. Donald MacDonald was slightly taken aback by his attire.

'You didn't go out stalking today, Mr Fular?' he began, thinking to himself that there was a fair bit of capital represented in the Lodge at that moment: this American seemed to exude wealth.

'No way, sir,' Clem answered loudly. 'Somehow, I'm just not with it today … got the Highland blues, I guess. Went out for a hike in the afternoon but sneaked back before the snow hit. Hell of a cold house, they've got here,' he confided. 'They seem to think central heating's something in science fiction!'

The Superintendent ignored this last remark, thinking to himself that the scrawny American looked very fit, and continued, 'Can you tell us where you went during your walk, Mr Fular?'

'Oh, just strolled up the trail a little,' he answered jocularly. 'I don't know what time that would be – was glad to leave that commodity back home.'

'Did you see anyone on your – er ... travels?'

'Not a soul, not a single automobile, Superintendent.'

'You seem an athletic sort of a chap, Mr Fular – you are President of American Copper, aren't you?'

'Correct, sir. But I do a lot of climbing and walking back home. You know,' he confided, 'I sure would like to get to grips with Scottish ice sometime.'

'You should manage that here. I understand this is one of the best climbing centres in Scotland.'

The American was asked the other routine questions and was eventually allowed to take his leave.

'Sorry I can't help you guys more,' he said.

'No, thanks.' Superintendent MacDonald raised a heavy hand. 'And thank you for your time, Mr Fular,' he continued. 'Will you ask Mr ...' he paused for an instant, '... Mr Spielman to come in?'

'Sure.' He moved to the door with the parting words, 'Take care.'

'What me old dad would have called a natty dresser,' Archie Campbell observed dryly when the door had closed.

'Just so,' the Superintendent commented. 'An interesting man ...'

Karl von Spielman could add little that wasn't already known. He claimed, emphatically, to have shot the hind. It was only later when Penelope Almen came into the room, followed by a wake of powerful perfume, that a spark of interest was aroused. She has a strong personality, Archie thought – as pervading as her scent.

'My, that's quite an incinerator you've got there, Sergeant,' she observed, wrinkling her nose for the room was already heavy with smoke.

'I'll put it out, Miss Almen,' he said hurriedly. 'I seem to light it, not thinking. Margaret, my wife, was getting at me only this morning at breakfast about it.'

'No, don't bother, Sergeant,' Penelope laughed. 'It grows on one – like a London fog.'

'Ah, weel, it's a rare Herbal Mixture, this stuff,' Archie confessed with a slow smile. He took out a handkerchief and wiped his mouth. 'And I'm not so sure but that it even does me good!'

'Nonsense, Sergeant,' the Superintendent retorted. 'You must be corroding your inside like the guts of a silencer.'

Penelope trilled with laughter and looked at each man in turn. She found these policemen charming, in striking contrast to the automatons she had grown up with. 'Well, I'm sure you want to discuss something other than the pollution of the Highlands, Superintendent?' She arched her eyebrows inquiringly.

'Well, yes, Miss Almen. Just a few questions about the stalk. I understand you accompanied the main party today?'

'Yes, I did,' she fingered her necklace and looked directly at him. 'But I doubt whether I can add any observation which hasn't already been volunteered.'

'That remains to be seen,' Donald MacDonald returned kindly. He liked this long-faced woman; she had a frank look about her and, though he didn't quite approve of her dress, he accepted that city females were a breed apart, and got away with behaviour which would be unthinkable for a Highland lady. Working through his list of stock questions, he thought Penelope Almen singularly unobservant until she confessed that her eyesight was impaired.

'Did you hear two or three shots?'

'I imagine you heard about that other shot, but I've been thinking about it and, honestly, I can only recall there being two shots – they were so deafening at close range, but the second one did seem louder.'

'Did the laird appear upset this morning?' Donald MacDonald asked.

'Well,' she hesitated for a moment. 'I only saw him fleetingly. He and Kenneth had a monster of a row last night. Ken hates shooting, you know.'

'So I gather ... Was that what it was about?'

'It was just a father and son argument – probably didn't mean much. I expect they'd had similar ones before; they seemed familiar with the salient points and stalking's not a recent pastime in this place.'

'Nothing else?'

'No, I'm sorry I can't help more.' She shrugged her bare shoulders.

'Well, I think we'll call it a day, Archie.' The Superintendent stretched himself when she had left the room.

'What about Watty's wife?' Archie asked. He had replaced his notebook in his tunic pocket.

'Aye, she looks an observant woman.' The Superintendent pondered for a minute. 'Yes, fetch her in, Archie, we'll have a quick word.'

'I'll ring the bell for her,' Archie replied and pressed the button by the empty fireplace. 'It's surprising that Penelope Almen goes stalking at all,' he mused, 'if she's as blind as she makes out to be!'

'Her eyesight's good enough to see the bottle o' Talisker,' Donald replied. 'I think she likes a dram.'

'I wouldn't be surprised.'

'What do you make o' the argument between Kenneth and the laird, Archie?' Donald MacDonald sat down heavily, his 15 stones threatening to demolish the chair.

'It's common knowledge in these parts that they didn't

see eye to eye. I knew myself even before it was brought up – and their politics didn't mix either ... Could it be that Ken was getting more bitter about it?'

'Just what I was thinking,' his superior agreed. 'I suppose Kenneth will be running the estate now.'

'Aye, probably, but I'll check wi' Hector MacAndrew, the family solicitor, in Kinlochsanda ... Are you wanting to see the missus tonight – the Honourable Mrs Dewar?'

'No, I won't disturb her,' the Superintendent answered thoughtfully. 'Perhaps you could come down tomorrow and have a word with her, Archie?'

'I'll do that, sir,' the Sergeant returned and continued, 'you'll be calling in the Regional Crime Squad, I suppose?'

'We may have to if there was foul play – which I doubt, but I'll see that our own lads are well to the fore.' The weight of 50 years seemed to bear heavily on the big man's shoulders. 'Inspector Wilson will be in charge of the investigation initially, but there'll be hell to pay if he doesn't get anywhere ... First he'll have to determine if there were actually three shots and then find that blasted bullet. We don't seem to be getting anywhere at the moment!'

'If he gets enough men on to it, he may find the bullet,' Archie volunteered optimistically. 'The doctor said it went right through the side of his neck and severed the main artery.'

'By the way, Archie, take all the firearms back with you.'

'I'll see to that, sir.'

Kirsty Gilchrist came into the room. She had changed and now wore a clinging knitted dress which seemed moulded to her body. A bonny lass, the Superintendent thought to himself, not many of her sort about – funny how she came to marry a gamekeeper when she could have had her pick from a dozen glens. He stood up.

'I don't think I've had the pleasure of meeting you, Mrs

Gilchrist, though I have seen you, of course.' She flashed him a ready smile he saw that her teeth were small and even.

'I think I met you at the police ball a few years ago, Superintendent,' she replied with a trace of amusement. 'You seemed to be ... enjoying yourself!' The Superintendent's normally ruddy face darkened somewhat and he gave a nervous cough as he sat down again.

'Well, you know, it is one of the few occasions when we policemen can let our hair down, Mrs Gilchrist, and, after all, we are all driven home that night ...' Archie stifled a broad smile with his hand. 'We won't keep you long, Mrs Gilchrist.'

'Kirsty, please, Superintendent.' She gave another smile. 'Calling me Mrs Gilchrist makes me feel a calliach.'

'All right, Kirsty ... Just a few points we want to clear up. Was the routine of the house normal over the last few days or was there anything unusual you noticed?' She thought for a moment, a slight line forming on her forehead.

'No, no, nothing of consequence that I can remember. That German chap always seems to be complaining, but we do get these types in the stalking season. They expect everything to be done for them and I'm supposed to do it single-handed.' There was a hint of exasperation in her voice.

'It must be difficult for you, Kirsty. Don't you have any help?'

'Well, Jean McBain comes in each day, but she would spend all the time gossiping if I didn't keep her at it.'

'Did Kenneth get on with his father?' The Superintendent asked the question casually, but he noticed a hesitation as she ran her tongue lightly over her lips. Archie turned a page of his notebook and glanced up, studying the woman. A bundle of goodies Watty has for himself here, he thought. He felt secure in the fact that no-one in their right senses would waste covetous glances at his wife Margaret.

'Not really.' She patted her hair self-consciously. 'They were always at each other's throats about something; usually politics or stalking.'

'They had an argument last night?'

'Yes, they had, but what's that got to do with the laird's death?' She gave him a puzzled look.

'Just the usual inquiries, Kirsty. We always go into the background of any accident.'

'Well, I can't see what you hope to gain by digging into regular family feuds, but Kenneth doesn't know how to behave himself, if you ask me!' She was slightly flushed. Archie noted it and wondered, then risked a question.

'Do you like Mr Kenneth, Kirsty?' She whirled on him then, standing up, looking both flushed and attractive as she demanded:

'Just what do you mean, Archie Campbell?'

'Nothing, Kirsty, nothing. I was just under the impression that you, er, respected young Dewar.'

'Well,' she answered, somewhat mollified. 'There's nothing wrong with Kenneth, I suppose, but his father was a gentleman, despite his blunt ways.'

'Did you happen to see Mr Fular this afternoon, Kirsty?' the Superintendent asked.

'Yes, he never went on the stalk; he'd been drinking too much whisky last night.'

'Did you see him go out?'

'I saw him come back.'

'What time would that be?' the Superintendent asked interestedly.

'Let me see now,' she pondered, a line again forming across her forehead. 'About three o'clock, I think. Yes, it was, for I was upstairs in the wee box-room when I saw him from the window. He had Gealeas the dog with him. I remember looking at the grandfather as I came back down the top landing.'

'Well, I don't think we'll detain you any longer, Kirsty,' Donald said, winding up the interview. 'Thanks for your time.' He got up gallantly and opened the door for her. As she went out she flashed him another smile.

'Well, well, Super, she seems to have taken a fancy to you.' Archie gave his superior a wink and shook out his handkerchief and blew his nose loudly.

'It's my personal charm.' Donald MacDonald picked up his cap and put it on, then glanced at himself in the mirror. 'What gave you the idea there was something between Kenneth and her?' He jerked a large thumb in the direction of the door.

'Just a hunch. Ken has an eye for a beautiful woman; he sees plenty of them in his job.'

'Even though she's married to the estate's keeper?'

'Of that I'm not sure, sir. But I must admit Kirsty's a bonny girl and it surprises me that she married Watty. He's not exactly God's gift to a lonely maiden ...'

'You know, Sergeant, I can appreciate now why St Columba didn't want cows or women at his monastery on Iona all those years ago.'

'Did some Viking or other spear the laird?' Archie asked, tongue in cheek.

'No, nothing like that, Archie. But he knew women caused trouble and if he had cows on the island he would have to have women to milk them, so he had neither. But it looks as if we're stuck with at least two women in the case, and one of them a stunner at that!'

'For a senior police officer, sir, you'd have made a good abbot,' Archie said with a grin.

Chapter 5

On the descent from the rescue the Inspector was in touch with the Superintendent by radio. He envied his boss the warmth of the Queenshouse where he had installed himself after concluding the interviews at the big house and where, no doubt, Willie Fyffe would be acting the ever-attentive mine host.

'I'll be wanting a word with you when you get back, Angus,' his boss spoke through the static. 'And can you make sure Watty comes.'

'I'll see you at the hotel, then sir,' he had replied 'And I'll make sure that Watty goes to Queenshouse, too – he usually does after a rescue, anyhow.'

It was 1 a.m. when the rescue party returned. The girl was in a state of exhaustion by the time they reached the road and was immediately bundled into the waiting ambulance. Dr Khan saw her before she departed and gave the driver instructions to take her to Kinlochsanda Hospital. The body, Angus decreed, could wait until morning and could then be taken down to the local morgue in the Land Rover.

In the hotel kitchen Superintendent Donald MacDonald gave his Detective Inspector the run-down on the investigation so far. They continued to drink their soup for a few minutes deep in thought. Eventually Angus spoke. 'It certainly seems odd, Watty not making any mention of three shots.' The others were through in the bar, talking loudly, and voraciously eating sandwiches prepared by Mrs Fyffe.

'Yes,' the Super returned, looking over his plate. 'You can't tell me that a keeper with Watty's experience can't distinguish between a high velocity report and an ensuing ricochet. I'm going to suggest to the Chief that you take on this case, Angus.'

'That's good o' ye, sir; I'll certainly do my best. There's probably a simple explanation of the whole thing ...'

'There may be an explanation, but the fact remains that the old boy was killed and at present we don't know by whom. You'll have to make a detailed examination of the locus as soon as you can.'

'I think I'd like to have a word with Kenneth as well as Watty before they leave,' Angus mused, putting his empty plate on a shelf by his elbow and giving his mouth a wipe with the back of his hand.

'Well, Archie and I had better be getting back now,' the Superintendent said. 'You can see Ken and Watty yourself, but I'll leave Constable Munro to give you a hand. Report back, Angus.'

'I'll do that, sir.'

'Good luck, then. By the way, we've taken all the firearms for forensics. They're in the car. Watty will have at least one rifle, but we didn't take his.'

'I'll look into that, too, sir. Goodnight.'

'Sorry we have to do this at such an ungodly hour, Watty –

if I can say that without Isaac hearing.' Angus opened the interview.

They were seated in the 'wee lounge', as Willie Fyffe called the small room in which Chris had earlier changed his clothes. PC Munro was stifling a yawn from the depths of an armchair close to the door. An electric fire glowed in the broad stone hearth. 'There have been some developments concerning the death of your late boss and I want to clear up a few points.'

'Is that so, now?' the keeper replied. He was feeling a bit hung over after the previous night.

'Some of the party thought they heard three shots, yet only two were fired by the guests.' He considered the situation justified bending the truth. Angus gazed at the narrow nose of the keeper, now a bright red from the combined effects of an Arctic wind and Ben Nevis whisky, but didn't fail to notice a slight hesitancy.

'It's difficult to say,' the keeper answered carefully. 'I was deafened mysel' by Spielman's shot; he seemed to just drop down on the ground and fire ... No wonder he can't hit anything,' he added. 'He seems to think it's a guided missile he's firing!'

'So there could have been three shots?' the Inspector persisted. 'I need hardly waste my breath saying this is most important, Watty.'

'Aye, there could have been,' the keeper admitted grudgingly. 'But I wouldna swear to it, ye ken; that's why I didna mention it at the time.'

'Would it have been possible for a ricocheting bullet from your party to have killed the laird?' Angus raised his bushy eyebrows.

'No, I wouldn't think so. Ye'll see for yersel' when you take a look. Unless, of course, Karl Spielman's bullet ricocheted from the gully, but I don't think it did; he was certainly firing in the general direction o' the hinds – I saw that.'

'And Chris?' Angus asked.

'Miss Almen was near him, but he's a good shot. And if you think he could have bumped the old man off, have another think, Angus. It just wasn't possible for Chris to see the laird's position from where he fired. But we could all have seen it from a wee way back along the strath.'

'Somebody shot old Horatio,' Angus said in irreverent tones, clenching his hands. 'And I intend to find out who! Did you see anybody else on the hill?' He barked the question at Watty and, again, both policemen noticed a tension in the keeper's manner, though his reply came easily enough.

'No, I never saw anyone other than our party and Ian Cuthbert, the gillie, way back towards the Lodge wi' the garron. I had a walkie-talkie wi' me for keeping in touch wi' him.'

'Aye, I know that,' the Inspector nodded. 'Where was Kenneth when you were out on the stalk?' He looked keenly at Watty.

'I suppose – if he'd any sense – he'd have been by the fire,' the keeper returned.

'And if he didn't have any sense?' The keeper just shrugged his shoulders.

'I've been informed that he went out for a walk,' the Inspector stated.

'Well, all ye have to dae is to ask him yersel'.' Watty's voice had a truculent edge.

'That I'll certainly do, Watty. As a matter of fact, I'd better do it before he goes back down the glen.'

'I'll go and fetch him,' Bookam offered and sidled out of the door.

'How many rifles are there at the Lodge, Watty?' The keeper did a mental calculation.

'Eleven, including the guests' guns and my own.'

'Yours are what calibre?'

'Both .275s. You've got all the details of them on file.'

'Were they kept locked up in the gun room?'

'Of course, but I keep mine in my cottage.'

'Just so,' the Inspector rumbled. 'check to see if one is missing will you?'

'OK.'

'Will I wait until ye finish wi' Ken?' Watty asked. 'He'll be coming back wi' me.'

'Do that.'

'Nae bother, Angus. Pity I can't help more.'

'Kenneth, I'm just sorting out some further details of the shooting fatality.' Thumper opened, once Ken was seated. 'The Super's reporting to the Chief, Mr Templeton, this morning.'

'John Templeton knew Dad,' Ken replied.

'That's one o' the reasons we want to give as full a picture as possible of what really happened,' the Inspector returned. 'The boss is very interested.'

PC Munro had returned to his easy chair and was obviously fighting a losing battle against sleep. He had been up most of the previous night with a drunk-in-charge whom he had to escort to Kinlochsanda. Kenneth seemed shattered, thought Angus. He studied the younger man before taking up the questioning.

'When's your sister coming?' he began conversationally.

'Today. I pick her up at the station.'

'She'll take it hard, I would think,' the Inspector commiserated. 'She was always a favourite with her father.'

'Yes,' Kenneth replied. 'Deirdre will be heartbroken.'

'I'm no' going to keep you, Ken. I know you want to get some kip, like the rest of us. James here looks as if he's been on the bash for a fortnight.' The constable jerked upright with a guilty start and his notebook fell on the floor. 'But we're trying to account for everyone's movements yesterday afternoon.' Angus looked from the fire to Kenneth who still wore his anorak, now damp with melted snow.

'Let me see,' he mused, rubbing his chin. 'I wrote a letter just after lunch. Then I went out to take a few photographs; there was nice, flat lighting, with brewing clouds and all that.'

'Where did you go?' asked the Inspector.

'Oh, just behind the house, up the hill above the glen road.'

'Did you see the stalking party?'

'To begin with, yes. They were walking slowly up the strath with Chris and I think it must have been Penelope on the left. It was difficult to tell since they were a fair way off.'

'Did you see the gillie?'

'Yes, I saw Ian as I left the house. He was just at the edge of the deer park, beyond the fence.'

'When did you get back?'

'I'm not sure; certainly before it started to snow. I got the pics I wanted.'

'I'd like to see them sometime,' Thumper remarked. 'I'm fond of that kind of shot; sort of depicts the Highlands for me – stainless steel clouds and off-white snow.'

'I'll run off a copy for you when I process them, Angus. You're quite a poet.'

'Just one more point, Ken. About the gun room. Is it usually kept locked?'

'No, the room itself isn't, but the gun lockers are, and father kept the bolts in his office safe. He was most careful about firearms; rather ironical, really.'

'Well, I'll probably be down at Grey Corries tomorrow to have a look around,' the Inspector informed him. 'I don't want anyone to leave before I give the word.'

'Well, if you say so,' Ken agreed reluctantly. 'Though they're not my choice of house guests.'

'It'll only be for a few days,' the Inspector said sympathetically.

As Kenneth rose, Angus spoke to Bookam. 'I'd better see Chris before he goes; then we'll call it a night – and what a bloody night it's been!'

Chris had been about to leave, having accepted a lift from the Kinlochsanda police, when Constable Munro collared him.

'One minute, Chris. The Inspector wants a word with you.'

'Tell him I'll give him a report on that fatal tomorrow; I'm bushed.'

'It's no' aboot that,' the policeman returned firmly. The geologist reluctantly followed him along the corridor towards the front door of the hotel.

'Ah, Chris.' Angus sounded disgustingly fresh to the geologist. 'Just a few wee details on that stalk – for the record. I have to get some things sorted out for the Chief.'

'Bloody late hour to start asking questions,' Chris muttered ungraciously as he sat down. 'Well, fire away, then let's get to bed.'

'Do you think there were three shots?'

'Yes, I guess there were,' the team leader replied promptly. 'But I didn't think so at first; it was only on reflection that I realised the last report was actually two –

to use an Irishism. It was too loud for one and, besides, the
echo wasn't right for a single shot. But it was confusing ...'

'I can well imagine,' Angus agreed. 'And you couldn't
see old Horror from where you fired your shot?'

'If you mean did I shoot him? the answer is no! And I
couldn't see him, anyhow,' he added. 'You'd have to be a
billiards champion to have bounced a bullet off some rock
and actually hit him.'

'I'm no' suggesting any such thing,' Angus returned
soothingly. 'But you know I've got to look at all the aspects
of the case.'

'Aye, I know, Angus. I guess we're all a bit tired.'

'Did you know that Ken and his old man had a set-to
the previous night?'

'Yes, I did, and if you think there's any motive there,
Angus, you're shinning up the wrong mountain. Ken and
his old man were always arguing the odds. That's what kept
them going. They're both a bit cantankerous – at least his
old man was when he was alive.'

'Did you see anybody else on the hill?'

'Not a soul. Bare as a badger's arse as far as humans
were concerned.'

'Penelope Almen was with you going up the strath,
wasn't she?'

'Yes, she's probably the best company in the whole
group. Von Spielman's a headcase, a Teutonic Walter
Mitty.'

'And Fular?'

'He's not too bad – a bit strange though for a climber.'

'What's your explanation of the incident, Chris?' Angus
asked, looking at his fingernails.

'I haven't one – but until there's more evidence, I'd
rather not think it was murder.'

'What do you think of Kirsty Gilchrist?' Angus asked the question quietly but it seemed to take the geologist off-balance.

'Kirsty? What's she got to do with it?'

'Nothing, only we got the impression that she doesn't like Ken very much.'

'Nonsense! Everybody likes Ken; he's a bit of a maverick – got a heap of chips on his shoulder – but otherwise he's okay.'

'Well, that's all, Chris If you could jot down a few notes on the Eagal Mor fatal in the next couple of days, I'd be obliged.'

'I'll do that, Angus.' Chris got up and left the room.

Willie Fyffe must have been hovering in the vicinity and now put his head round the door post.

'Can I get you anything before you go, Angus?'

'No thanks, Willie. What I need you don't serve in a bottle, and I'm going home for four hours of it!'

'Ah, it's been a long night, a long night,' the publican echoed. He glanced then across the foyer, observed that Chris and the Kinlochsanda police had left and slid surreptitiously into the room, closing the door behind him as if setting a mousetrap.

'Just a wee chat, Angus, a wee chat.' He glanced at Constable Munro with suspicion. 'And I don't want any of this breathed outside this room, Angus, no, not outside this room, for I have good relations with the Grey Corries and they give me a fair bit o' custom, aye, a fair bit ...'

'... o' custom,' James Munro couldn't resist the temptation. The publican gave him a withering glance, raised himself up to his five feet eleven inches and licked his lips before commencing.

'I liked Mr Dewar, you know, Angus. Puir man, puir man, and anything I can do to help, I will ...'

'Well, let's have it, Willie Fyffe; your hospitality is more forthcoming than your havering.'

'Just so, just so. No time these days at all. It's just that I heard there were moves afoot to get the laird to sell land down in the strath, at the bottom end.'

'Why shouldn't he sell land if he wanted to?'

'That's just it,' Willie Fyffe replied confidently now, his eyes shrewd. 'He didn't want to sell, from what I heard!'

'You hear a lot, Willie, you must have good ears,' the Inspector remarked dryly.

'That I have, Angus, that I have. It's amazing what one hears over a counter, so to speak; it's a sort of confessional sometimes.'

'And what would this party be wanting the lower strath for? It's not even good for sheep,' the Inspector retorted, rather tired of Watery's dramatic portrayal of simple facts.

'Copper.'

'Are you referring to me, derisively, or talking about the mineral?'

'The mineral, of course,' the publican answered.

'What's copper to do with it, Willie?' The policeman's voice was impatient; he didn't like talking in riddles.

'I don't know exactly, but there used to be an old copper mine down there, way back.'

'How did you come by this, Willie?' The publican seemed to be reluctant to disclose this information. Angus waited for a reply.

'It was from Horror himself,' Willie stated. 'One night on his way back from Glasgow he came in on his own and had a cider – that's about all he drank. He said: "Willie, imagine all those years and the water from Loch Gorm going to waste, then the Hydro Company comes along and builds that great pumping station and ruins the loch and some of the best fishing in the area; and the old mine which has been closed for generations, now they are wanting to re-open it and make more mess." That's almost his exact words, Angus, I remember well. Then we got talking aboot the mines over in Ardgour, the lead ones, ye ken, and I also mentioned the old copper mine on his own ground. "That's what I was referring to earlier," he said. Those were his very words, Angus, and he continued, "It would seem that they're once again a viable proposition but imagine, Willie, open-cast mine workings on the estate! Oh, we're a company now, Willie, but development won't be in my time." There may be a pickle o' money in it for ye, sir, I suggested and he replied, "I've enough to get me by until I reach for my tarpaulin jacket. I won't agree to selling, don't you worry!" And, do you know, Angus, I don't know exactly what he meant by that jacket bit; the gentry usually get buried in their kilt jackets ... I speired Chris Watkins aboot it, but he said he didn't know anything aboot any interest in the mine, though I have my doubts.'

'Did he give any hint of who was wanting the land?' Angus asked, his interest now aroused.

'No, he didn't. But from his manner I understood that he was totally agin' it – totally agin' it. He called them slick talkers and seemed a wee bit het up aboot it.'

'We'll look into it, Willie, have no fear.'

'I just thought it was my duty, Angus, my duty as a ratepayer and a' that!'

They were going outside towards the police car when the Constable spoke.

'I dont know if the Superintendent mentioned it, Angus, but that chap Fular – the one with the bright clothes – is the big wheel in American Copper Incorporated.'

'How aboot a lift doon the road?' The deep voice of Duncan MacGillvery reached them as they were about to drive off. James lowered his window.

'We thought you'd gone with the Kinlochsanda boys; jump in.'

'Isaac's here, too,' the poacher added as he came over, his large frame silhouetted against the entrance light. 'Come on, Rev,' he called to the dark figure which had just emerged from the doorway. 'We don't want to walk back on a night like this.'

'You did a lot o' work up there, Duncan,' said Angus as they passed the Eagal Mor.

'And lucky to be alive!' Isaac added.

'All in the day's night,' the poacher replied.

'Less fruitful than some of your nocturnal ploys,' Bookam retorted. 'I'm thinking of when the fish are running ...'

'Aye, you would, James, but we don't all get a steady wage with a pension after 20 years loafing aboot!'

'Two deaths in six hours or so,' Isaac murmured, ignoring the banter. 'It's a sad place.'

'Aye, we get our quota here all right, Rev,' Angus agreed.

'You seemed to be asking a lot o' questions about old Horror's death, Angus,' Duncan ventured, slightly distracted by the Constable's carefree driving, the car was waltzing all over the road.

'I don't suppose you were on the hill today, Duncan?' The Inspector turned round.

'Just for a wee walk before the snow came, Angus.'

'Where to?'

The poacher thought furiously. He had been seen crossing the Glen Liath road that afternoon by Donnie the Post; he knew Donnie wouldn't normally say anything but with the laird being shot, one could never be sure ... The postman was an Elder in the Kirk and a staunch Free Presbyterian into the bargain. He decided to make a clean breast of things for, after all, he had nothing to hide.

'I was going to see you aboot that in the mornin', Angus. I felt it was a bit late the night.'

'You knew damned well – excuse me, Isaac – that it's never too late for the truth! Give ...'

Duncan gave him a quick run-down of what he had seen, omitting the fact that he had his rifle with him.

'So you just went for a stroll, Duncan, over several miles o' peat hag, to see if the Glen Liath guests were enjoying themselves?'

'I never dreamt there were any guests there. Imagine, selling the hind shooting and the estate keeping the beasts. It's Highland robbery!'

'Some people enjoy fishing, shooting and stalking legally,' Bookam observed as he took a corner as if he were in the RAC rally.

'And you only saw the stalking party, no-one else?'

'No, no-one, but of course I couldn't see into that big gully.'

'How many shots did you hear, Duncan?' Angus continued, watching the road ahead.

'Three.'

'Are you sure?'

'Of course I'm bloody well sure. Do you think I'm deaf?'

'Watty Gilchrist wasn't so definite.'

'Weel, Watty should have his ears examined. Anyhow you can't tell me that that keeper didn't hear all three shots. Why, he can detect a car back-firing in Kinlochsanda from his shithouse. Mind you, if he was alongside one o' the guns at the time it might have been more difficult.'

'Do you have a rifle, Duncan?'

'No, Angus, the police relieved me o' it a while back. Pity that, for it was father's and I cherished it.'

'I can imagine,' replied Angus briefly.

'And you've fine lungs for that .270 folding magnum blowpipe of yours,' Bookam observed wryly.

'Did you hear a ricochet?' the Inspector asked the poacher.

'Aye, I did. I thocht at the time it was bloody dangerous wi' all those fools on the hill. That's when I decided to head for quieter places.'

'Well, I'll have to get a written statement from you tomorrow, Duncan,' Angus said. 'Hey, Constable,' he addressed James in terse tones. 'Take that big foot of yours off that bloody accelerator or we'll be joining the all-night party in the morgue.'

They drove in silence until Duncan spoke again. 'I hear Mrs McWhirter is poorly,' he observed to no-one in particular.

'The doc was in seeing her yesterday, is that right, Isaac?' The Constable spoke as he slowed down for some deer which were crossing the road.

'I'm sorry to say that is the case,' the minister replied gravely. 'She is getting rather frail now.'

'The old lady has been a great benefactress to the village,' the Inspector interjected. 'But it's strange,' he continued, looking at the bank of snow alongside the road, 'that your cousin Chris never got on with her.'

'I was just saying to Chris a short time ago that both he and our aunt are too stubborn. There seems to be a line of pig-headedness in our family.'

Bookam said under his breath – you can say that again.

Chapter 6

Sergeant Archie Campbell and Inspector Thumper Wilson were in a police car heading round the edge of Loch Sanda towards the village of Faileadh. A long, low light gave the loch a metallic sheen and the snowy hills completed a picture of arctic sobriety. Archie, who was driving, took this for granted. The road had been re-gritted that morning and the rustle of sand could be heard chortling in the wheel arches.

'The Super asked me to have a word with the Honourable Mrs Dewar this morning, Angus. Are you wanting to handle that?'

'Yes, I'd better, Archie. I'm having a look at the bealach anyhow. I think I'll take Duncan along.'

'Good idea,' the Sergeant agreed. Angus had already brought him up to speed with the late night developments on the case. 'He's a reliable bloke, Duncan. Straight as a caber and would give you his last penny and he's quite a brain box, he's a district chess champion.'

'Pity there's no' more like him aboot,' the Inspector

agreed, thinking of all the neds with whom he had to deal. 'A bit o' poaching never did the estates any harm. Mony's the time I took a beast mysel' when I was younger – he must be bright to keep one step ahead o' the keepers.'

'Is PC Munro coming wi' us?'

'No, we'll leave him be, he needs his sleep. Let's see what he can dig up locally; not much, I'm thinking ... Old Hector MacAndrew gave us the run-down on the will this morning,' the Inspector continued.

'And ...?' The Sergeant glanced at his colleague.

'Well, the estate is owned by the company. Horatio had it for his lifetime and the old dear stays on at the Lodge if she so desires until she also kicks the proverbial bucket. She's plenty of money of her own, I gather. There's an allowance for Deirdre. Watty gets £1,000.'

'And Kenneth?'

'Ten grand, seeing how he does all right with his photography and he and Deirdre will inherit from their mum.'

'So both Ken and Watty will have benefitted from the old man's death,' Archie observed.

'Aye. People have been murdered for much less,' the Inspector agreed.

Duncan was cutting firewood when the two policemen arrived.

'Mornin', MacGillvery. Fine day.'

'It is that, Angus. Seems as if we're going to get a thaw, though.'

'Aye.' The Inspector looked up at the clouds to the west; they appeared to be smothering the hills like wet sphagnum moss. 'We could do with a bit o' soft weather to find the rifle and that bullet.'

'You heading there now?' Duncan leant on his axe and brought a hand over his brow.

'Would you care to come and gi' a hand? I'd like to see where the laird was shot.'

'Just wait till I get my jacket, then,' the poacher replied and went into the house. He lived alone in his small, ivy-covered cottage, prim and fresh with its white painted windows. Smoke trickled from the chimney and the fragrant tang of peat reached out to the policemen.

'He keeps his place nice, does Duncan,' Archie observed.

'Aye, a bonny hoose,' Angus agreed.

'See that wee shed up the back there?' Archie pointed towards a clump of trees at the bottom of the garden.

'Aye.'

'Well, he's got a 30 cubic foot freezer in there, and the number of butchered beasts he can stuff into it, including salmon, is certainly not our business!'

'But he's a big man, Sergeant, with a big appetite!' They were both laughing as Duncan came back along the path. Angus noted that he had already repaired his jacket in a series of long racing stitches.

Miss Deirdre was with her mother when the two policemen were shown in. Duncan waited in the car. The Inspector introduced himself and Archie. He didn't fail to notice that the daughter had dark circles round her eyes. She was an attractive girl, he mused, sort of bambi-like. Once seated, Angus cleared his throat.

'I'm sorry to have to bother you at such a time, Mrs Dewar, but I would like to ask you one or two questions.'

The second day widow was a woman of ample proportions; her grey hair was immaculate but thin. She wore a plain dark green dress which matched her fading, but still compelling, green eyes. A pair of glittering earrings adorned her small shapely ears. She looked haughtily at the two

policemen as if they were beings from another planet. The
Honourable Mrs Dewar was a woman of fortitude and
breeding. Though she had passed a sleepless night, she had
quickly accepted the situation. She had married Horatio more
than 58 years previously, when she was a slip of a girl, and
had become inured to his long absences at sea. Since his retirement they had seldom stirred from Glen Liath. Now she came
straight to the point without any show of emotion.

'Kenneth tells me there seems to be some confusion over
which shot killed my husband?'

'That's just the trouble, ma'am,' Angus replied, regarding
a fine piece of Dresden china on the table beside him. 'We're
trying to shed some light on the matter.'

'Well, it's not much use asking me about it. I'm not up
in ballistics and I have never stalked in my life.'

'I realise that,' the Inspector ventured. 'But perhaps you
can give us other details?'

'For example?' She looked severely at the policeman
and her slightly irritable tone didn't go unnoticed by the
Inspector.

'Did you know that your husband had been approached
to sell part of the estate?'

'I knew that a London agent had asked him if he was
interested in selling the old Glen Liath mine, but that was
some time ago. And, of course, Horatio would never have
dreamt of disposing of any of the land. Probably the company was wanting to ...' she paused for a moment and
added, '... jump the gun!'

'How did they find out about it?' Angus persisted.

'That I don't know. I do remember some reference to
old records which one can still obtain on mining concerns.
I think they quoted from those. Isn't there a Department of
Mines, or some such bureaucratic place?'

'But surely they must have had someone to have a fresh look at it; why, the mine could have fallen in by this time. After all, it hasn't been worked for 60 years!'

'Young man,' the Honourable Mrs Victoria spoke with ill-concealed impatience, 'as far as I know, no-one has been in the old workings for ages and there are such things as the Ordnance Survey and a geological survey of the valley.' The Inspector swallowed. He felt he wasn't handling this interview too well and out of the corner of his eye he fancied he saw a smile playing round the silent Sergeant's lips.

'He didn't ask Chris Watkins for his opinion on the matter?'

'He did not. What was the point? He wasn't interested in developing it and he had the last say in any such matter. But I recollect that Chris did bring the matter up not so long ago; just a comment I overheard that the mine might be worth looking at one day.'

'Was this remark made to your late husband?' asked Angus.

'Yes. It was just a vague statement to no-one in particular, but Horatio thought it was directed at him, and he suggested that Chris might have a look round it if he wished. "Have to be careful, though, Chris," I remember him saying. "The old shaft's in a bad way, now." Horatio put a fence across the entrance after the Second World War, but that's fallen down. "I must tell Watty to repair it sometime, Victoria," he said to me at the time. But it was never done ...'

'Did Chris Watkins inspect the workings?'

'I don't really know, Inspector. I certainly never heard any more about it.'

'If you'll excuse me, Inspector,' Deirdre interrupted with a wan smile, 'I'll go and finish unpacking. Ken picked me up from the station only a short time ago.'

'Certainly, Miss Dewar.' The two men rose as she left
the room.

'Did your late husband know that Mr Clem Fular is the
President of American Copper Incorporated?'

'That terrible man? I have never seen anyone so desecrate
the national dress; he wears a kilt, would you believe, and
the Campbell tartan to boot.' She spoke vehemently and
gave a sidelong glance at the Sergeant. 'Horatio didn't
bother much about the occupations of his guests,' she
added in aloof tones. 'He only tolerated them because he
felt that the estate should be run as a business nowadays,
due to the crippling taxes.'

'Did you have any conversation with the stalkers
yesterday?'

'No, I didn't, Inspector.'

'Did you go out at all?'

'I went for a short walk, Inspector, but I'm not as young
as I used to be and seldom manage more than a hundred
yards. I didn't see any sign of the stalking party, though I
did see the gillie.'

'Kenneth was out as well – did you see him?'

'So he told me, Inspector, but I didn't see him.'

'We will have to consider that your husband's death was
not necessarily accidental,' Angus told her gravely.

'I should think that's an obvious conclusion from what
I've heard, Inspector.'

'Well, many thanks, madam. We will try to be as unob-
trusive as possible in our inquiries.'

'Well! She kept you on your toes, Angus.' Archie gave a
short laugh as they went down the stairs to the main hall.
Six mounted stags' heads adorned the wall on their right.

'I notice you weren't loquacious, Sergeant,' the Inspector

retorted dryly. 'She probably thought you were the original dumb policeman! Ah, Watty,' he addressed the keeper who was just going out the front door, putting on his cap.

'So it's you, Angus. Are you wanting to go up the hill?'

'Aye. I've got Duncan here, too – he's in the car.'

'Duncan?' the keeper queried.

'He saw the shooting yesterday and he'll show us exactly where the laird was lying.'

'And I know what he was doing up there. I'll get him one o' these bloody days.'

'Where are the guests?' asked Archie.

'They've gone over to Kinlochsanda, shopping, I think. If you'll just hold on a meenite, I'll fetch my stick.'

The four now followed the same line as the stalk of the previous day, Watty leading over the rough ground. Eventually, he stopped at the place where the shots had been fired.

'I was standing right here and Spielman dropped doon jest by that rock there.' He pointed to where snow was melting off a granite boulder. 'Chris and that titless Sassenach were over there, aboot a couple o' hundred feet away, by the clump o' heather.'

'Where exactly was Dewar lying?' Angus screwed up his eyes, for the sun was slanting low over the peak to their left and it was difficult to see well.

'See the bealach?'

'Yes.'

'Weel, come doon this way, a wee bitty left, and there's a flat area of ground below that blackish cliff. Well, it was aboot there – ye can't quite see it from here though. What dae ye say, Duncan?'

'That's the place all right; we'll spy it better as we go up the slope on our right,' the poacher affirmed.

Watty's Jack Russell was digging under the snow; quantities of peaty earth were cascading upwards.

'That dog's got a good nose, Watty,' Archie observed.

'Aye, Gealeas is a terror for the foxes; but she'll be after voles the noo ... I must go doon to the den by the auld mine: there's a vixen there that's been dodging me this last couple o' years; she moved her cubs twice this year. Chris was going to give me a hand.'

'Talking about Chris,' Angus said. 'Was he using one of the Lodge rifles yesterday?'

'That's right,' Watty affirmed. 'The old .303; he likes that gun.'

'And von Spielman's was a big calibre rifle: a .375 Mannlicher?'

'Aye, he says he used it to shoot a wild elephant once. A'm thinking that's the size o' target he'd need; the man's glaikit.'

They spoke little until they reached a gully. Duncan, in the lead, glanced upwards into it. From it spewed a large boulder field, running out on to the snow-covered peat and heather of the strath. He turned to Angus who was already studying the terrain.

'How about you two going up there and finding the best spot for a shot at where the laird was lying?' Watty gave him a quick glance.

'It's no' my line o' country: shooting lairds, Angus, but I ken what yer after. Come on, Duncan.'

The two men trudged off, their movements deceptively easy and swift. Archie realised just how much they had slowed their pace for himself.

'Good idea, that, Inspector.' There was a touch of admiration in his voice.

'As I said, Archie, I've done a bit o' stalking in my time,

but these lads have a better eye than me ... What did Watty say about the rifles at the Lodge?'

'There's one missing.'

'You get the details of it then, this could be important?'

I have a copy with me. By the way Angus, what did the Chief have to say this morning?'

A shout came from above, 'Angus!'

'Come on, Sergeant. Looks like they've got something.'

'It could be anywhere aboot here,' Watty said to Angus when they arrived, moving his stick in a wide semicircle. 'Duncan favours up the hill a bit, says there's more cover for getting into the gully from over the top.' The poacher was standing about a hundred feet above them.

'We'll just go up that bit further and see, Watty, but this is a likely place.' They moved up and joined Duncan. Angus looked back towards the col.

'You can see the laird's flat bit of ground now, Angus.' The Inspector followed Duncan's outstretched arm.

'This is where I'd have shot the old bugger if I did that sort of thing,' the Sergeant observed.

'So this spot is your hot favourite, Duncan?' Angus asked.

'Aye,' Toń confirmed. 'It gives a better angle than Watty's place. It offers a fine view o' the laird's position, I must say.' He swept his eyes upwards to the top of the low ridge. 'Hmm,' he pondered. 'It wouldn't be difficult to keep under cover coming down to here.'

'That's what I thought, Duncan,' Angus affirmed. 'Watty's place is just that wee bit more exposed to the strath ... Archie,' the Inspector addressed his colleague.

'Yes?'

'I want a thorough search made of this whole gully, starting with Watty's position and working up past here to

the top. Better get that police dog – Carl, I think he's called
– he might turn something up other than a fox turd.

'I'll see to that, sir,' Archie replied. 'But I think I'll give
up my pipe if I've much more o' this hill bashing to do,' he
muttered, taking out his tartan handkerchief. 'It's no good
for man nor beast.'

'It doesn't do the beasts any harm, nor you neither, I'm
thinking, Archie Campbell!'

'You may be right at that, Duncan.'

'Watty,' Archie addressed the keeper. 'Did you know
that rifle No. 6500321 is missing – the .270?'

'Is that so, Archie? From where?'

'The Lodge.'

'Oh?'

'Yes, a high velocity one. A Weatherby magnum' The
keeper looked at him in astonishment.

'But it was there yesterday; I saw it. As a matter of fact,
I was going to give it to Penelope, but she didn't want to
shoot.'

'It wasn't in the gun room last night, when we removed
the other rifles.' The Sergeant cut in.

'Well, well,' Watty mused, pushing his fore and after up
and rubbing his nose. 'A powerful gun that. It has a good
scope as well. I was going to make a check on the gun
cabinet today.'

'A bit late' the Sergeant retorted.'

'I think we're going to be lucky to find whatever gun
may have been used, even if it's up here' Angus said. 'We
have to get the bullet as well Archie, we'll start a sweep for
both this afternoon. Now, let's go down and inspect where
Dewar was found.'

He was shown the place to which the laird had rolled
and where his rifle was found by Watty. Then they went to

the heathery ledge under the small cliff, but the Inspector kept them away from the place where the laird had been lying in wait, according to Duncan.

'I don't want everyone tramping over the snow here, like Hannibal's elephants,' he explained. 'I've an idea but we may have to wait until the snow has melted. Make sure those buggers with the big feet from Kinlochsanda don't stampede up here, Archie.'

'Right, Inspector.'

'Now, Duncan, just explain to us how Horror was lying, will you?'

'Dr Khan speaking.' The chubby Pakistani doctor spoke rapidly; indeed he seemed to do everything rapidly, even the most demanding consultation.

'It's Chris here, doctor. I was wondering how my aunt was?'

'Not too good, Chris. She's an old woman, you know.'

'I heard that, doctor. Perhaps I had better call and see her.'

'Why not?' the Pakistani replied instantly. 'Why not, she is your aunt after all. But don't stay long, Chris; she's not a well woman and the laird's death has hit her more than she'd like to admit.'

'I won't. Maybe I'll go with Isaac. He's visiting her today.'

'Good idea.' Dr Khan abruptly put the phone down; he was already thinking about his next patient.

Chris declined a lift on the pillion of Isaac's motor cycle when he went up to the manse. He persuaded Isaac to go in his car. They were silent as they drove to their aunt's house, a large rambling mansion hidden amidst a profusion of trees. As they turned into the long drive between the rhododendrons, Chris broke an awkward silence. 'I hope this isn't going to be unpleasant, Isaac. Dr Khan said she's in a bad way.'

'It doesn't have to be, Chris,' the minister replied evenly. 'When did you last see her?'

Chris screwed up his eyes, glancing at the sky, as if reflecting on the question and its implications. 'It must be 18 months, I guess.'

'Don't you feel a bit guilty?'

'Not really, Isaac. We were never close, as you know.'

'Both Chris and Isaac's parents had been killed in the same car crash when Chris was at primary school. He had been brought up in England by a friend of the family, while Mrs McWhirter had more or less adopted Isaac. They had seen little of each other in the intervening years, until Chris came to stay in the village.

'It seems a pity, Chris. Let's hope she recognises us; she didn't know me when I was last here.'

'I didn't know it was as bad as that,' the geologist murmured with what, Isaac felt, was real concern.

'Oh, some days she's as right as rain,' Isaac said as the car drew to a halt. 'Other days ...'

Duncan was up late and he was in deep thought. The peat fire had been smoored to a warm heap of aromatic embers awaiting to be revived at dawn with a few prods from an old World War One bayonet which in retirement served as a poker. It was when holding this survivor of more turbulent times that Duncan paused. It made him think of another war souvenir which had been lying in an old tin trunk under his bed for years. His logical brain of a chess expert clicked into gear and in a flash he had resolved in a course of action which would be put in operation at 8.30 a.m. that morning – when the school at Kinlochsanda opened its gates.

John Cassidy, a science master at Kinlochsanda High School was surprised to see Duncan in the staff car park when he arrived. The poacher was leaning on the bonnet of his van.

'Good morning, Duncan, you are a bit early to enrol for our archaeological group – it won't be up an running again until spring.'

'Well, John, indirectly, that's what I'm here about, but I may be back later to help on your excavation of the old dun.'

John, who cycled to work each day dismounted and pushed his bicycle into the adjoining bike shelter and came over. He had great respect for this big highlander.

'Rather a strange request, John,' Duncan straightened up. 'I'm here to borrow your group's metal detector. Let me give you a quick run down of events.' He then outlined the circumstances of the death of Captain Horatio Dewar.

'So your wanting to find the bullet?'

'Just so,' Duncan returned. 'I have been helping the police in a small way and the rescue team seems involved even if we don't want to be.'

It was exactly 10.40 a.m. when Duncan reached the point where he had judged the fatal shot had been fired from which killed the laird. There were a couple of small marker flags left by the police. He hadn't seen a soul since parking his van at the layby far. There was no sign of police activity either. But he could see yellow police marker tape indicating Horror's position below. He put his rucksack on the ground, which was still partly snow-covered and took out a telescope and a pair of Bosch and Lomb 7 x 50 binoculars. Then he carefully laid out an old Team bivvy bag on the ground behind a boulder. 'May as well make myself comfortable,' he muttered to himself, 'this may take some time.' Duncan realised that the visibility was almost perfect as he checked every rock in the close proximity of where Horror had been positioned when he was shot. Any sign of a recent mark on bed rock or boulders was then double checked by using his powerful telescope with the stone in front of him acting as a tripod.

After over two hours his eyes were getting sore with the strain of concentration of the meticulous search when he noticed a lighter mark on a rock. It took some time to find it again using the telescope despite the fact that he had memorised positioning clues.

'Good God,' he shouted out loud, 'I've found it.'

He was right as he confirmed a short time later. The location was about 50 feet from the yellow markers at the laird's position. The high velocity bullet had sheared a shard out of the surface of a rock, leaving a distinct groove indicating that the round had deflected at a tangent of about 40 degrees towards the side of the ridge, towards where the laird had been waiting.

Duncan sat down for minute and surveyed the ground below. He could see the path stamped out on the snow below by many police boots, but there was still no sign of them returning so far. 'Now for the long shot,' he mused as he reached into his rucksack and pulled out a case in which was a powerful Zeiss sniper sight, souvenir present from his brother when he returned from war in 1946. It had resided beneath his bed for years for he never had an inclination to use it as he felt it would have given him an unfair advantage over the deer. With difficulty he positioned himself so that the top side of the scope was resting on the rock groove and when he looked through it he was amazed at the clarity of the 50mm objective lens. It showed the exact position where he estimated the laird had been lying. Beyond this a tiny rowan sapling was framed protruding from the snow like a symbol of spring and hope. It took some time to verify the samplings location with the binoculars and then he prepared to set off on the last phase of his plan. It was an experiment he realised, with odds stacked against it, he knew that the bullet could have continued through the side of the lairds neck on its trajectory from the rock, arse over tit as they would say in the Team, and be a long way from that vibrant little rowan. Before leaving the rock he put a strip of fluorescent marker tape which they used on rescues alongside with a stone to hold it down and took a close up photograph of the scar with his camera.

Twenty minutes later he had found the rowan and took the metal detector from his rucksack and assembled it. The next part of the search process was familiar for him, from avalanche work, only instead of using a probe or an avalanche transceiver he would use the metal detector. First he marked the slope out in 50 feet squares using small stones as cairn markers, then methodically grid searched each designated area. The light was beginning to fade before he heard the positive bleep over the headphones and in seconds he had pinpointed the spot. At exactly 4.15 p.m. he dug out a bullet with his ice axe and lay back in the snow elated. Deep down he never thought this scheme would work and was amazed that the bullet was only a few feet from the rowan. Quickly he put the round in a small plastic bag and stowed the equipment back in his pack. Despite the distortion, he was sure that it was the bullet. It had fresh scars on the casing. He finished off by marking the spot with the fluorescent tape and took a further photo for good measure.

By the time he had fed the cat and had a meal he concluded that it would be better to get the bullet to the Inspector ASAP. He uncovered his old typewriter and spent sometime composing a detailed account of the day's activities.

When he read it over he put into an envelope with the bullet and the roll of film and addressed it to the Inspector, then phoned Angus, who was back home.

'This is Duncan, Angus,' he stated when the big policeman answered.

'Well what can I do for you, Duncan? Don't tell me it's another call out.'

'No, some good news for a change, I found the bullet...'

'What the hell, where, how?'

Duncan gave him an account of his morning's activities and concluded: 'I've typed a full statement and I'll drop it off with the bullet and the film at the police station in about half an hour.

'Right,' the Inspector returned, taken aback at the news. 'I'll get forensics onto it right away and have the film processed. 'I'll see you tomorrow morning.'

'That's a date, Angus.'

It was a fine morning and Duncan thought he would do some shopping after seeing the Inspector. It was after midday by the time he drew into the police car park in Kinlochsanda. He didn't come any earlier as he knew that the Inspector would be still dealing with the information from last night.

'Good morning, Sadie,' Duncan greeted the secretary. 'Is the boss in?'

'He certainly is, Duncan.' She gave him a warm smile. 'I'm sure he'll be glad to see you.'

'Is that you, MacGillvery?' Angus's voice bellowed from the open door of his room. 'Tell that girl o'mine to bring some ritual tea in, will you. You've got some explaining to do.'

'I can hear even if you whisper, Inspector,' she shouted back, 'and the kettle's on.' She raised her eyes to the ceiling and gave Duncan a smile and drew her hand across her throat.

'Aye, I guessed that, Sadie,' the big man whispered and gave a chuckle as he moved to Angus' office.

It was an hour and a half later before Angus was satisfied he had gleaned everything from Duncan.

'MacGillvery,' he addressed the tweeded figure, 'I don't know if I should recommend you for an award or throw the proverbial book at you.'

'The charge, Inspector?' Duncan grinned. 'Saving police time? You know, Angus,' he continued, 'I thought I was being a fool trying to find that bullet. That high velocity round could have gone over the ridge to Faileadh. As we know, the area was far too big to search at random with a metal detector and I would have looked an idiot waving that poncy wand round that huge corrie.'

Chapter 7

Thomas 'Tombstone' Kirkpatrick had a job to do that morning. There was a grave to dig or, as he professionally termed it, a lair. It was for a deceased pensioner who had been a drinking crony of Tombstone's for many years. As he spat on his hands and took up his spade, he thought of past times, lingering regretfully over the qualities of Bob's missus; Beryl was a fair lass in those days ... Bob Scott had been awkward though, even in death. Here he was, having to clear away the snow before he could even get at the ground. After a few minutes he took up a half bottle and fortified himself with a dram. Then he picked and cursed at the old glacier moraine which lay under the sparse turf. It took four hours to reach the regulation depth of six feet. Then he straightened up, feeling every one of his 68 years in successive stabs of pain. Taking a last medicinal swig, he wiped his mouth with the back of his hand. Then he gave a drawn-out sigh, placed his spade against the wall of the grave and, using it as a step ladder, extricated himself from the hole with a stiffness painful to watch. Someone did watch – from a distance – and turned away thoughtfully.

'Is the Reverend in, Mrs Watt?' The Inspector asked the prodigiously fat housekeeper.

'Yes, Inspector, he's in his laboratory. He's lost something, I think; he said he was looking for more BHP, whatever that means!'

Angus gave a wry smile. 'I'll just go and have a word with him. Thanks, I know the way.'

As Angus made his way along the snow-covered pathway which led round the back of the house, then on to the church, he met 'Hellfire' McColl, an Elder of the Church, and general factotum of this place of worship. He glared at Angus as if the Inspector had just strangled a new-born child. His fresh-coloured complexion was in contrast to his tight-lipped expression.

'And what does the Law want with my kirk?' he demanded with hostility. Hellfire was a tall, bony man, clad in black, with a stiff stoop, like a part-open pocket knife. He held a gardening fork.

'I'm here to see the Reverend, Elijah,' Thumper replied civilly, using the verger's proper name.

'He'll be tinkering with that devil machine, no doubt,' Hellfire replied, spitting out the words.

'At least it allows him to get round his parishioners,' the Inspector defended the absent minister.

'In my young days the minister walked round his flock!' Hellfire retorted, driving the fork into the edge of the snow-covered lawn with a flourish. 'They didn't rush aboot on chariots of fire!'

'Well, it didn't cost the congregation anything ... It was very generous of Mrs McWhirter to buy the motor cycle for him,' said Angus.

'It will bring hellfire in its wake,' Hellfire himself predicted. 'That infernal machine ...' He raised a dramatic skeletal finger in the direction of the sombre granite church. 'Other meenisters have served oor kirk since 1897, withoot them needing motor cycles.' As the Inspector had already heard of the motor cycle controversy he refused to be drawn into it now.

'Well, I'll be seeing you, Elijah,' he said pleasantly as he skirted round the Elder. 'I want a word with the Reverend Isaac.' Hellfire extracted his fork as if drawing a claymore from its scabbard and headed in the direction of the peat stack.

Isaac's laboratory – as he liked to call his workshop – was a low wooden structure behind the manse. Just as Angus was entering, the morning was fragmented by a roar: a strange sight met his gaze. The minister was dressed in immaculate white overalls, with a chequered flag monogram over the breast pocket. He still wore his dog collar and also an ancient pair of headphones; a wise precaution, thought Thumper, to prevent premature deafness. A look of concentration was etched on his sharp features and there was an oily mark above his moustache. The motor cycle was mounted on a robust steel stand with the rear end of the machine pointing out of an open window. He was busily adjusting the exhausts. Suddenly, he noticed the open door and gave a start before quickly shutting the engine off. The building still seemed to vibrate with the noise. He removed his headphones and placed them carefully over a small bench anvil. He was very methodical. Angus looked round the lab. It was well fitted out with tools, presses, a precision lathe, vertical drills and a milling machine.

'Good morning, Inspector,' the Reverend greeted him. 'A social call?'

'Sort of, Isaac. That thing makes more noise than Concorde!' He cleared his ear with a large forefinger but the ringing persisted.

'I was tuning the pipes, as they say, Inspector – it was suffering from megaphonites,' the minister explained defensively. 'Of course, I don't take it out on the road like this!'

'Of course not, Reverend,' Thumper smiled. 'I'm surprised that the late parishioners don't complain!' He nodded towards the small graveyard behind the church which could be seen through the open window.

'I'm getting about 100 BHP out of the engine, now, Angus,' the minister enthused. 'And I've got 110 degree overlap cams fitted. That, with the compression ratio up to 10:1, should make it the most potent motor cycle on the west coast of Scotland.'

'Aye, it's quite a machine.' The Inspector looked at the gleaming array of pipes and polished alloy. 'It's a pity there's a statutory speed limit, now,' he added dryly with a twinkle in his eye.

'Uhmm, quite so, Inspector – quite so,' Isaac replied, slightly embarrassed.

'I was just wanting to have a few words about Horatio, Reverend,' Angus said. He perched himself on the edge of a long bench on which was an array of tools and testing equipment. 'How well do you know the Dewar family, Isaac?'

The minister, who had picked up a pair of pliers, idly toyed with these and put them down again before replying.

'Not all that well. Horatio did come to church on occasion, but he was not a member. From time to time I called in to see them and like yourself, Inspector, I know Kenneth quite well. I'm afraid I can't be of much help to you. But why these questions? Surely the laird's death was an accident?'

'I hope it was, Isaac. But we're not so sure now. You see, only two shots were fired by the stalking party and neither of these shots could have killed him, yet a further shot was fired.'

There was a look of concern on the minister's face. 'I

gathered that from what I heard in the car, when you questioned Duncan MacGillvery. Is it murder?'

'Too early to say, but we'll have to conduct our investigation with an open mind until there is some satisfactory explanation. As that bullet removed part of his neck it's going to take some explaining!' Angus moved to the door. 'Well, thanks, Isaac, we'll no doubt get to the bottom of it. Did you detect any friction between Ken and his father?'

'No, Inspector. I thought that they were on good terms. As a matter of fact I'm sure they were, though they didn't see eye to eye over the "exploitation of the estate", as Ken called the stalking. But he has my sympathies there.'

The policeman, as he looked at his fellow rescuer, realised that he had never got to know this small, alert cleric very well; the chilly barrier of his extreme views on matters of religion had seen to that. Angus himself had been more or less ostracised by his father – who was of the same church as Isaac – and the Inspector had developed a subconscious antipathy towards the sect. He thought now of all the hours spent listening to protracted sermons on hard deal pews, and of his father's remorseless piety, whence the family had been denied even the simple comforts of life. Isaac wasn't as hard as his father had been but there was still a fanaticism evident which reminded him of a snappy dog. He wondered what suspicions of old Horror's case the minister really harboured – if any.

'What about Mr Fular, Reverend?' Angus picked up a micrometer and fiddled with it, at the same time glancing at the minister.

'I wouldn't know about that American,' Isaac replied distainfully. 'I only saw him once – the other day. His choice of attire reflects a sad defect in his make-up.'

'A coat of many colours, Isaac?'

The minister placed a hand on the seat of his motor cycle and looked evenly at the Inspector. A glint kindled in his dark eyes and he spoke as if reiterating his weekly purges on the sins of the world and Faileadh in particular. 'They stripped Joseph out of his coat, his coat of many colours that was on him; and they took him and cast him into a pit.'

Those words of the minister proved to be remarkably prophetic ...

Anyone walking past the graveyard of Faileadh that night would have been astounded upon hearing the strange noises emanating from the freshly dug grave. Its very live occupant was wielding Tombstone Kirkpatrick's pick, surreptitiously 'borrowed' from the tool shed by the gate. As he dug, he considered the risk he was taking – a grave risk, he thought, giving a tight smile.

Not long after the nocturnal digger had finished his task, Duncan arrived back home from a late visit to the hill with two hinds safely in the back of his van under an old tarpaulin. He reversed the vehicle alongside the house. The south-westerly wind had now brought snow and it was warmer. A dreich night, he thought to himself as he carried the hinds to the shed close by his house.

Isaac had finally completed his fire and brimstone sermon when he heard a tap at the window. He looked at the clock; it was well after midnight – he hadn't realised the time. 'Who on earth can that be?' he muttered. 'Bit too late for kids to be playing pranks.' Putting on his slippers, for he always went about the house in stockinged feet, he opened the back door. There was no-one there. He walked along to the window on the east side, from where he had heard the tapping. It was in a narrow passageway between the house wall and an outbuilding, leading to the coal-house. It was bleak and he looked down the alley – no-one there either. Strange, he thought. He was about to turn to go back to the house when a blackness darker than night descended. He didn't fall to the ground for he was caught by powerful arms.

Thomas Kirkpatrick was in the habit of 'taking a bit of air', as he phrased his constitutional to his cousin with whom he lodged. She was a staunch member of the church and a distant relative of Hellfire McColl. To Mairie MacIntyre it would have been more acceptable to have a case of TNT in the house than a bottle of whisky. Tombstone had to exercise the most artful deceit to pursue his hobby ... Even his shed at the kirk yard wasn't safe enough to keep a bottle. No, he had his own hidey-hole, so his amble that night, like many a night before, took him in the direction of the churchyard. Mairie was always in bed by midnight and there was no fear of her smelling his breath when he returned. Some locals, occasionally espying his slow and dedicated nightly tread to the last resting place of the populace of Faileadh, thought he was endeavouring to make peace with his Maker or contemplating where he would eventually be taking his own long rest; others knew the truth.

It was raining steadily and the gate of the churchyard was ajar, so no familiar creak came from it. He could see a light at the back of the manse and was surprised to see Isaac up so late. Working on his sermon, no doubt; this was the night he wrote it – more references to the evils of drink, he thought glumly. If Hellfire saw a light burning at this late hour in the manse he would be surely gathering his brows, condemning the minister's extravagance.

The 'new' bottle which Tombstone had secreted under the

wire mesh of a galvanised flower container on the grave of the
late Lachy MacMaster – who, incidentally, had died from
cirrhosis of the liver – was more than half full. He unscrewed
it with a sigh of anticipation and had it poised at his lips
when he heard a scraping noise nearby, What little hair he
had left stood to attention on the back of his neck and he
felt his long flannel shirt soak up a cold perspiration. He
stood motionless, unable to move, even to have received a
free gift of a distillery! The noise came from the fresh grave.
He could see it only dimly: it was a dark night and his eyesight wasn't that good – he really should have worn glasses
but, like his false teeth, he usually left them on the wee
dresser beside his bed.

The prospect of savouring his whisky had caused
Thomas to emit a loud belch. It had a dramatic effect: a
phantom-like figure leapt out from the grave and ran
between the gravestones to the boundary wall of the
churchyard, disappearing over the wall. Later he swore that
it didn't ever touch the ground ... Swallowing most of the
contents of the bottle in one long, frantic gurgle, he moved
unsteadily over to his day's labours and saw in the dim light
that the boards he had placed over the grave had been
removed. He cursed in a most unchristian manner and
peered inside. He could just discern his pick and the gleam
of his spade. He had put them away in the shed – he
remembered that distinctly – for he had cleaned them and
given the spade a polish, maintaining that a polished spade
made light work.

Had it not been for the fortification from the Talisker,
he would have turned tail and run when he heard the moan.
But Bob was not yet buried and, anyhow, the crateur was dead
and lying in his front parlour; he hadn't taken up permanent
residence. So he took a box of matches from his pocket and

after several attempts succeeded in lighting one. The shake in his hands was not only attributable to his 68 years or the whisky ... Directly below him were two feet, or rather the toe of a slipper and on the other foot a toe sticking out of a black sock. He blinked and stared until the match eventually burned his fingers. Then, letting out another oath, he struck another match. This time the moan that came from under the earth and stones sounded human enough. There was no doubting that, so he lowered himself into the grave, with his feet astride the victim, and gently removed the covering of earth and stones with the spade. He finished off the job with his bare hands and he could feel first smooth cloth, then a face ... Slipping his hands underneath the armpits, he slowly lifted the buried victim into an upright position. In so doing he fell back so that he was sitting on the still covered legs. There was a spluttering and retching as the exhumed man spat out grit and earth.

After a few minutes the coughing became more controlled and Tombstone was greeted by semi-delirious ramblings. They sounded strangely familiar and he recognised them as snatches from the Bible. Eventually, he asked in an unsteady voice:

'Is it you, then, Reverend?'

'Where am I?' Isaac's voice was high-pitched with a hysterical edge.

'Ye're in the grave, man,' Tombstone informed him. 'Where dae ye think ye are?' His hands were still supporting the other's armpits.

'The grave?'

'Aye, Bob's grave. The yin a' dug today!'

'Who are you?' Isaac's voice seemed suddenly cool and calculating, suspicious. Too many thoughts were crowding in and his mind couldn't take it.

'It's me – Thomas Kirkpatrick. I heard a noise here at the new lair, so I came over and I saw someone – or something – going away like a bat out o' hell.'

'A grave?' Isaac repeated, putting a finger in his mouth and removing a small stone. Like a blind man, he felt the walls of the grave with the backs of his hands. Suddenly, he panicked, but was too weak to struggle much; with Thomas still firmly astride him, it was impossible for him to move.

'Now wait a minute, Reverend,' Thomas spoke soothingly. 'Let me stand up first and get this muck off yer legs. My ... you've been buried alive, man; you've had a gae lucky escape, if ye ask me!'

Isaac allowed him to clear the soil and slowly his reasoning power returned. But he had suffered a violent shock and started to shiver uncontrollably. Eventually, Thomas propped him up and, not without a great deal of trouble, he climbed out of the grave. He then realised that it was almost 18 inches deeper than when he had completed it earlier. Once out, he placed a board across the top, bridge-fashion, and reached down to get a hold of the minister's jacket.

'Now hold on to the plank, Reverend, and I'll gie ye a hand up. Easy now. That's right– get yer feet on the walls, that's it, man – just as if ye were backing up a chimney!'

The minister emerged and lay gasping on the fill at the side, damp from the snow. Tombstone went over and rescued the whisky bottle from the top of a headstone. There was still some left and he could smell the delectable contents. But, showing great fortitude, he resisted temptation and staggered back to the minister who was lying prostrate on the pile of earth. Tombstone eased back his head and forced some of the liquid into his mouth. The effect was electric; it was as if the minister had been touched by a cattle prod. He leapt to his feet, spitting furiously.

'The curse of the Lord on you, Kirkpatrick! How dare you pollute me with the devil's water!'

'Sorry, Reverend – but I thought you were in a gae bad way. I was only trying to help ...' Isaac, now on his feet, albeit unsteadily, lurched on to the granite chip pathway between the graves. Tombstone followed, dropping the bottle as if it was contaminated. He took the minister by the elbow and gently walked him back to the manse.

Mrs Watt was surprised to find the kitchen of the manse occupied by Constable Munro. He had propped his feet up on the Raeburn and taken his cap off; his bald head gleamed above a copy of a popular paper referred to by Hellfire as the *Daily Trespass*. A mug of tea stood on the stove beside the constable's large feet. He glanced up in time to catch the look of astonishment on the housekeeper's face.

'Mornin', Mrs Watt. Looks as if we've had the last of the snow for a bit, doesn't it?' He reached up calmly and took a long draught of strong tea.

'I hope you are quite at home, Constable,' she remarked in a heavily sarcastic voice, noting the muddy footprints, not to mention bits of gravel, on the linoleum. 'What's been going on?' She threw him an accusing glance as she went over to the sink and placed her shopping bag on the draining board.

'There's been a slight accident.' The policeman got up and held up his hand when he saw alarm registering on her face. 'Oh, it's a' right, Mrs Watt, dinna fash yersel' ... It's just that the Reverend had a wee mishap last night. He, er, fell into a hole. But he's a' right. Dr Khan was in to see him and gave him a sedative – he'll be waking up ony time noo, I hope.'

'Fell in a hole, you say? But how ... where?'

'Into the new grave – he must have decided to go out for a breather last night and fell in there. Thomas Kirkpatrick found him.'

Mrs Watt gave him a withering look as if to say 'tell me another'. 'There's something strange going on in this district just now, Jamie Munro. We were just talking aboot it the ither night at the WRI. It's not good enough; it's getting more like Glasgow every day. It's time ye did something aboot it, other than reading comics.' She gave a venomous glance at the newspaper. Putting on her apron, her lips now firmly sealed, she started to clean up the mess in the kitchen and Bookam, with a yawn, returned to his lonely but comfortable vigil.

Isaac hadn't slept well and as soon as he got up he prayed earnestly before doing his morning ablutions. The trauma of the previous night flooded his thoughts and he still felt the flavour of earth in his mouth which made him realise how close he had been to death. Looking out, he could see the sunlight kissing the hillside high on the slopes of Bheinn Bruhm. He yawned, stretched, then closed his eyes again, for a moment, thankful that he could still witness such things as the mountain, though both eyes still felt gritty as he asked once more for guidance. Then he put on his dog collar and his black suit, the only one he had, reminding himself to ask Mrs Watt to repair a small tear at the elbow of the jacket.

He walked downstairs shakily and was taken aback when he opened the kitchen door and saw PC Munro occupying his chair by the Raeburn. The policeman stood up as Isaac entered.

'It's good go see you back on the surface of the earth again, Reverend,' Bookam said heartily. 'We would have missed you.'

'Er, thanks, Constable. It was a nasty experience. I'm still not clear what happened.'

'It appears,' Bookam said, folding up his newspaper, which he noticed the minister had spotted, 'that person or persons unknown wanted to expedite your departure from this previously tranquil community. You were clobbered and dumped into the grave earmarked for old Bob Scott, which, I may add, had an extension excavated so that Bob wouldn't object when he took up residence. You were to have been rendered incognito with a layer of soil.'

Mrs Watt, who had come out of the back kitchen, had her mouth open upon hearing this. 'It's the work o' the devil,' she said hoarsely.

'Aye, a devil wi' size nine feet,' Bookam observed mildly, picking up his unfinished cup of tea. 'It was Tombstone Kirkpatrick who saved your life, Reverend. He scared the de'il away and got you out.'

'Do you want your brose, Reverend?' Mrs Watt's practicality came to the fore.

'Thank you, yes.'

Just as he was about to expound on the carnal sins to the apprehensive policeman, who knew the signs of a hot sermon, Mrs Watt handed him his bowl.

'Er, thanks,' the minister said, suddenly put out of his zealous stride. There was silence as he morosely ate his breakfast standing, a habit inherited from his father which, he thought, had some obscure claim to religious discipline. When he finished he asked, 'Could you mend the tear in my jacket, Mrs Watt?'

'I saw it a few days ago, but never got around to it,' she remarked. 'I'll do it right now – just take it off; there's a clean collar for you on the sideboard.'

'Yes, I saw that,' he acknowledged gratefully, placing

the plate on the stove and, removing his jacket, gave it to the small, plump woman.

Mrs Watt lived out. Her husband, who had worked on the roads all his life for the Ardkyle County Council, had died some 10 years previously and she had taken on the meagrely paid job of attending to the needs of the minister and cleaning the church once a week. Hellfire, though an Elder, looked after the exterior, whilst Tom Kirkpatrick tended to the needs of the dead, at least in digging their graves. Mrs Watt had seen him pass the kitchen window a few minutes before en route to his (usually) unresponsive charges.

The policeman finished his tea with a gurgle and put the empty cup in the back kitchen, then, taking up his cap, he said to Isaac, 'Now that you are up and about, Reverend, I'll be getting along. The Sarge or the Inspector will be along shortly for a word.'

'Well, thank you for the vigil, Constable,' the minister returned, 'but it really wasn't necessary. I have the utmost faith in the Lord.'

'Aye, that may well be,' James replied as he opened the back door, 'but it must have been His night off last night. I suppose I had better tell you the rest of the bad news, minister; trouble never comes alone … Dr Khan told me that your aunt, Mrs McWhirter, passed away last night. He asked me not to tell you until later. I'm sorry.' The policeman quietly made his exit, donning his cap.

Mrs Watt, like Isaac, was obviously shocked at this news and worked away on the sleeve by the window with renewed concentration. They didn't use the electric light during the day if they could avoid it. Isaac quietly knelt by the stove and prayed. Eventually, he stood up, his face ashen.

'You won't be doing your veesiting today, Reverend?'

'Yes, I will. I can't let such incidents interfere with my work. I'll be seeing some of my older parishioners and later consulting with Mrs McLeod about the sale of work she's organising and I must make arrangements for Aunt Beth.'

'Your tea is mashing on the stove,' she instructed the minister. 'If you would care to help yourself, I'll just finish this off. My eyesight isn't as good as it used to be,' she added unnecessarily, holding the sleeve some three inches away from her face.

After his frugal breakfast, Isaac went out and surveyed the snowy scene in front of the manse. The hills had come to life after a blizzard on the tops and the air was crisp. Hellfire came up the path which led from the road to the front door. A parallel narrow drive led to the side of the manse and round to Isaac's lab. The Elder was armed with a large shovel which he affectionately called his 'shovel mhor'.

'Good morning, Elijah,' the minister greeted him.

'Morning,' the Elder replied grudgingly with the enthusiasm of a miser confronted by a charity collector. 'I'll get the path cleared to the house, the thaw didn't last long.'

'That's good of you,' Isaac replied. 'If you could do the church entrance as well, just in case there's a visitor … and round the back of the house, too.'

'Aye, but I'll no' be clearing roon' to yer labooritory,' Hellfire answered with ill-concealed disapproval. 'I'm sure ye'll be able to walk wherever ye have to go and there are black forces at work round here.' He looked at the minister without a trace of compassion, though he knew of his ordeal.

'Well, if that's how you feel about it, Elijah, I won't argue.' With that Isaac strode off irritably and almost did a somersault, slipping on a patch of slush. His mountain skills came to his aid, fortunately, and with certain gyrations he

managed to keep his feet, though his dog collar took up a
new jaunty angle.

By the time he reached the one and only street in
Faileadh he was reorganised and passed the time of day with
several of his flock. He crossed the road, the kerb of which
was piled high with snow, and walked along the opposite
pavement until he reached Duncan's house. There was no
sign of life so Isaac assumed the big man was still in bed.
However, upon investigation he found the poacher devouring
a huge meal of eggs and venison in his trim little kitchen.
The poacher had bellowed, 'Come awa' in' when Isaac
knocked on the door.

'Oh, it's you, Isaac.' Duncan sounded surprised. 'Have
you recovered? I was told you had a narrow escape.
Anyhow, come ben. Have ye had breakfast?'

'Aye, thanking you, Duncan.' Isaac was somewhat
taken aback by the quantity of food piled in front of the big
man; it would have lasted him a week. 'I've had my brose.'

'Brose! Good God, man, ye need more than brose!'
Duncan expostulated, buttering a slice of wholemeal bread
at least an inch thick. 'They only ate brose in the bad old
days when it was mixed wi' whisky or blood; injected some
life into it!'

'You needn't try to bait me, Duncan MacGillvery,' Isaac
spoke sharply, his temper rising at the mention of drink and
the thought of the previous night. 'I'm not here for evangel-
istic purposes, but to seek advice ...'

'Well, if you're not wanting breakfast, how can I help
you?' Duncan said quietly, spearing a hunk of meat expertly
with his fork. Isaac didn't reply and the poacher, sensing that
the minister really had something on his mind, asked, 'Well,
what is it, Isaac? I was only pulling your leg, you know.'

'It's about last night ...' Duncan didn't comment, but he

gave the minister a sharp look. 'I'm worried, Duncan. Why should someone want to kill me?'

'Tell me everything you can remember of last night, Isaac; don't miss out anything.'

The minister went through the sequence of events leading up to the time he lost consciousness.

'Umph,' the big man murmured and absently stroked his cat which was rubbing against his leg. 'And you say James Munro mentioned a size nine print?'

'Yes, it was found on the soil.'

'I had a word with Tom Kirkpatrick before breakfast,' the poacher said. 'He told me about last night – it was as if he had won the pools. He certainly didn't recognise the ghostly digger, but I wonder if Watty noticed anything as he was going back home – he was visiting his sister last night and he usually stays late playing cards. I must ask him,' he mused.

As he poured himself a final cup of tea, he said deliberately, 'Isaac, I've got a few suspicions, but I'll have to delve a bit deeper than your vacated grave before I can give these an airing. By the way, how are the plans for the orphanage?'

Isaac's eyes took on a fresh gleam at the mention of his pet scheme, a home for coloured orphans in the district.

'The usual search for funds, Duncan. My aunt was most helpful.'

'Was?' the poacher queried.

'She passed away last night, Duncan.'

'I'm sorry to hear that, Isaac,' Duncan said quietly. 'She was a fine woman.'

The minister then took his leave and walked down the path to the main street.

His stride didn't have quite its usual spring.

Chapter 8

The Fiscal got into the police car with Angus Wilson. He had been told that morning of Isaac's narrow escape when he reached his office at 11 a.m.

'Morning, Inspector,' he greeted the policeman.

'Morning, sir. Good of you to come.'

'Strange business!' he replied as the car swept round the bends towards Faileadh. 'You say the Reverend was being buried directly beneath where another coffin was due to repose?'

'That's right, sir. Old Robert Scott's. The grave had been deepened and when Tombstone Tom found the minister, he was already partially buried. I guess that when the job was completed to the satisfaction of his assailant, the pick would have been driven through Isaac's chest for good measure. Save making a mess anywhere else. I'm sure he wasn't simply to be buried alive.'

'Yes, I think you're right, Angus. I remember once as a boy reading that tale by Edgar Allan Poe: it gave me the horrors!'

'Me, too,' the Inspector agreed. 'I think that it was statuary reading for juveniles when we were young.'

'Yes, I can think of better ways to go ...' his legal companion stated.

'I left PC Munro on guard in the house until Isaac got up this morning, sir. Just in case.'

'Good thinking. The minister will have to watch his step.'

'Well, we'll try to squeeze what information he has out of him, sir. I couldn't do much last night; Tom Kirkpatrick phoned Dr Khan and the Rev was given a sedative before I got there. But the doctor said he was too shocked for questioning, anyhow.'

'Let's hope he feels a bit better today,' the Fiscal replied. 'What I can't understand is, how – what's his name – Tombstone ...?'

'Yes, Thomas Kirkpatrick, the gravedigger.'

'... how it is he went to the churchyard so late. It happened after midnight, you said?'

'That's right, sir,' Angus answered with a low laugh. 'I was a bit suspicious myself, but Bookam – PC Munro – who was first on the scene after the doctor, explained. Tombstone keeps a bottle at one of the graves, since his housekeeper can't abide drink!'

'I'm beginning to think, Inspector, that the motto of the Highland Police should be "Cherchez le dram". Drink always features somewhere, somehow, in Highland crimes ...' and he added with a laugh, 'there's often a clue in the nicknames!'

'As Sergeant Campbell would say, there's more than a drop o' truth in that!'

'By the way, Inspector, did you know that Mrs McWhirter passed away last night?'

'Yes, I was informed sir. She was a nice old dear and very generous. The minister will take it badly,' the policeman added. 'She was his aunt.'

Mrs Watt answered the doorbell. A couple of minutes later the Inspector and Procurator Fiscal followed her into the room. Angus greeted Isaac who was writing a letter at the desk in the corner.

'Good to see you after your ordeal, Reverend. This is Mr Frew, the Fiscal. I think you've met before?'

'Er ... Yes, of course. How are you, sir?' Isaac offered his hand.

'I must admit you show amazing fortitude after your escapade, Reverend.'

'I've lit a fire in the drawing room,' Mrs Watt cut in. 'You can do your talking in there.'

'Good idea,' Isaac replied.

'Thanks,' the Fiscal added. 'That was most thoughtful of you.'

Once the two lawmen were seated, Angus opened the questioning. Isaac insisted on standing.

'Well, Reverend, can you tell us what happened?' Looking pale, but otherwise appearing normal, Isaac went over the events of the previous night, ending with what he knew of Tombstone's discovery of him and subsequent rescue. 'Yes, I spoke to Thomas Kirkpatrick last night,' the Inspector continued. 'It looks as if you were lucky.'

'Have you any idea at all who your assailant might be?' the Fiscal asked, watching the small man in concern. Peter Frew now noted there was a tremor in his hands.

'I haven't the slightest notion, Mr Frew,' the minister replied unhesitatingly. 'But I can only pray whoever it was may be forgiven.'

'I don't think there's any great likelihood of that if we

get hold of him,' the Fiscal spoke with feeling. 'What time did you hear the noise at the window?'

'Probably about midnight, but I can't be sure.'

'Isaac, with all due respect,' Angus began. 'When we talked yesterday about Horatio Dewar's death, I thought you were holding something back.' He arched his bushy eyebrows so that they rose high on his forehead. The minister gave him an uneasy look.

'You must be mistaken, Angus.'

'I have to be blunt with you, Reverend,' Peter Frew interrupted with deliberation. 'Whoever buried you last night intended murder. Obviously somebody thought it more expedient to finish you off in the grave – we might never have found your body!'

'That seems possible,' Isaac replied. 'Whoever it was wasn't playing sandcastles!'

'So you've nothing more to tell us?' the Inspector asked a trifle petulantly.

'Nothing, Angus,' the minister repeated firmly.

'Well, so be it,' Angus said, rising as if he had been sitting on his crampons for the past week. 'But I must warn you that whoever attempted to bump you off may try again. We can't give you indefinite protection, but I'll arrange for a policeman to be on duty here for a while, anyway.'

'No thanks, Angus. I don't want any molly-coddling. My protection will come from the Lord.'

'We have warned you, Reverend,' the Fiscal stated with finality. 'It's up to you.'

'I appreciate your concern,' Isaac replied, unbending a fraction. 'But I have my work to do. I have to make arrangements in respect of my late aunt and I can't have a policeman, even a plain clothes one, hovering around.'

'Yes, I understand,' Peter Frew acknowledged. 'It could be difficult.' He paused for an instant. 'Couldn't you go away for a week or so after the funeral? We could arrange somewhere where you'd be safe.'

'I don't run away from anything,' Isaac retorted. 'So if you gentlemen will excuse me, I've a christening this afternoon and must prepare …'

After leaving the manse, the Inspector and the Fiscal went over to the churchyard. Archie Campbell was there with a number of constables who were searching the area. The police dog which had been called in earlier had succeeded in following a scent between the headstones, over the boundary wall and then back into the village. But it had lost the trail at a point where water had been flooding over the road from a blocked culvert during the overnight thaw, close to Duncan MacGillvery's house. Another print had been found outside the cemetery wall where the man had jumped down on to mud. Archie was holding a newly made cast. He passed it to his Inspector, after reporting progress.

'Size 9 boots, Sergeant,' the Inspector spoke. 'Or so I was told.'

'Yes, that's correct – standard cleated climbing sole. Probably about five million of them made every year.'

'Nothing else, Sergeant?' the Fiscal inquired.

'Not so far, sir. Pity that the scent petered out; it might have been a good lead but the thaw messed things up. Hell of a lot of slush now.'

'What size of feet has Duncan MacGillvery?' Peter Frew asked.

'Nine,' the Inspector replied concisely. 'Same as Chris and Ken, amongst others.'

'He was seen over at the manse earlier,' the Sergeant added.

'Umph,' the Fiscal grunted.

'It was I who suggested he should do that, to have a word with Isaac and try to find out what the minister was worried about, even though he had spoken with him earlier.' Angus explained.

'Got anything in the village?' the Fiscal asked.

'Not a great deal so far. Basil Thorndyke was in Faileadh last night, visiting Chris. Ken called in to see him, too; they were there until 9.30 p.m.' Inspector Wilson tugged at his ear absently before continuing. 'Watty Gilchrist visited his sister, Mrs Black, in the village and played pontoon with Jack Black and Molly – that's his sister – until about one o'clock. But he says he didn't see anything when he went out to his car. Kirsty, his wife, didn't come with him.'

'She doesn't get on with Molly,' the Sergeant cut in.

'Mind you,' the Inspector continued. 'Watty could be keeping tight-lipped: you spoke with him, Sergeant, and you thought he was a bit hesitant.'

'That's right, sir,' Archie nodded. 'I had a feeling there was something, but it's hard to say. The fact is he usually has something to drink at his sister's, and he has to drive back home.'

'Yes,' the Fiscal murmured. 'There seems to be a certain amount of Free Masonry amongst the witnesses in this case, or rather these cases.'

'I think you're right, sir,' Angus agreed. 'Clem Fular went to bed early – or so he says – but a call came through for him from the States and he couldn't be roused. His door was locked.'

'What does Fular have to say?'

'He told me he sleeps soundly.'

'Isaac slept soundly, too,' the Fiscal observed dryly.

* * *

Isaac felt tired when he returned to the manse. The activities of the previous night were now telling on him. He removed his clerical collar and vest stock and hung them up. Then he went into the kitchen to look through his mail. Mrs Watt put her head round the kitchen door.

'There was a call for you a couple of minutes ago from Queenshouse; an accident on the east side of Bheinn Bruhm. There's someone critically injured up by the Dubh Burn. I told them you'd had an accident yourself and couldn't go out.'

'What? Why on earth did you do that?' he snapped, annoyed at her presumption. 'I'm always fit to help someone in need. How long ago was this?'

'Just two minutes ago. I'm not sure who phoned, but they said it was most urgent. I gathered that the police and the rest of the team have been informed.'

Without another word Isaac took his boots from a locker by the Raeburn and deftly laced them up before running out to his laboratory where his motor cycle was housed. Quickly, he put his helmet on and, shouldering a rucksack which was always packed for an emergency he wheeled his machine out. It roared at the first touch of the starter and, putting it in gear, he moved up the path to the road. The gate was open.

Isaac hadn't yet replaced the cones in the exhausts, so he went easy on the throttle until he cleared the village. The revs rose and he felt the punch of acceleration as the megaphones cut in and the needle jumped to 7000 rpm. The salt which had been applied to the roads had cleared the last of the snow but the surface was still damp. He was in fourth gear on the short straight leading into the last bend before the descent to the bridge under which Duncan hid his van on his poaching expeditions. The tight left-handed hairpin would force him down into third. He knew which gear to take – he had the changes on every corner in the district down to a fine art. The roads were dry here and he drove with a verve that sent thrills down his spine. He had always dreamed of competing in the Manx on the Isle of Man and of coming down the mountain: this was the closest thing to it, locally. Here was the first right-hander. He changed down, a one-two on the foot lever to activate the close ratio box. The big twin disc brakes on the front wheel were the best anchors the minister had ever used on a motor cycle, grabbing the machine as if it were attached to powerful catapult elastic. But now, when he operated the hydraulic hand-lever, nothing happened. He was doing over 95 mph and the corner seemed to rise up as if someone had hurled it towards him. He leant the bike over until the centre rest scraped the tarmac, sending up a tracer-like line of sparks. Still he couldn't get round: the bend was just too tight. He managed to change down to second, but by then he was off the road, running up the snowy bank and taking off over the top like a ski jumper. The powerful quartz headlamp spiralled a beam of light to the heavens. He rose 50 feet in the air, hanging there for an instant, still astride his machine. Then, as if in slow motion film, the light swung down steeply and he dropped in a half spiral on to the jagged boulders of the stream. The death of the Reverend Isaac McMillan was certainly dramatic.

Chapter 9

The lights were out at the manse when Duncan called on the minister. He tried the back door. It was open. He looked in and gave a shout.

'Isaac, are you home?' There was only silence. He closed the door again and was heading down the footpath when on impulse he turned on his heel and went round to Isaac's lab. The door was open and he switched the lights on. The place was as normal … 'No,' he muttered, 'his bike's gone – must be out visiting some poor body!' he thought. There was a predominance of old folks in Isaac's congregation. But then it occurred to him it was rather late for that. Isaac's flock did not burn the midnight oil. Looking behind the door, he saw that the minister's rescue gear was not on its usual peg, but he knew that he sometimes kept in it the manse. He paused for a minute, then, putting the lights out, he decided something was wrong. Mrs Watt lived up past the police house; when he got to her place it was in darkness. Regardless, he hammered on the door and after what seemed about 10 minutes, a hall-light came on and he heard the sliding of bolts and the turning of a well used key. It was as if a top security cell in Barlinnie was being opened. The housekeeper, resplendent in a tartan night robe – barely big enough for her – squinted through the slit, for the door was still safeguarded by a chain.

'Who is it making such a commotion in the middle of the night?' Her voice sounded hoarse.

'It's me, Duncan MacGillvery.'

'I might have known! Only the sinful and degenerate are abroad in the streets at this hour.'

Mrs Watt,' Duncan replied exasperated. 'It's only nine o'clock and there's only one street in Faileadh, and no-one in his right senses would roam it unless he was courting and rest assured I'm on no such mission. I want to know where the minister has gone.'

'On a rescue – where you should be … The man's not fit and well and here you are hanging about and keeping the righteous awake. You've no sense of responsibility, Duncan MacGillvery.'

'What rescue?' the poacher barked. Mrs Watt, taken aback by his sharp tone, condescended a trifle.

'On Bheinn Bruhm. The call came about five past seven, I would think.'

'There's no rescue on Bheinn Bruhm,' the poacher snapped. 'Who called him out?'

'Well …' she faltered for an instant. 'It was mysel' got the message. It was from Queenshouse and said that he was needed urgently.'

'Willie Fyffe?'

'No, it wasn't Mr Fyffe's voice. I didn't recognise it – one doesn't on these call-oots; they fair give me a turn, they do. It was just a voice and I didn't think aboot it. You see,' she hurried on, now almost apologetically, 'I didn't think the Reverend would consider going out anyway, with his aunt dying and he was so shook up after that terrible experience last night.'

'Wasn't he in then, when the call came?'

'No, no, he was visiting Mary MacFadyen after the christening – her young boy's back from hospital – he's called Kenneth ...'

Duncan never even said good night, but ran – ran to the police cottage. PC Munro was still up, of course. His wife Jeannie had just put their lad to bed and the policeman had his feet warming by the fire. He was watching his favourite programme: the saga of a London bobby. His wife answered the door.

'Oh, it's you, Duncan. Come on in. Jamie's watching *Handcuff*.' The Constable turned away from the screen when the poacher entered.

'Have a seat, Duncan. Jean will get you a stroupach ...'

'I'm worried, James,' Duncan said tensely.

'Never thought you had a care in the world, Toń,' the policeman replied, one eye still on a car chase.

'It's Isaac.'

'Isaac?' Bookam pricked up his ears. 'Don't tell me he drowned in the baptism font just for a change.'

'He's not at home.' James Munro immediately favoured Duncan with his full attention as the poacher outlined his discoveries. 'I think I'll give Fyffe a ring, or perhaps you'd better do it,' Duncan suggested finally.

The Constable got to his feet and reached for the telephone extension from his office. He dialled the Queenshouse number.

'Is that you, Willie?'

'Aye, Jamie.'

'Right, Willie. Can you tell me, was there a call-out on Bheinn Bruhm?'

'A call-out, you say, a call-out?' The Constable didn't comment on this useless observation; Watery had a condenser between his ear and his brain and a repeater from the same organ to his vocal chords, he thought bitterly. 'No, man, there wasn't,' Watery continued. 'Is there somebody missing?'

'There could be, Willie. By the way, Isaac isn't up there, is he?'

'No, he's not exactly a regular customer,' the publican replied with a chuckle. 'I hear he had a nasty experience last night, very nasty ...'

'Thanks, Willie.' The Constable hung up abruptly.

Without another word to Duncan, he phoned headquarters. One of the new constables was on duty: a Sassenach, and Bookam couldn't abide the southern English.

'Get me the Inspector, if he's in, will you? Constable Munro, Faileadh, here.'

'I think he's out with the Sergeant, but I'll try his office. Oh, hold on, he's just coming in.' There was a pause and then Angus came to the phone.

'Well, James, what is it?' Bookam quickly related Duncan's discovery. The Inspector acted decisively. 'Go with Duncan and have a look for the motor cycle at Bheinn Bruhm, by that last layby. That's where he'd have gone to, I imagine. Take a radio and keep in touch. I'll call out the team and take some of the lads from here as well.'

'Right, Inspector.' James hung up. 'Angus is calling out the team. We've to go and have a look at the top end o' the glen. Let's go, Duncan.'

'Good,' the poacher replied. 'Where's Chris, by the way?'

'He went down to Glasgow. He won't be back until tomorrow.'

* * *

It wasn't till the early hours of the following morning that Isaac was found. A rescue searchlight had picked out the tyre marks high up the snow bank on the corner. They saw his helmet first – a shredded mass of glass fibre.

'Well, at least he died instantly,' Archie observed as they gazed down between the boulders at the crumpled mess that had once been the fiery preacher.

'I suppose it was inevitable, the way he drove,' Douglas observed. 'Just look at his bike, though; it's hardly damaged.'

True enough, the motor cycle, apart from a dent in the petrol tank and a twisted handlebar, didn't look much the worse for the accident. Though Isaac had landed amongst the boulders of the stream, the machine had bounced off a grassy tussock and now lay amongst rushes. Duncan went over and pulled it upright.

'Well,' he observed, his headlamp lighting up the machine. 'It's still worth over a grand, even in this state, I suppose. Changed days from when my old A.J.S. used to fire every second telegraph pole if I was lucky, and it cost a fiver.'

He peered over to see which gear it was in: second. He was surprised since, the way Isaac drove, he would have been more likely to have taken that bend in third. But then he was in a hurry, thinking it was a call-out, not a hoax, and probably came into the corner too fast. It was blatantly obvious, he observed, that he had gone too fast from the state he was in! Funny there'd never been a hoax before, Duncan mused, and idly rocked the machine with the clutch out, fingering the front handbrake. He was still abstractedly thinking of the hoax and who might have done it, when suddenly he realised that something was amiss: the brake wasn't working. By the light of his lamp he inspected the callipers on the front discs. Yes, they were working all right … Funny, he thought to himself and bent down to look more closely at them to see if oil had got on to the discs. But there was no oil there. He touched one of them with his finger and felt a filmy deposit, invisible to the eye. He then put finger and thumb over the disc, drawing them down towards him. 'Yes, by God,' he exclaimed aloud. A slippery coating was on both sides of the gleaming and perforated discs. Both discs were affected.

'You thinking of putting in an offer to the Church Committee for the Laverdo, Duncan?' the Inspector inquired, coming over. The others were crowded round Isaac's body.

'Not me, Angus. I've given them up – these things are too dangerous. At least the bike isn't, but these bloody tourists and their caravans are as unpredictable as black-faced sheep.' He glanced at the rest of the men who were about to carry Isaac's body up to the road. 'Angus, a word wi' you, before the others are back ...'

'What, Duncan?'

'Somebody's tampered with the bike.'

'What do you mean?' Angus demanded, his voice terse.

'Run yer fingers owre the front discs.' The big policeman did so without a word, then stood up, frowning, as he tasted the deposit.

'What is it, Duncan? A fine oil?'

'Could be, Angus. But I'm thinking it's something else, possibly silicon.'

'Silicon?'

'Aye, I used an aerosol of it once when I was sawing logs; stopped the blade sticking a treat, it did. There's next to no friction wi' it.' The Inspector tried the brake, using all his force on the hydraulic lever and rocking the machine.

'It's quite a stiff brake that, onyhow,' Duncan said. 'But I know for a fact it's one o' the best stoppers on any motor cycle ever made ...'

'That brake is now about as effective as a carton of salt on a chicken's arse!' the Inspector said grimly. Duncan examined the rear brake.

'The back one has its adjuster slackened off as well, Angus. It works, but it wouldna be very good; anyhow, the back brake would never stop the bike, not the way Isaac drove it.'

'Could be a murder case, Duncan. When the hell is it going to stop?' he muttered. 'Here are the others now. Keep your mouth shut about this for the time being, Duncan.'

'What about the bike?' Douglas asked as he came over. 'We've got Isaac in the back of the Land Rover.'

'That's all right, Doug,' Thumper replied. 'We'll call it a night, or rather, a morning. I'll arrange for the garage to get the bike out. You can tell the others to go back now, and many thanks.'

When the Sergeant returned, Angus took him aside and told him to get the motor cycle back to police headquarters, using Constable Munro and the police rescue team members for the job.

'Right,' Archie replied obediently.

Peter Frew wore a grim expression when Angus entered his office later that morning. He indicated a chair to one side of his desk and put a file away in a cabinet beside the window as the Inspector sat down.

'Well, I've heard from the Chief a summary of the night's activities, Inspector. Fill me in on the details.'

The Inspector gave him all the facts available, adding, 'I've put Sergeant Archie Campbell and PC Munro on to obtaining statements on the movements of various team members yesterday. Doctor Grieve estimates the time of death to be about 7.30 p.m., give or take an hour. The

Reverend was lying in a cold stream among boulders so it was difficult for Grieve to give a more specific time of death.'

'When did Mrs Watt say he left the manse?'

'Sometime after seven so it ties in quite accurately.'

'I don't imagine it would have taken him long to cover those few miles on that machine.' Peter Frew frowned. 'I always considered the man a menace on the road.'

'Oh, he was a good enough rider, sir,' Angus defended the late minister. 'It's just that he went about 60 mph faster than fast drivers ...'

'Umph,' the Fiscal grunted. 'You say it was MacGillvery who discovered the stuff on the discs?'

'Yes. Duncan was playing about with the machine after we found Isaac and was amazed to find that the front brake wasn't working.'

'Quite so,' the Fiscal replied. 'That man seems to be able to show the Force a few things, Inspector. I don't wonder he's never been convicted of poaching!'

'He's quite a canny man – Duncan,' Angus admitted graciously. 'And as far as poaching goes, he never sells the meat and many o' the old folks o' Faileadh rely on Duncan for their weekend joint. He never accepts payment or even payment in kind and he never gives it directly to any o' the pensioners either. It's left in a biscuit box, or the mail box for them, where the cats or dogs can't get at it.'

Peter Frew didn't keep Angus long; he knew the Inspector had a great deal to do.

'I gather you're working closely with MacGillvery, Inspector,' the Fiscal remarked finally. 'Good idea to have a local civilian ear to the ground.'

'I hope it is, sir,' Angus confided ruefully.

'Well, I won't press you for further details, Angus. I'll see it all in the reports. You must be getting stretched for manpower?'

'We're managing, sir.'

'Have you had a report on the brakes yet?'

'Yes, sir. It's silicon all right. I've told the Chief Constable: someone tampered with them – the rear brake as well, but not a print anywhere except the Rev's and our own.'

'Darned cunning business with the brakes,' the Procurator Fiscal replied, a trace of admiration in his voice. 'It would seem that we have a mechanically inclined murderer, Inspector. Had you thought along those lines?'

'I must confess I had, sir, but it might be worth pursuing further,' Angus agreed.

'Well, off you go and keep me informed.'

'I'll do that, sir.'

Back at the station the Inspector called on the Sergeant. Archie was on the phone and motioned Angus to sit down.

'Right, many thanks. Let me know as soon as you can, will you?' He turned to Angus. 'That was Sergeant Quigley of Strathclyde,' he explained. 'He's checked further on Chris's movements for us.'

'All above board?'

'Yes. Chris was apparently at a geological conference at the University ... Was there all the late afternoon and most of the evening. He told me that himself, of course – says he went out to the toilet during a break in the evening lecture, but wasn't sure of the exact time. Quigley can't find this out.'

'And the others?'

'Any one of them could have used the phone. We're not getting anywhere!'

'What about silicon spray?'

'I asked locally. None of the ironmongers had even heard of it. It's sometimes used as a do-it-yourself spray for re-proofing garments. You certainly can't buy it locally, but probably in Glasgow. Willie Fyffe says he remembers seeing a silicon aerosol spray at the hotel a while back; one of his fisherman guests left it. But he can't find it now.'

'What was Clem Fular doing?'

'Both he and Spielman were playing chess before dinner, but either one of them could easily have slipped out to the phone; it's in the hall, as you know.'

'Basil and Douglas?'

'The same – both had the opportunity – Ken, too, I gather – he could have phoned. Kirsty said he was in his room for part of that time and he has an extension there.'

Chapter 10

Watty and Ian Cuthbert, the gillie, had been shooting hinds at the foot of Glen Liath and were now returning to the Lodge in the Range Rover.

'Well, Ian,' the keeper remarked as they garaged the vehicle. 'It's a lot less bother getting the hinds on our own than with bumbling guests.'

'That it is, Watty. They're naething but vermin.' Watty wasn't too sure if his companion was referring to the deer or the guests ... 'When's Horror's funeral, Watty?'

'We're no' quite sure yet.'

'Ah, it's tough. First the laird, then the Rev. Whit dae ye think's going tae happen to the estate noo?'

'Oh, I suppose Ken will manage it for the Company meantime. Oh, blast it,' Watty expostulated. 'That bloody dog!' I bet she's away to the fox's den at the old shaft.'

'Ye know, I felt there was something wrang – we forgot all aboot Gealeas!' Ian observed, shaking his head.

'Well,' Watty said determinedly. 'A'm no' going doon to fetch her till I get a bite. I micht tak' the 12 bore wi' me and see if I can get a shot at that bitch of a fox.'

'Dae ye want a hand?' Ian didn't sound too enthusiastic. He had a date that evening with Janet Smith, the new waitress at Queenshouse.

It wasn't until 11 o'clock that Watty left his cottage. He drove down the glen and parked at the nearest point to the old mine. Taking his shotgun and a powerful headlamp, he set off on foot. The night was damp, yet the dark had a mystical quality. It's often like this with a westerly, soft, he thought, as he moved up stealthily towards the old mine talus, now heather-and birch-covered, spreading downhill to his right. There was a constant spray of water above the shaft entrance, for the hillside rose a thousand feet at this point. He could smell fox, that pungent aroma which clings round their dens. He waited a few minutes, then gave a high pitched whistle. It wasn't loud, but it carried and he knew that if Gealeas heard it she would let him know. A few minutes later, he whistled again. There was a faint bark from the depths of the shaft; it was more of a whimpering. Watty was alarmed; he knew there was something wrong. He was fond of his dogs, though he never gave a dog a pat of affection in its life.

He propped his shotgun under the overhang at the entrance because he thought it too dangerous, even if there was a fox, to risk a shot in the tunnel and climbed over the skeleton of wood which once had been a barrier. He switched on his torch, realising that the vixen had won this round, but consoling himself with the fact that Gealeas would still flush out many more foxes. His light stabbed the blackness. Suddenly, it was cold and clammy. It was ten years since he was last in this tunnel. He whistled again and the whimpering, though still faint, seemed closer. She must be trapped somewhere up by the first chamber, he decided, by the sidings. The track was still in fair repair and he followed the rusty lines, in the centre of which was an old wire rope. The shaft steepened. He called again to Gealeas and an answering whimper came down the tunnel. There was occasional fallen debris, but generally the shaft appeared in good shape and a channel alongside the track carried drain water. He was pulling himself up the long slope, using the rusty wire rope as a hand line, when unexpectedly it fell slack. Above, a piece of rotten wood, which had been acting as a chock under one of the wheels of a bogey on to which the rope was attached, snapped.

With seeming reluctance, the old steel wagon started to move, slowly at first, then, as if annoyed at being roused from its slumber, it gave a deep, rumbling roar and accelerated. This was a noise which Watty couldn't identify at first and stood stock still before he realised what was happening. There was no escape. Although he had seen the old bogey on his last visit, he thought that it was the roof of the tunnel that was collapsing ahead. His knees felt weak but a voice from within urged him to run: run as you've never run in your life, Gilchrist!

As a puppy Gealeas had been a compulsive chewer. She had never really grown out of that habit and Watty seldom successfully tethered her except with a chain. She normally lived with the two collies in the gamekeeper's barn. The dog had now been chewing for several hours at the piece of nylon rope that secured her to the turntable of an old crane in the underground siding and a few seconds after the bogey had started its descent, the dog broke free, with a short length of the hawser laid nylon rope still attached tightly round her neck. Gealeas scampered down the shaft in the wake of the runaway vehicle with short but rapid strides. She knew her master was below, somewhere in the dust.

Next morning Ian Cuthbert was skinning hinds for half an hour before he decided it was odd that Watty hadn't arrived to help. Thoughtfully, he wiped his hands on a piece of rag and went over to the keeper's cottage. Kirsty was returning from the big house. He shouted, 'Where's Watty?'

'He's not back. I was just coming to see you about him. Once he goes after foxes, nothing else matters,' she answered heatedly. 'He's more interested in a vixen than his wife!'

'But it's unusual for him to be oot sae lang; it was Gealeas he was worried about.'

'No doubt! You'd better have a look for him,' Kirsty replied, 'instead of talking ... I've got work to do, if you men folk haven't! It was only a month ago that he spent the night at that den above Queenshouse and never even saw a fox!'

Ian returned to the barn where he kept his small motor cycle and in a few moments was burping down the narrow road in the direction of the lower strath. At the entrance to the shaft he saw the 12 bore propped up against the rock and, squinting inside the tunnel, he called out:

'Watty, where the hell are ye?' A tumult of barking greeted him and he heard the scampering of Gealeas as the dog rushed down the tunnel, still with the short length of rope round her neck.

'Hallo, lassie. Where's that bloody boss o' yours – eh?' The dog jumped up, yelping excitedly, then ran back into the mine.

Ian cursed because he hadn't brought a torch, but timidly made his way forward, then up the angled shaft. He fumbled his way along, guided by the damp, cold rails. After what seemed ages and when he was beginning to regret his impetuosity in venturing inside, the dog, which was ahead, gave a warning bark. Ian stopped, straining his eyes, but it was pitch black. With an outstretched hand he felt the pitted, rusted steel of the bogey which had slewed sideways across the shaft when it had left the rails. He squeezed his way past it and over loose rocks, almost stumbling over the unconscious figure of the keeper.

The Jack Russell was excitedly giving whimpers and short barks. Reaching down between the rails, Ian felt rough Harris tweed.

'Watty, Watty!' His voice was urgent. 'Are ye a' richt? The keeper moaned, then relapsed into silence. The gillie was scared. What if Watty snuffed it? he thought. What will I do? 'Watty!' he repeated urgently.

Just then the keeper came round. 'It's hellish dark!'

'It's me, Ian. Ye're in the old mine, Watty. Are ye all right?' Relief surged into Ian's voice.

'Aye, I think so, Ian. What the blazes happened?'

'You tell me, mon! Did ye get hit by a rock or something?'

The keeper sat up, rubbing his head and felt a great lump at the back of it, sticky with blood.

'Gie me a minute, for Christ's sake,' he muttered, prodding himself to see if there were any bones broken. 'Ah seem tae be a'richt, Ian,' he reported. 'Bloody miracle! It was that bogey. It came doon like a tube train. I only knew what it was when it was on top o' me.'

'It's jammed here beside us.'

'I fell flat between the rails,' Watty continued. 'I must have tripped. Come tae think o' it, I've still got my head-lamp roon' my neck ... Have a feel aboot and see if ye can find the lamp battery; it's popped oot o' the case.'

They both started to feel about between the rails. Gealeas, thinking this was a fine game, ran from one to the other.

'That bloody dog,' Watty muttered. 'Here, Gealeas, find it, find it, lass.' The terrier stopped playing when she realised her master wanted her to find something and started sniffing around. In a few minutes she nuzzled her master and Watty reached down.

'She's got my fore and aft; that's something, at least,' he said thankfully.

'I've got it!' Ian spoke triumphantly. 'Here.' He handed the battery to Watty and seconds later a cutting beam lit the shaft.

Watty glanced at his pocket watch. 'It's midnight, Ian.' He sounded puzzled. 'But I left the hoose aboot 10 o'clock; I musta hae been unconscious for an hour!'

'It's midday the next day!' the gillie replied.

'Well, well, what dae ye ken aboot that?' He ran his hand gently over the wound on the back of his head. 'We'd better be getting oot o' here, Ian, before something else happens. There's something aboot this place. I felt it last night when I came in: kinda sinister-like.'

They squeezed past the bogey and, seeing it now by torchlight, Ian shuddered. It looked as if it might easily fall from where it was jammed; there was only loose rock supporting it on one side. The haul wire was wound round the rusty contraption as if it were a large parcel. They slid past without saying a word and breathed with relief only when they emerged into daylight. Ian picked up the shotgun.

'Here, Gealeas,' he called to the terrier. 'Let me tak' that stupid rope off yer neck. Ye'll trip up. How the hell did you get it round your neck, anyhow, dog? Bloody strange!' Watty was still trying to refocus on events and gazed about in a dazed fashion. Ian didn't bother him about the dog's strange tether.

'I'll drive you back in the Rover, Watty. I can pick up my bike later.'

'Right,' the keeper answered automatically.

Duncan MacGillvery's old green Ford van drew into a layby to let the estate Range Rover past. Ian leant out of the window to pass the time of day.

'I'm just on my way down to Paddy MacManus at the tailrace,' the poacher informed him. 'I've promised to go down and see his mother for months.'

'Gie the auld dear my regards, Duncan. She's a great calliach!'

'I don't often see you driving that machine,' the poacher observed curiously, seeing Watty in the passenger seat.

'Watty had an accident in the old mine. He was looking for Gealeas – the dog seems to have been tied up somehow in the shaft – when the bogey came doon the tunnel. He's been knockit oot a' nicht.'

'You don't say,' the big man replied, concerned and, raising his voice, asked, 'Are you okay now, Watty?'

'Feeling a bit coorse, Duncan, but I'll survive.'

'Ye'd better go and see the doc if you've been unconscious a' that time,' Duncan suggested forcefully. 'Concussion can gie serious effects, as ye well know.'

'Well,' the keeper replied reluctantly. 'I suppose I'd better get home; Doc Khan's getting plenty o' custom at Grey Corries the noo!'

'How did that bogey run away?' Duncan leant out of the van window with a puzzled expression. 'It's been there for ow'r a quarter a century and I didna think it would be exactly ready for a sprint at this time of its retirement.'

'I'm no' sure,' the keeper answered, feeling suddenly tired. 'I just remember pulling on that old wire rope when doon it came at me … It's strange that Gealeas had that bit of nylon rope round her neck.'

'Well, well,' Duncan said. 'I'll no' keep you, but you make sure that Kirsty calls the doctor right away, Ian.'

'I'll do that, Duncan.'

Duncan MacGillvery was going to deliver a haunch of venison to the MacManuses, but on impulse he decided that a slight detour would be in order. Something was very odd about this mine business. After all, he had his rescue gear in the car and the late Isaac's lamp was still in his rucksack – he won't be needing it now, Duncan thought, visualising the minister sporting a pair of swept-back wings.

Detective Inspector Wilson hadn't been so busy for years. Extra help had been allocated to him for the case. The police surgeon's report lay in front of him now, in his office at Kinlochsanda. The Procurator Fiscal had asked for a post-mortem on Horatio Dewar and Dr Grieve, the police surgeon, had completed this in conjunction with Dr Isa Khan the previous afternoon. In simple language, he had been killed by a bullet passing through the side of his neck, severing the carotid artery. Death was due to a massive loss of blood. There was also a medical report on the laird from his doctor in Edinburgh but, other than mentioning a heart condition and arthritis of the hip, the old man had appeared healthy enough for his age.

Archie came in and he put the report down.

'If I'm as fit as old Horrible was when I'm 78, I'll be happy, Archie!'

'Aye, I'm only 48, but I find it hard enough going up to that bealach, without having a wonky hip!'

'You should be getting used to it by now, Sergeant!'

'We're fair wearing a channel up that slope, Angus ... When's the body being released for burial?'

'He can be taken away any time now,' the Inspector replied, shuffling through a pile of photographs on his desk, taken by the police photographer. Beside them lay one of Glen Liath, taken by Kenneth Dewar on the day of the shooting.

'He's a good photographer, is Ken,' he remarked to the Sergeant, taking the photograph to study it again. It had been given to PC Munro for the Inspector that day when the Constable was down at the Lodge. The Sergeant walked round the desk to take a look at it over the Inspector's shoulder. A winter's scene, taken above the Lodge near the road, he thought.

'I'd rather see it in the spring,' he remarked. Angus put the print down on his desk, then picked it up once more. Something bothered him about it and he couldn't quite pinpoint what it was.

'Did ye hear about Watty?' Archie asked now.

'What about him?'

'He had a nasty mishap in the old mine. He was in after a vixen – his dog, actually, I think. She was missing, but there's a den there and he's been after the vixen for some time. Anyhow, an old ore bogey ran down the tunnel and clobbered him. He was lying in the mine all night, unconscious. It was Ian the gillie who found him.'

'Looking for his dog, you say?' The Detective Inspector looked up at the Sergeant.

'Aye, that wee terrier he had oot wi' him when we went to the bealach; the Jack Russell.'

'Yes, I remember it. A bonny wee dog ...' Angus' interest was aroused and he continued. 'A bogey, you say, Archie? Now how could a thing like that suddenly rush off without any motivation?'

'There was an auld hawser on it; he was pulling on that to help him up the slope. The dog was way back o' the shaft somewhere.'

'These keepers will do anything to get a fox,' the

Inspector muttered in disbelief. 'They stay out for nights, watching dens.'

'Mind you, Angus, they cause an awfu' havoc – the foxes, I mean,' Archie added with a disarming grin. 'I ken well, back home in Glen Dale, we lost mony a lamb.'

'It's a debatable point, Archie,' Angus argued. 'Naturalists tell us foxes would reach a natural population level, no different from killing them every year. There's only enough food for a certain number, anyhow.'

'I don't believe a word o' it, Angus, not a word,' the Sergeant retorted heatedly 'If they weren't kept doon at lambing time, there'd be wholesale slaughter!'

'Just then there came a knock on the door. Duncan MacGillvery looked in. 'I thought there was only one man shot and one killed on a bike, yet I hear talk o' wholesale slaughter!'

'Just talking about foxes, Duncan,' Angus said. 'I think they should be let be, and Archie here is all for the extermination of the species.'

'Aye, weel, there are arguments both ways, you know,' the big man agreed. 'But I don't want to trespass on your valuable time,' he added.

'Just as weel there's no trespass law in Scotland, as far as you're concerned,' Archie retorted, a hint of humour in his eye.

'It's aboot Watty that I came.' The poacher closed the door and took a seat opposite Thumper.

'What about Gilchrist?' Angus demanded.

'You heard o' the accident?'

'Archie was just telling me …'

'Well, it's a strange thing,' Duncan said, clasping his hands over the knees of his plus-fours. 'You see, I've just had a look in the mine mesel'.'

'You've been in today?'

'Aye.'

'Why?' the Inspector asked with interest.

'Jest a few things … I met Watty and Ian as I was going down the road in my van. Ian told me about it. The point is, I was probably the last person known to have been up to the siding which is at the top o' the first tunnel. When I was there,' he paused, 'and that must have been aboot three years ago, I remember seeing that old bogey. I thought it could be a good bit o' scrap, so I had a close look at it, but it was badly rusted and I remember there were some big boulders in the front o' it. It couldna have gone doon that slope, even if it was pulled by a bulldozer!'

'What are you suggesting, Duncan?' the Inspector asked quietly.

'That it was moved deliberately, or fixed in such a way that when the rope was pulled it would run down the rails.'

'But that's havers, Duncan!' Archie put in. 'Who'd want to bump off Watty?'

'I canna answer that, Archie. I only deal in facts …'

'But he was looking for his dog. Nobody knew he was going back there, did they?'

'Oh aye, Ian did, but he'd naething to do wi' the accident. I've been having a talk wi' them both, before I came to see you. But going back to the dog … That's what first made me interested, apart from the rusty bogey. When I got into the gallery – and it's no' very safe getting past that bogey, I can tell ye – I found an old bit of nylon sling, a bit that used to lie aboot in our rescue truck, if I'm no' mistaken. It had been chewed through by the dog.'

'Had the dog been tied up then?' Angus asked.

'Aye, but not by Watty.'

'But who'd want to tie that wee beasty in there?' Archie

asked, puzzlement stamped on his face. Duncan made no reply.

'So the dog was tied up in the gallery?' the Inspector recapped. 'Yes, Gealeas was with Watty who was unconscious by the bogey when Ian found them. Watty had been hit by it but no' cut bad; his hat saved him, no doubt – the dog still had a noose o' the sling round her neck, chewed through.'

'What does Watty say about all this?' Angus asked, looking down at his nails.

'He remembers hearing the dog barking and, as it wouldna come to his calls, he went in after it. Next thing he knew was a rumble like a train and, Bob's your uncle, he thinks he must have fallen between the rails as he ran downhill, but was probably hit by the axle o' the bogey when it passed over him. It went off the rails just where he was lying.

'He didn't see anybody, or hear anything else?' Angus looked quickly up at the poacher.

'Not a sausage.'

'Well, it's odd,' the Inspector admitted, 'but I don't see what it's got to do with the case o' the dead laird, or Isaac. I'm sure there's some simple explanation. Someone playing a practical joke on the keeper, or do you think there's a homicidal maniac on the rampage?'

'It's a funny sort o' joke to put some o' that rust-removing fluid on the axles; then move the boulders and substitute them wi' a wee bit o' woodwormed timber that wouldna stop a draught!'

'You saw that?'

'Aye.' Duncan regarded him evenly, his blue eyes steady.

'Did anyone ever tell you that you should have been in the force, Duncan?' asked Angus.

'I like it better on the other side, Angus – in an honest way, so to speak.'

The poacher got up to go. 'If you want, I'll go in with you, Angus, but it's no' very safe.'

'I'll take you up on that.' Safety never worried the Inspector when there was a job to do. 'We'll go right now.'

'Oh, another thing. It might be as weel to take one o' those forensic men, or whatever you call them; I found some interesting footprints on the ground up by the old crane. The man who tied that dog up had very big feet.'

The back end of the year was usually a quiet time for Queenshouse, but because of the late laird's sudden demise, the place was suddenly inundated by reporters. The police had issued the usual non-committal statements saying investigations were continuing but, despite pressing questions, Superintendent MacDonald had not yet admitted publicly that they were investigating a murder – or murders. But several of the national dailies, interested in the spate of accidents, had dropped hints that certain country forces took upon themselves tasks which were much better suited for the experienced Regional Crime Squads. Isaac's sudden death had spread jam on this slice of Highland drama.

In deference to the guests and the Grey Corries household, the Inspector had posted a man at the gate and no-one was allowed in except on legitimate business. One female reporter, however, showing considerable ingenuity, had penetrated the grounds by posing as the sister of Kirsty Gilchrist from the Island of Eigg, and had succeeded in interviewing Kirsty in her cottage, unbeknown to her husband whom Dr Khan had packed off to bed, seeing that the keeper was unwilling to go to Kinlochsanda for observation.

* * *

John Templeton, the Chief Constable, and Peter Frew, the
Procurator Fiscal, had lunch together at least once a week
at the Masonic Arms in Kinlochsanda. They would often talk
shop over the meal and today the subject was inevitably the
recent sudden deaths. These had received wide coverage –
John Templeton knew only too well that publicity could
either be good or bad. The press traded in extremes ...

'Was Inspector Wilson in to see you this morning?' The
Chief opened the conversation over soup, which was their
usual starting point for any item of importance.

'Yes. Good man that, John. Never knew him properly
before; does a lot of mountain rescue work, I gather.'

'He's on most call-outs; fit chap, despite his size ...
They've got the bullet now,' he added as he reached for the
salt. After sampling the venison broth which was to his satisfaction, he continued. 'It's a strange business. The forensic
squad have still to confirm it, but I think we can assume that
it was the .270 which was found in the earth that killed him.'

'It was a remarkable bit of detection on Duncan
MacGillvery's part. Quite remarkable – bit of a one man
show,' the Fiscal said dryly, 'don't you think?'

'Yes, even the forensic boys agree. There may a bit of
luck in it, but he got results – the bullet, a high velocity one
– was the same calibre as the missing rifle, a Weatherby
magnum, and had particles of rock on it compatible with
the rock scar.' The Chief appeared to speak to himself as he
continued. 'As both forensics and Duncan pointed out, the
trajectory of a bullet fired from high up that gully was a
likely one for entry into the late laird's neck after a ricochet
with Dewar lying down in his shooting position. This has narrowed down now with the location of the ricochet point
and the final resting place of the bullet.'

Peter Frew finished his soup in silence, then wiped his

lower lip with his napkin. 'Yes, I agree also. Wilson seems to be handling things well. Has the Inspector enough manpower?'

'He's asked for two more police dogs from the city to help in the search for the rifle. We also had about 20 men on the ridge today, much to the annoyance of our own dog handler.'

'And he's probably right, John. You're a great advocate of dogs – I remember your saying that one dog is worth 40 men in certain circumstances ... Though Carl, your own official dog, hasn't done much so far, has he?' Peter Frew smiled. A look of annoyance crossed John Templeton's normally serene face for an instant.

'We're doing our best, Peter, and I'm sure we can handle it. We're a big region, as you know, but I think our resources are more than adequate.'

The Procurator Fiscal laughed. 'Don't get me wrong, John! I'm as much for keeping it in our own backyard as you are. Let's hope we dig up something more ...'

Angus wasn't exactly digging at that precise moment, but he was removing moss and earth from the butt of a rifle which the police dog had just located, high in the strath gully. Though Carl and his handler had been over the spot many times before, it was not until the snow had finally melted from all the crevices between the boulders that enough scent from the gun had enabled the dog to find it. Even now there was a trace of ice on the barrel.

'Good bit of work this,' the Inspector addressed the handler. 'Get it down to Kinlochsanda as soon as you can, will you. I'll have MacMatthews examine it. It's the missing one with a telescope, all right and the serial number corresponds.'

'I'll do that right away, sir,' the Constable replied and took the rifle which Angus had wrapped in his rescue cagoule.

'Don't smudge it, lad.'

'No, sir.'

The Inspector had been on his way to see Watty, prior to visiting the mine with Duncan when word of the find came over the walkie-talkie. He had come up immediately after picking up the poacher. They now stood gazing down to the fatal, now fenced off, ledge below the cliff with crime scene tape connecting steel stakes on three sides; the remaining side was the drop down which the laird had rolled.

'You were right, Duncan,' he remarked. 'Only a few yards out, from the point from where you thought the shot was fired and the rifle found a stone's throw away.'

'Aye. I guessed it would have been about here, assuming that whoever fired it came down the ridge.'

'Have the boulders marked where the Weatherby was found, Archie, will you?' he addressed his Sergeant. 'It won't be any good looking for any other evidence, I shouldn't think. It's like the floor of a cattle market after all the searching that's been going on ...'

'Have the place where the rifle was found marked as well, Archie.'

'I'll do that, sir.'

'Well, come on, Duncan. Let's get down to that mine; a couple of our own men will be meeting us to take photographs and a cast.'

There was a discreet knock on the darkroom door and Kenneth gave a groan.

'Go away! I'm busy ...'

'It is me, Herr Dewar.' Von Spielman's voice reached into the inner darkness. Kenneth paused for an instant.

'Come in, then.'

The German entered, brushing aside the back curtains and stood in the dim light.

'What do you want?' Ken demanded curtly.

'Ah, how do you say?' the business man replied. 'A delicate point, Herr Dewar … Your father, he vas interested in disposing of the old mine in the lower strath, it is called, but, unfortunately, he is no more … I had wished to come to an agreement with him. Perhaps, when you have time to settle down, you vill discuss the matter – yes?'

Chapter 11

It wasn't until after five that the Inspector and Duncan drove back up the Glen Liath road after their visit to the mine. One of the constables had refused point-blank to go past the bogey, but his bolder colleague obtained photographs and a fine cast of the large prints. Angus mentioned them now to his companion.

'As you saw, Duncan, I put my foot alongside one o' those prints and it was as big as mine. Watty's potential assassin has large feet!'

'It seems a bit too obvious,' the poacher remarked reflectively. 'An outsize visiting card and it doesn't tie in with the print at the grave!'

'The same thing occurred to me. If I didn't know Munro was busy last night, I'd say he was having us on. I don't know of anybody else here with feet our size, not even Willie Fyffe.'

As they approached the turn-off to Grey Corries Lodge, the Inspector said, 'We'll nip in and have that word with Watty and see that bit of rope.' He paused first to exchange a word with the Constable on duty at the entrance to the drive.

Watty was up, talking with Ian the gillie, when Kirsty

led them into the kitchen, a large, stone floored room, with a stove, hot and snug against one wall, a rack of clothes hung above it.

After preliminaries, Angus said to Watty, 'Now about that bit o' sling that was round your dog's neck, Watty. I want to see it and I want to know everything you can remember about your visit to the mine.'

'It's over there, on the dresser. Give it to the Inspector, Kirsty.' His wife went over and handed the piece of cord to the policeman. Duncan, who was standing beside him, took a step forward to have a closer look.

'There seem to be bloodstains on it,' the Inspector observed, studying the rope.

Ian said, 'It was tied with a bowline round the dog's neck.'

'Aye, and the other bit round the crane was one o' them grocer knots – the kind that slips when you tighten it and then locks,' Duncan informed him.

'I ken that knot fine,' Watty responded. 'I used to use it for tying up wool bags at the clippings.'

'It's no' used by mony people, though,' Duncan mused. 'That bloodstain now. Gie me a look at it, Angus.' He examined the dirty nylon carefully, then gazed at the keeper. 'Are ye thinking the same as me, Watty? … that rescue the other night?'

'Jest my thoughts, Duncan,' the keeper responded, casting bloodshot eyes over the exhibit.

The poacher turned to Angus. 'If you think back, Angus, slings were used to drag the body doon after I lost the stretcher on the Eagal. And this looks like one o' them!'

The Inspector was thoughtful. 'You could be right, Duncan. I'll have it checked. For a generally law-abiding area we're working forensics overtime!'

Watty had nothing new to add about his narrow escape, so Angus wound up the interview.

'Someone knew you were down in lower Glen Liath and took advantage of it – and I suspect it was someone who knew your dog. You can't just pick up a man's dog like that and wheek it away. The beast would have to know the person. When did you realise she was missing, Watty?'

'Hard tae say, Angus. Ian and I discussed that very point. I came tae the conclusion that it must have been when I got back to the road. There's a fair bit of cover there – birch and rhoddies.'

'Well, we'd better get going, Watty.' The Inspector stood up. 'You take it easy for a bit.'

'Aye, well, we'll see,' Watty replied.

As the Inspector drove Duncan home, the poacher said, 'I think I'll have a look round that birch wood sometime, Angus. I'm used to spotting things in what they term nowadays "the natural environment" – what I call the countryside!'

'Good idea, Duncan. My boys can have a check over afterwards, if you keep me informed.'

'That I will, Angus, rest assured now.'

For some reason the photograph which Kenneth had given him had been preying on Angus's mind; something didn't seem right. 'Blast it,' he muttered as he returned to Faileadh. 'Just one of those quirks; probably nothing in it ...'

'Sadie said you'd be over, Angus,' PC Munro greeted the Inspector at the gate. Angus had already dropped Duncan off at his house. They made their way into the small police office which was built on to the side of the house. The linoleum floor was polished to a mirror finish by Jeannie, his wife.

'Any developments on the case, sir?'

'Nothing much, James. You know about Watty's narrow escape?'

'I did; strange affair that. I heard Duncan found prints the size o' my feet.' Bookam gave a laugh. 'The only other person I know who can compete is 'Nessy' Newton, a constable from Inverness – he has feet like the monster!'

'It's about that I came over, James. I brought the cast with me.' He laid a brown paper parcel down on the counter and unwrapped it. 'It occurred to me that you usually keep your Wellingtons in the back of your own van, don't you?'

Bookam shot him an apprehensive glance. 'Aye,' he admitted.

'Do you always keep it locked, James?'

'Well,' the Constable replied, flushing a deeper red than normal. 'Not always, sir. It's my own van, as you know, and I always take the ignition key oot,' he added defensively. 'The back door never locked properly since the night o' the last ceilidh at Queenshouse, way back when I gave Duncan a lift home.' Angus gave a puzzled frown and the Constable continued hurriedly. 'He was a bit fu', ye ken, and I wouldna let him drive his own van, so I told him to jump into the back o' mine. He's an awfu' powerful beast, Duncan, and he didn't realise that the back door was locked! I don't think he even remembers it to this day …'

'Go and get your boots, James. We'll have a wee look … Meantime, I'd like to use your phone. What's Watty Gilchrist's number?'

'It's on the rescue call-out list by the phone, sir.'

'Thanks.'

'I'll be back in a jiff,' the Constable said.

Minutes later, the Constable was back, a puzzled frown on his face. 'You know, sir,' he began, a wary look in his eyes as he fingered his moustache with his free hand. 'I thought there was something familiar aboot that cast when you unwrapped it ... I know why now.' He turned one of the boots upside down to reveal the sole. It was identical to the cast. 'I was jest joking when I said they were aboot my size, sir!'

'Well, well, James, the plot thickens ... But why would someone want Watty bumped off?' Angus asked quietly. 'Why, James?' he repeated.

'I canna think, sir, but I would imagine it's something tae dae wi' the decease o' the laird.' The way he pronounced 'decease' sounded like 'disease'.

'Nice way you put it, James, the decease o' the laird. I suppose we'll all decease one of these days. Or could it be something to do with Isaac's decease?'

'Tempus fugit and a' that, sir!'

'It doesn't make sense,' Angus continued as he went out. 'Have the boys check your wellies for prints and soil from the mine, Constable.' He added, 'Whoever took your wellies ran a double risk in returning them.'

With the passing away of the laird, Grey Corries Lodge seemed to mourn. There was an atmosphere of gloom about the establishment; the guests sat about morosely, only occasionally venturing out. Deirdre's presence brightened things slightly, but she didn't mix with the guests. Clem had climbed Eagal Mor that morning in good time. Von Spielman was becoming progressively more impatient and had started muttering about going back home.

'The relaxation will do you the world of good, Karl,' Penelope said. 'Get rid of some of that hypertension.'

'All the tension is in this house, not of me, and I have no desire to be permanently relaxed.' The fat German pointed to his chest. 'The polizei are feruckt. They cannot even speak English!'

They were all sitting in the drawing room, awaiting the call for dinner. Torrential rain was beating a tattoo on the windows. Clem appeared in a new jacket of black and white check, having forsaken tartan for the evening.

'You really do look like a chessboard in that jacket. You should have a game with Duncan MacGillvery!' the Honourable Mrs Victoria had commented with distaste when they met on the stairs. Penelope shuddered when she saw it.

In an argumentative mood Ken was trying to raise a conversation on the merits of nationalised industries, but this fell on deaf ears.

'I'm trying to relax, too, as Penny has suggested, Ken,' Clem retorted. 'Anyhow, I'm not getting into an argument.'

'I think,' Spielman said, looking up, 'money and politics is, how do you say,' he turned to Penelope, 'the odour of the people?'

'You mean opium, Karl,' Penelope corrected him sweetly.

'Nein, the people smell it and, how do you say, get to like it.'

After dinner Kirsty left Jean MacBain to wash up.

'I'd better go and see Watty, Jean. He still looks gae glaiket.' She put on an oilskin coat.

'My, he's verra lucky, Kirsty. Mr Horatio was going to fence that mine off years ago. I heard him saying so mysel' – and if he had put netting over it at the same time, it might have prevented the accident and kept the foxes oot o' the mine.'

Watty was scanning the *Highland Journal*, the Kinlochsanda weekly rag. His wife had just come in.

'I see that they're laying off 20 men at the Highland Smelters in Kinlochsanda,' he greeted her. 'It was only aboot a month ago I read aboot that big order from China for aluminium. I canna understand it. I hope Dougie Stewart doesna lose his job; he's a fine man in the team.'

'Dougie's too good a worker to be paid off,' his wife replied.

Just then there was a knock on the door. Watty got up.

'Oh, it's yersel', Deirdre, come away in – it's a terrible night.' The daughter of the house had draped a coat over her head; it gleamed in the light of the hall.

'I'm not coming in, Watty. Ken wants your walkie-talkie. There's been an accident on Ben Deurach. He's getting ready. That American climber is going with him.'

'You tell Ken I'll be with him in a brace o' shakes, Deirdre. I can at least operate the base radio.'

'Well ...' Deirdre hesitated, obviously unsure of the wisdom of this. 'I'll tell him certainly, Walter, but you know what he'll say ...'

'You must be mad!' Kirsty said as he came back in. 'And on a night like this. There you were, unconscious all last night and now proposing to go out on a stupid rescue. Dr Khan told you to rest. Whoever it is has probably only got cramp or a sprained ankle ... And,' she added as an after-thought, 'he's probably drowned by now, anyway!'

'Well, we'll see, but I'll no' go up the hill. I'll stay wi' the radio and it'll free someone else for the sharp end.' He went next door to collect his gear and in a few minutes was out of the house, heading for the garage. The rain angled down with ferocity.

The Range Rover was already running when Watty entered the garage. Ken almost exploded.

'You get back to bed, Gilchrist! You're not coming.'

'Yes, I am, Ken. But I'll stay at base.'

'I heard about your close shave, Watty,' Clem cut in. 'But you should take it easy!'

'I'm coming,' Watty repeated, and slid into the front seat.

'Idiot!' Ken replied, but shrugged fatalistically.

'Isaac would no doubt have had a few words for a night like this,' Ken said as he took the vehicle through what appeared to be a channel of water and what was in fact the glen road. 'I remember him once before on a call-out quoting that bit from the Flood: "the waters prevailed exceedingly upon the earth; and all the high hills that were under the whole heaven were covered."'

'I didn't think you were a great churchgoer, Ken?' The keeper sounded amused.

'I'm not, as you're well aware, Watty. I had it drummed into me at school in Edinburgh. One of my masters had a passion for the Old Testament, but we all enjoyed it – there are a few spicy bits, it should have an x certificate.'

'I sure was sorry to hear that the preacher met his end on that hot-rod,' Clem said.

'Yes, we'll miss him – he certainly got round his flock "with celerity", to use his own words,' Kenneth replied.

'Where's the rendezvous?' asked Watty, changing the subject.

'Up at the aqueduct outfall at Loch Gorm. I was speaking to Basil Thorndyke. He says we'll be able to drive up the main tunnel to the upper catchment area and get to the kid that way. That'll save some time.'

'Aye, it'll be handy,' the other agreed. He was feeling slightly nauseous, but certainly would never admit it. 'At least this rain will shift the remaining snow,' he added.

'It'll cause flooding, too,' Ken replied, concentrating on driving since the road was now worse beyond Queenshouse. 'When we get rain like this on top of snow, it can play havoc.'

'It's a young lad, you say?'

'Yes,' Ken replied. 'One of a school group. He's a broken leg; fell through a snow bridge into a gully. It must have been thawing like springtime in Hell even up near the summit of Ben Deurach.'

After 20 miles they left the main Glasgow highway and turned in a shower of spray on to the narrow track leading down Glen Uisgich and eventually left this to pass through a pair of white painted gates.

'Is the Inspector coming?' Watty asked.

'No,' Ken replied. 'It's his night off; he's having a meal out, I understand.' The headlights picked out a large sign which declared it was 'Forbidden to Unauthorised Vehicles'. Ahead the mouth of a tunnel led down to the underground pumping station, but he swung the vehicle left on to a narrow tarmac road which he knew was the beginning of the steep ascent to Loch Gorm.

'That's someone waving a torch,' the keeper remarked.

'It's Basil,' Ken answered, changing down. 'I know that old cagoule.' The Range Rover stopped beside him.

'Wanting a lift?'

'The others are just behind,' the boss of the Hydro project told them. 'They should be here any minute.'

He squeezed into the back of the vehicle with his rucksack.

'I'm sure you don't get rain like this in the States,' Basil said, mopping his face with a handkerchief.

'Don't you believe it, Basil,' the American retorted. 'We get our share of flash floods.'

As they rounded the shore of Loch Gorm, they caught a glimpse of lights behind.

'Those must be the other vehicles,' Watty observed.

'Probably be the police,' Basil added, then continued. 'Go up into the bottom of the Recorder House, Ken. There's a ramp and a right-angled turn into the main tunnel.'

'Are we using the tunnel?'

'Yes, the mountain road is impassable tonight, I'll turn the water off, but there's so much flowing just now that I'll have to let it run back through as soon as we get up. That cold spell a few weeks ago didn't help the water level, but there's plenty now. Also there's an emergency down at the tailrace tonight,' he added. 'The staff are all there, but I'll operate the gates myself. They're power-operated.'

By the time the Range Rover had stopped inside the mouth of the tunnel, the police Land Rovers were coming up the ramp behind them. Lights blazed in the entrance. Basil was pointing out the layout.

'The water coming down the tunnel goes through the gratings up ahead there, then into Loch Gorm,' he explained. 'And there's one hell of a lot coming down just now – about 500 cubic feet per second. The tunnel is three-quarters full.'

'The Recorder House is directly overhead, isn't it?' Ken asked, now putting on his climbing boots; he didn't like driving in them.

'Yes, that door leads to it. I'll go and shut off all of the sluice gates.'

'What happens to the water then?' Clem asked, taking his baseball cap off and putting it in the Range Rover.

'It goes where it went for millions of years, Clem, before this place was thought of – down its old course.'

'You must be bloody mad, Watty Gilchrist!' Duncan's voice boomed from a side window of the police vehicle. 'What the hell are you doing here? You should be in intensive care, not in a Land Rover.

'I'm only going to the top o' the aqueduct,' the keeper retorted. 'We'll need someone to operate a base radio.'

'Aye, but not a corpse! ... Chris!' the poacher shouted

to the team leader. 'Why don't you order the silly bastard to stay down here, or to get back to bed?' Chris came over, adjusting his headlamp as he did so.

'Duncan's right, Watty. I heard about your accident. It's stupid to be here after that crack on the head.'

'It's hardly cut,' the keeper replied, 'and what about your escapade on Eagal Mor, Duncan,' he responded, fingering Dr Khan's dumb bell stitches.

'You know perfectly well that you might have a relapse. Duncan tells me you were unconscious for most of last night.'

'Well, there was most likely a bit o' normal sleep thrown in as well,' Watty returned. 'I can kip anywhere!'

'You're impossible, Gilchrist – but if you insist, you may as well operate the radio relay in the Land Rover. You can stay up there as well as here.'

'Hello, Clem,' Chris shouted. 'Come to try your hand on a wet Scottish mountain?'

'Sure, I've mentioned to Ken a couple of times that I'd like to help you guys out,' the American drawled. 'You always seem short-handed.'

'That's good of you,' Chris replied. 'We'll take the three Rovers up the tunnel.' Chris shouted above the din from the water. 'That okay, Basil?' He had just returned from closing the sluices.

'Sure. The aqueduct's eight foot six high by seven foot wide. OK for the Rovers but a bit too tight for a rescue truck.'

'Right, then, as you've turned off the tap. We'll go up with Basil in the first vehicle and ...' he paused for an instant, 'Clem, PC Munro, Ken and me, plus some gear. Watty, Duncan and Ian Wright in the second with the rest of the equipment. The police Rover can follow up with the others.'

'The tunnel's steep,' Basil shouted as they all piled into the vehicles. 'Keep in low ratio!'

Soon the thunder of thousands of gallons of water subsided and an uncanny silence seemed to flood the vault ahead.

'Queer place, this,' said Robert MacNish, the big Kinlochsanda policeman. 'One minute it's like a flooded boiler shop and the next it resembles a cathedral in need of a damp course.'

'Okay, Chris, let's go,' Basil called. 'Leave ten minute intervals between the vehicles.'

The first 4 x 4 rolled on to the grating and into the tunnel. As they moved slowly up the steep incline, Chris felt like a worm heading upwards in its well-lubricated passage towards the surface of the earth. The floor of the tunnel was of concrete with deep transverse ribbing so that the tyres got a good purchase despite the steep angle.

After what seemed ages, the hypnotic symmetry diminished as they passed side tunnels which led in from other catchment aqueducts, each with its own power-operated sluice gate. Presently, they drove out into inky darkness and the headlights descended to the horizontal, revealing a wide concrete area. On Basil's instructions Ken parked the machine on a ramp beside the top valve house.

'When Watty comes up he can stay here,' Basil said as they got out. 'There's a heater and stove, so he can make a brew. I can also operate the sluices from here.'

'Great,' Chris observed. 'We can't usually drive most of the way up a bleeding mountain on a rescue!'

PC Munro and Ken were scanning the darkness above. Suddenly Ken saw a light.

'Hey, look, lads, there they are!' They crowded round to the front of the Land Rover and Ken flashed the headlights off and on. There was an immediate pinpoint of light from above; then a series of long and short flashes, the International Distress Signal.

As the Land Rover driven by Duncan was creeping up the tunnel, Watty felt sleepy; he yawned widely. His first warning of impending disaster was an almost casual remark made by Duncan.

'Bloody funny, Watty!'

'Eh? What was that?' The keeper rubbed his eyes.

'Look at the water.'

In seconds the floor of the tunnel, which had only been damp a moment before, was streaming with peaty black water; it was rising at an alarming rate.

'For Christ's sake, get into reverse, Duncan. Someone's opened the bloody sluice gates.'

'How's the missus?' Archie Campbell asked Robert MacNish, the young Constable from Kinlochsanda and a member of the police rescue team. They were awaiting their turn to go up the tunnel. The second Land Rover had already departed.

'A bit better, thanks, Sergeant. She came out of hospital last week. You know,' Robert observed, cocking his head. 'I could swear that the water has started to flow again.' They all listened attentively.

'I think you're right, Robert,' the Sergeant agreed, looking alarmed as the noise increased. In a flash he disappeared up into the top Recorder House. Though he hadn't been inside before, a rapid glance was enough for him to spot, to the right of an array of dials, a red button marked 'Emergency Sluice Closure', beside which were two telephones. He saw one was marked 'Aqueduct only'. He picked it up and could hear a ringing tone, but there was no reply.

Robert MacNish burst in. 'Quick, there's something bloody strange going on! The water's rising every second.'

Without any further hesitation the Sergeant punched the red button and wiped the sweat from his brow. 'I sincerely hope, Constable, that I haven't sabotaged the National Grid!' The policeman didn't say anything but he looked pale.

'It's going doon,' Robert observed when they joined the other two policemen. 'Weird business, this!'

They all paused since a loud scraping noise now emanated from the tunnel. They ran over the concrete to where the heavy grating spanned the floor, through which the tunnel water dropped down into the pipelines. The lighting was poor, but they saw ahead, in the dark, peaty water of the tunnel, two red lights. A Land Rover bounced and scraped with a graunching of metal, from one side of the tunnel to the other.

'I hope to hell they're all right,' Archie shouted in alarm. The vehicle didn't cease its rapid backwards motion until it shuddered over the grating beside them; they narrowly missed being mown down. It rocked as it stopped. Robert's large hand gripped the passenger's door handle, where he could see Watty sitting, white and shaken. But the side of the Land Rover had been so distorted that the door refused to budge. Duncan, on the other side, sat as if paralysed.

'Wait till I get these bits o' glass removed,' Archie shouted and used his ice axe to break off the offending fragments from the broken window. A few seconds later the keeper came out head first, assisted by Archie and Robert. The other constable, helped by Duncan, succeeded in wrenching open the other door.

'What happened?' Archie asked Duncan, when they had got their breath back.

'You tell me!' the other returned. 'One minute all was well, and the next somebody pulled the chain …'

At the top of the aqueduct the others were preparing to

set off up the mountain. It was Basil who first noticed that the next vehicle seemed to be taking a long time. He went over to the top valve room and picked up the telephone. When it had rung previously there was no-one there when he picked up the receiver. Eventually, his call was answered by Archie.

'What's the matter, Sergeant? Where the hell has everybody got to.'

'Duncan's Land Rover has been caught in the water, Basil!'

He explained briefly what happened.

'Did anybody turn the water on down there?' Basil's voice was tense.

'No, we were all outside.'

'Well,' the engineer said at length. 'This is serious. They can go down to my place until we finish; the missus will look after them. Meanwhile, I'll stay inside here until the rest of you are up. I'll make sure nothing else happens,' he added grimly.

'Okay, we'll be up right away.'

Chris came into the concrete room. 'What's up, Basil? You look as if you've seen the ghosts of those Poles who died drilling the tunnel!'

'There were nearly three more to join them,' Basil answered quietly. 'Someone turned the water on.'

'What!' Chris exclaimed in disbelief. 'Bugger me. How, in God's name?'

'By pressing the master button.' He pointed to the button. 'One opens and the other closes the main water gates. This is a bad business, Chris,' the engineer added tersely. 'I should never have allowed you all to go up without extra official help; it's against regulations.'

'This isn't the first odd happening, Basil. Someone

seems to be wanting rid of Watty at least and they don't seem to mind whom they dispatch with him ...'

'What's all this, Chris?' Basil asked curiously. 'How come?'

'The mine,' the team leader said. 'Somebody tried to put out Watty's light for good and auld Horrible's death was strange, to say the least. And after a dress rehearsal Isaac went out with a bang!'

'But the shaft – that was an accident, surely? Why, we were only talking about it at the bottom a short while ago.' Basil's voice trailed off uncertainly. 'And – and Isaac, he surely died in the motor cycle crash?'

Constable Munro came to the door and spoke, impatience evident in his voice.

'Where the hell are the others – we'll be out all night!' In a few, well-chosen words Basil told him what had happened.

'It must have been an electrical fault, Basil,' the Constable spat out. 'In any case, it's no use going into it further now; there's a lad injured up there.' He pointed in the general direction of the high peak of Ben Deurach.

A few minutes later the throb of a Land Rover engine was heard and then its headlights swept down through the night sky, like long white arms lowering in prayer. It rocked to a halt and its occupants spilled out.

'What in hell's going on, Archie? Are the others all right?' Chris asked.

'They're fine,' the Sergeant replied, taking the stretcher out of the back of the vehicle. 'But they'll be none the worse o' a cup of tea at Basil's place, but Duncan's here with us; the man's incorrigible.'

'You use awfully big words since you were on that last course at Police College, Sarge, just like Bookam,' the poacher said.

'Let's move and get that lad down before he dies from exposure or old age!' Chris urged them.

'I wish to hell someone had called me!' The Inspector brought his fist down on the table. 'I was bored stiff at Erchie Robertson's anyhow, and the meal was terrible! Go over the whole thing again, Archie, would you?' he asked his colleague.

The Sergeant obligingly reiterated all he knew of the previous night's events. Angus Wilson's face was impassive in concentration, though he wasn't really listening to Archie – the Sergeant was providing the background theme. The Inspector was attempting to compose a logical pattern from a mass of disjointed events.

When Archie had finished, there was silence in the Inspector's office and only the discreet knock of Sadie Murcheson, bearing two cups of tea, broke the spell.

'I've typed the letters, Inspector.'

'Aye, thanks, Sadie. I'll sign them presently. I think we can rule out the possibility of the water being switched on from below, Archie. Only Clem was missing for a couple o' minutes and, as you said, he went to relieve himself. Unless he was telling a lie ... I wonder,' the Inspector mused. 'No, Sarge, it was probably up at the other end that the villainy took place. But, for the life of me, I can't think who could have slipped in to do it. It could have been any one of them, I suppose. But,' the Inspector continued as he blew on his tea,'it was one of four: Basil, Chris, Clem or Kenneth. Goddammit, man, it must have been one of them and I can't see Basil as the villain of the piece, he doesn't fit into it. You say, Sergeant, the door and window of that top valve room are on the side – not visible from where the vehicle was parked. Also it was dark, of course?'

'That's right. It may have nothing to do with that earlier attempt on Watty, Inspector,' Archie added. 'It could be a different motive entirely, but I can't think what. I had a word with Constable Munro,' the Sergeant went on, 'and he thinks the most likely chance for doing the job was when they spotted the lights o' the party on the hill, as they were standing round the Land Rover at the top. They were all distracted then.'

'There was a 10 minute interval between the vehicles?' Duncan asked for confirmation.

'That's right, and it takes about a quarter of an hour to get up the tunnel. Clem had plenty of time to have his wee-wee and rejoin us. Nobody else from our group went wandering off at all.'

'Where did Clem release his transatlantic water?' asked Angus.

'I think it was just at the mouth of the ramp, where you arrive at the Recorder House. I'd have noticed had he gone inside.'

'Umph,' the Inspector rumbled, deep in thought. 'We'll try both the top and lower rooms for prints, Archie. It's two buttons, that operates the valves?'

'Yes. I'll see to that, Angus. I asked for both places to be kept locked until we had finished our inquiry, unless it's an emergency and then only with two of the staff.'

'I don't think there'll be much gained in my going down there, but keep your eyes skinned when you do, Archie, won't you?'

'Aye.'

'We'll have to delve a bit deeper into the background o' some of the lads,' the Inspector continued. 'PC Wright is from Glasgow, and he's been with us for about a year.'

'Basil's from Manchester, isn't he?'

'That's right,' Archie confirmed. We may as well make a thorough job of it; ask them if he's kept to the straight and narrow. But, come to think of it, he must have – he's in too responsible a job. Funny thing how Clem Fular seems to keep popping up, isn't it?' the Inspector went on quietly, then added, 'I think I'll contact the LAPD and see what they can tell us about him; he may be the President of a Christmas Club for all we know … How's the boy?' he continued abruptly.

'Fine,' Archie replied. 'Broken femur, and he was suffering from exposure, but they recover easily, like stirks, at that age.'

'Watty, Ian and MacGillvery?'

'I phoned up the Lodge this morning and was told by Kirsty that Watty and Ian are away after hinds … Watty's a hell o' a man.'

'He's hard,' the Inspector smiled and, changing the subject, asked. 'How's the Land Rover?'

'It's in a bonny mess,' the Sergeant commiserated. 'Looks as if Glasgow wide boys were practising panel beating!'

The Sergeant rose. He paused at the door.

'You missed a good talk Dr Khan gave the other night, on first aid: "Trauma and the Patient". Makes one think on what our victims go through sometimes.'

'So I gather, Archie,' Angus returned. 'It seems we should make more use of laughing gas, nitrous oxide. I was under the impression that its principal use was for relief of pain in childbirth.'

'Aye, we've had that equipment for years and never used it much at all. I guess because it's a bit heavy. You have to mind to keep the cylinder wrapped up in the rucksack, though. The doctor told us it's possible for the gas to separate at low temperatures and then it's no joke.'

The Inspector went round the rescue team later that day, but he obtained little fresh information. Ken hadn't seen anybody going into the Recorder Room either, other than Basil, then Chris when the phone rang. 'And,' Chris added, 'I can't understand how anyone would have had the opportunity. On the face of it, Angus, I doubt Basil's assurance that an electrical fault is out of the question.' He continued, 'Even Bookam Munro suggested that – that such august bodies as the Electricity Pump Station Authority get their wires crossed.'

Angus next drove round to Duncan's. 'What's your considered opinion after yesterday's ablutions, Duncan?' The Inspector addressed the big poacher MacGillvery from his front garden fence. The big man looked up from a new shed he was building and came over to Angus. He pushed his fore and aft up and gazed at the policeman with this pale blue eyes.

'Strange business, that, Angus.' He dropped a claw hammer on the ground. 'I've been thinking aboot it off and on since I got back. One of several people could have done it, but I can't see why. There were three of us in that Land Rover so one of us, or perhaps two, obviously knows something which someone doesn't want us to pass on – there can be no other motive that I can see.' A puzzled frown creased his brow. 'I asked Basil how long it takes for the tunnel to fill to capacity,' Duncan continued. 'It's only a matter of minutes. And I had a look inside the Recorder Room or whatever the hell it's called after I came down from the rescue, and that was before anyone else had a chance to tidy up but I couldn't see anything amiss.'

'Do you think Basil is up to something?'

'No, Angus, I don't, but I suspect everybody else, "except thee and me."'

'And what have you deduced, under that fore and aft?' The Inspector smiled broadly.

'Nothing, Angus. Not a bloody thing. But I'll tell you who had the opportunity to switch the gates open.' He paused for an instant and a faraway look came into his eyes. 'I hadn't, for one, but Chris, Basil and that chap Fular – queer bugger that, Angus, if you ask me – and Ken had. Bookam was at the Land Rover to begin with so he couldna have made it … Anyhow,' he added. 'His feet are so big he'd have tripped in the dark.'

The Inspector paused before he spoke. 'Well, Duncan, the only conclusion I've reached is that the mystery of the second tunnel wasn't an accident, but a deliberate attempt to kill either Watty, Ian and/or yourself.'

'Did Constable Munro not notice anything?' Duncan glanced at the Inspector, an almost furtive glance, Angus thought.

'Well, he might have, Duncan, but it's my job to investigate and correlate information, not volunteer it!'

'I was only asking, Angus. Don't take me wrong; But Munro doesn't miss much!'

Chapter 12

For the rest of the afternoon Inspector Angus Wilson was engaged in routine jobs. He saw the Superintendent and made a verbal report on the investigations to date. Several of the guests at Grey Corries were getting desperate to be off; namely Penelope – who had to visit a sick relative. Clem Fular seemed quite happy to stay on for a day or so, but had suggested to Spielman that they should move to Queenshouse.

The Inspector shouted through to Sadie, generally finding this quicker than using the intercom: 'Ask Archie to come in, will you, lass.'

'Right.' Her voice came over the small loudspeaker on his desk. A few minutes later the Sergeant appeared.

'You wanted me?'

'It's just to say that we'd better let that woman with the face like a Shetland pony go to see her ailing aunt.'

'Penelope Almen?'

'That's her. Her aunt's sick.'

'What about the others?'

'Clem Fular and Spielman want to stay, but may move to the hotel. I think Willie Fyffe has offered them some stalking.'

'I'll tell them,' Archie promised.

'You know, Archie,' the Inspector ruminated, twiddling a pencil between his fingers. 'Duncan suspects something. I wonder what it can be.'

'Is that so.' The Sergeant was amused. 'I wonder if he got the tip-off from one of his cronies. They're a tight bunch, those crofters.'

'It's probably only my imagination; it could mean nothing, or a lot … Oh, and Archie …'

'Yes?'

'I want a check done on a plaster cast; the one on the table in the corner – there.'

The telephone rang; Thumper picked up the receiver.

'An emergency call from Queenshouse, sir.'

'A rescue?'

'Yes. I've got Water, er … Mr Fyffe, on the line.'

'Put him through, will you.' Angus looked up at Archie. 'A call-out … Hello, Willie?'

'Aye, it's another, Angus,' the publican's rolling voice boomed in the Inspector's ear. 'Up on the Eagal again; looks nasty.'

'Let's have it, Willie.'

'It's a girl, fallen on Red Wall. Her companion jest got doon to Queenshouse aboot 10 minutes ago. I've called out the team, Angus, and told Chris. He's having a chopper stand by for first light.'

'We'll be up shortly, Willie.'

'Ah, good. I asked PC Munro to raise Duncan, but he said he thought he'd gone.'

'It's on the Red Wall, Archie,' Angus stated as he hung up. Sadie came in with two cups of tea on an old Guinness tray.

'A call-out, Angus?' she asked, her sloe-dark eyes filled with concern.

'I'm afraid so,' the Inspector replied, taking a cup. 'Everything happens at once. We've been quiet for months. It's worse than Glasgow – the place is littered with bodies.'

'Red Wall could be difficult just now,' the Sergeant mused, blowing on his tea. 'Has Chris been told?'

'Yes, he's getting a helicopter for dawn.'

'Good,' Archie agreed. 'It could take some time getting folks off that face.'

'Isn't it strange,' Sadie observed, putting a plate of biscuits down on the Inspector's desk, 'how the weather always seems to get worse when there's a rescue? It's starting to snow again.'

'Sod's Law!' Angus muttered in disgust as he looked out of the window.

'Do you want me to stay on, Angus?' she asked.

'No, no,' the Inspector replied. 'You've got your Gaelic class tonight?'

'That's right.'

'Well, if I'm not back for nine in the morning, phone through to Inspector Mathieson of the Strathclyde Regional Crime Squad and tell him I'm much obliged for the help of his backroom boys and that I'll send him a telex shortly.'

'Yes, I'll do that, sir.'

There was a knock on the door. Three policemen entered, wearing anoraks and over-trousers.

'That didn't take long, Donald,' the Inspector addressed one of the men. 'Have you recovered from your last rescue, Constable Wright?' Thumper asked Ian, a regular member of the police team.

'Just needed a change of clothes, sir!'

'Well, the hill it is,' Archie chimed in, finishing his tea in

a gulp. 'And it's going to be gae coorse, as Watty says.'
Putting the cup back on the tray, he said, 'Thanks, Sadie.'
The Inspector didn't even bother finishing his, but collected
his rucksack from a corner of a cupboard.

'We'll take the long wheel-base Land Rover, Archie.'

'I'll get it,' the Sergeant offered. The other followed
him out.

'Good luck,' Sadie called as they filed out.

'I think the poor lass up the hill will need all of that,' the
Inspector replied, eyeing the heavy snowflakes.

Watery bustled out of the office where he had been trying
to chat up Janet Smith, the waitress.

'It's yourself, Chris. A terrible night now, terrible, is
it not?'

'Inclement, Willie,' Chris replied.

'The others are on their way,' the publican said. 'Come
away in.'

They had no sooner entered than there was a squeal of
brakes. The publican peered through the front door glass.

'It's MacGillvery,' he stated. 'With Doug and Basil, the
party from the Hydro.'

'Good,' Chris said, taking a seat and putting on his
snow gaiters. 'We can get off.'

The others entered in a cloud of snow and were momentarily dazzled by the light for it was already dusk outside.

'Hello, Willie,' Duncan greeted him. 'Any of the others
here?'

'Just Chris.'

'Hello, Duncan,' the geologist greeted him. 'Poor conditions.'

'Yes.'

'Hope she holds out.'

'The Inspector will be round shortly, Chris, and the rest o' the lads.'

'Right,' the team leader replied, standing and placing his rucksack on a chair. 'Where's the survivor?'

'In the back room. The missus is with him; he looks frozen. I called the doctor.'

'Good.'

'What happened?' Chris asked the ginger-haired youth. Annie, Watery's wife, had taken him under her generous wing and was fussing round the lad. He couldn't be more than 18, thought Chris.

'I was just telling him he should be in bed,' Annie clucked, looking with concern at the climber.

'I'm all right, really, Mrs Fyffe. Just a bit cold. I don't seem to get any warmer, despite the fire ...' He glanced at the team leader, remembering that he should have answered his question. 'It happened up near the top, on the Red Wall. Joyce peeled; fell off the fourth pitch.'

'Was she leading?'

'No, I was. But she pendulumed a fair way. There's a long traverse and I just couldn't pull her up after she'd come off.'

'So you left her hanging?' Chris' eyes narrowed slightly.

'No, I untied from the rope after a lot of trouble and went down to her. I got her back on a ledge, but she stopped breathing. I gave her mouth to mouth,' the lad added defensively, his eyes wet. 'But I'm not sure if she's still alive.'

'Did you take her pulse?'

'Yes. It was very weak and she was extremely cold. Joyce wanted to go back earlier when the snow started – I should have listened.'

Annie turned his anorak which was drying at the fire and gave Chris a questioning glance.

'My,' she remarked. 'I don't know why you folks go climbing at all. This place is like an A & E clinic.' Her bosom gave a quiver as she straightened up. 'I'd better go into the bar, Chris, as Willie's talking about going up wi' you.'

'Right, Annie. I'll be through in a minute. Now, I didn't get your name?' he looked inquiringly at the small wiry climber.

'Barry Hunter.'

'I'm Chris Watkins. I'm leader of the local team. I want to get the details right, Barry. I presume that she was near what's called Kipling Traverse on Eagal Mor when she fell?'

'Yes, I think that's the place – but we may have strayed off route.'

'Very likely, at this time of year. That route has only been done once before in winter, and that eight years ago! It's remarkable that you managed across that pitch.'

'It was hard,' Barry agreed. 'And I couldn't get any protection – or put a peg in.'

'Did you tie her on when you got her back to the ledge?'

'Yes, I also left my down jacket on her; she's in a plastic bivvy sack.'

'Good, we'll see what we can do. You stay here. The doctor will be up shortly.'

'Well, what's the score, Chris?' It was Kenneth Dewar. He was standing with Watty, Clem Fular and Deirdre. They were grouped round a table.

'Looks serious, as Willie Fyffe predicted. It may last into tomorrow … I don't know how the hell we'll get the girl off that terrace at the end of Kipling's in darkness.'

'Phew, what a ruddy place!' Watty expostulated. 'And on a night like this with the forecast for minus 20.'

'For your information, Watty,' Chris said. 'That's how that pitch got its name – it's Rud-y-ard.'

'But why on earth were they doing that climb?' Ken put in. 'It's serious.'

'That we know full well,' Chris responded. 'We had a desperate time when we tried it.'

'Have you done it then?' Deirdre asked, looking dazzling in a sheepskin jacket and red trousers.

'We tried,' Chris replied ruefully. 'But didn't make it.'

'It was one of my off days, I think. Either that or we weren't up to it.'

'Hey, Chris!' Duncan called from close by the bar. 'What gear do we need?'

'About the lot, Duncan … and you'd be as well to take up the oxygen and the nitrous oxide cylinders. She may still be alive.'

'Right. I'll get them out of the truck,' Douglas volunteered and went out of the door. Deirdre moved over to the door as well, but spoke first to her brother.

'Give me a ring when you want picked up, Ken, and I'll come up.'

'Right, sis, but you can sleep peacefully. It'll be a long night.'

'Good luck,' she called as she went out.

'I've got one of the team rucksacks for you, Clem. It's a bit smaller than the back-packing frame you have,' Ken said.

'Great!' the American returned. 'As I told you, I left my day pack in the States.'

'Let's get moving,' Chris called. 'We'll go up in two parties. Angus, will you take the second one?'

'Sure.'

'We'll see you at the top of Red Wall – round the easy way,' Chris added.

'I'll go with the Inspector,' Watty spoke. 'Seeing I'm no' quite mysel' yet.'

It was two hours later that the advance party reached the crest of Red Wall. The headlamps were appreciably dimmer.

'I'm no' sure where the top o' Kipling's is,' Duncan admitted, looking from under the shelter of the skip of his fore and aft.

'It must be about here somewhere,' Basil shouted, moving over cautiously to the edge of the face. A blast of icy air snapped at him and he hurriedly moved back.

'Better get a rope on,' Chris advised, putting down his rucksack. 'I'll abseil.'

'I'll give you a safety line,' Duncan volunteered. 'It's not a place to be on a night like this. I've a spare rope with me,' he added as he knocked the snow from his crampons with his ice axe.

'Any sign of the others?' someone asked.

'I got base on the radio a wee while ago,' Duncan advised. 'PC Munro's there now.'

'Ask him if there's confirmation for the chopper, would you, Duncan?' Chris asked.

'Aye, I will.' Duncan took up the microphone and blew the snow from it. 'Hello, base, come in.'

'Base here. Identify yourself, please … over.'

'Jimmy Munro's being a smart Alec tonight,' the poacher said to the other two. 'As if he doesn't know my bloody voice … procedure!'

'He likes to work by the book these days, Duncan,' Chris replied. 'It's these high-powered investigations that have gone to his head!'

'Duncan here, in the advance party. Can you advise if the helicopter is available for first light?'

'Stand by, advance party. I'll contact HQ and come back. Over.'

'Secure this rope, will you, Basil.' Chris addressed the

engineer. He knew that if Basil made the belay it would be a good one. 'Better take some pegs with you.'

'I've got some, thanks.'

Duncan had returned to the task of uncoiling another rope. He gave the end to Chris and the geologist tied it to his harness.

'I'll use my radio to keep in touch. It's too bloody windy to shout, Duncan.'

'Right, Chris.'

Basil returned in a few moments. 'Got a good rock bollard, so I didn't need a peg.'

'Great.' Duncan had the safety rope laid out on the snow and went back a few feet to where the ridge rose beyond the wall; sounds of a peg going in reached the other two. Then, Duncan's large figure re-emerged out of the maelstrom.

'That's your safety rope organised, Chris.'

'Right, I'm ready,' the geologist said.

'This bloody hill has grown since I last climbed it!' Willie Fyffe gasped. He was following in the wake of the rear party which had halted for a rest.

'I think it's you who have grown, Willie,' Sergeant Campbell observed dryly.

'Well ... I may have put on a wee bit over the years,' the publican confessed. 'Let's hope nothing else goes wrong tonight, Archie,' he added.

'What else would be going wrong, Willie?' the Sergeant replied.

'If somebody wants to kill off the team there are plenty of opportunities on a night like this.'

They were at the ridge which led directly to the top of Red Wall when the Inspector finally halted. By the light of his headlamp he could see the steps of the advance party. Here the ridge narrowed and formed a crest which reared like a rock fin to the top of the Red Wall. To the right lay the sinister depths of Cranberry Gully, a deep defile which severed the mountain from top to bottom for almost 2,000 feet.

'How are you faring, Watty?' Angus inquired.

'Fine.'

'Look – there are the lights of the others, directly above,' Willie Fyffe pointed. 'They must be at the top of the Wall.' The others looked up into a maelstrom of driving snow.

'No sae far tae go now,' Ian Wright said hopefully.

'I trust we've brought enough bivouac gear with us,' Willie remarked. 'I can't see how we can get that girl down tonight.'

'We've brought the big bivvy tent … You've got it, haven't you, Douglas?'

'That I have, Angus,' the climber responded.

Chris eased himself down the icy abseil rope. He couldn't see a thing, unless he stopped and swung his headlamp down. Basil was shining a light from above, but an overhang now frustrated this advantage. He gave a call: 'Hello, Joyce, where are you?' But his words were devoured by the wind. He kept edging down, looking for the terrace where the girl had been left, then stopped, his crampons scraping the iced rock as he locked the abseil rope off to his harness and was now secure. He swung his walkie-talkie round and spoke to Duncan as he could no longer contact him by shouting.

'How much rope, Duncan?'

There was a moment's delay, and he imagined the big man grabbing the microphone, but it was Basil who eventually answered.

'Basil here, Chris. Duncan's belaying you. He thinks there's 40 feet.'

'OK I'll move on down. Tell Duncan to keep me tight when I stop and until I call you, will you? I can't be far off the terrace.'

'Wilco, Chris. Standing by ...'

The slow descent continued. He angled his headlamp over to his right and, through the slanting snow, thought he saw something red. Yes, it was part of a cagoule. He swung over the face towards it. As he drew closer, he could see the girl, bundled up in an orange bivvy bag and partly covered by snow. It was a section of her hood that he had first spotted. He couldn't quite reach her on the first swing, so he returned across the face again secured by the rope above, until he was at the limit of the friction of his crampons on the hard ryolite. Then he started to run sideways, holding on to the ropes above him. He was 60 feet from the belay point; sparks flew from his crampons as they bit through the atmospheric icing which lightly covered the wall. His momentum was almost spent when he managed to reach the ledge and grab at a tape sling which protruded from the snow, hoping that it was tied off. It was. Gratefully, he pulled himself alongside the motionless girl.

Chapter 13

Douglas was the first to join up with the advance party.

'How is she?' he asked.

'Don't know, yet,' Basil answered. 'We're waiting to hear from Chris.'

'It's freezing, Doug,' Duncan greeted him. The Inspector arrived, breathing heavily.

'You sound like a grampus, Inspector!' Basil shouted.

'That creature has more sense than me!' the policeman responded. 'It doesn't climb bloody mountains.'

'Is everyone else behind?' Duncan asked.

'Aye, Watery's taking up the rear – like a brave gendarme!'

'Duncan here, Chris. Do you need help?'

There was the usual delay before the reply came, metallic and distorted.

'Hello, Duncan. She's in a bad way – unconscious. Bring some more pegs down with you when you come. It's grim down here.'

'I'll be with you shortly.'

'By the way, keep to your right as you descend.' Chris's

voice was now distorted. 'The ledge isn't in line with the top anchor; I've tied the bottom end of the abseil rope at the ledge.'

'Right.'

'Hello, advance party. Come in, please.' The Constable's voice was loud and clear.

'Reading you, base. Send your message,' Basil replied.

'Confirmation: the helicopter's ETA is 0800 hours.'

'Thanks, base. I'll pass that on to Chris. Out.'

'I'll tell him when I get down,' the poacher said to the engineer, 'but he probably heard it.'

'It's hell, Willie,' Watty addressed the publican as he loomed out of the darkness.

'It is that,' Willie agreed. 'My God, I'm getting a bit past this lark ...' He collapsed in a heap on the snow beside Ken. Clem arrived last, not because he was unfit, but because he was concerned about the publican who, he felt, shouldn't have been allowed on the hill in such conditions in such a condition.

PC Donald MacNish switched on a large fluorescent lantern.

'That's better,' said Archie thankfully. 'Now I can see to put a fresh battery in my headlamp.'

'I understand you may be coming to stay at the hotel for a few days, Mr Fular?' Willie Fyffe, having made a rapid recovery, was employing his business tone despite the blizzard.

'I sure hope so, Mr Fyffe. Karl Spielman and I would like to get some shooting in before we go. I don't seem to do anything but help you guys on rescues.' He gave an infectious laugh.

'Aye, it's no' often we get Ameericans helping us oot,' the publican agreed. 'But it's verra guid o' ye.'

'Oh, I get a kick out of it, Willie – it is Willie, isn't it?'

'Aye, but I'm often called worse than that ...'

'What I can't understand, Willie, is how all these dudes get into trouble. The hills aren't that tall.'

'I think we've more fools here than you have in America,' Angus interrupted. 'I'm no' a climber myself, but I should be, by the amount of time I spend off the level.'

'Base speaking, pass your message, Basil. I have the doctor here. Is there anything he can do?'

'Hello, James. I suggest you call Chris directly – he has a radio, but may be too busy to talk. Duncan's also descended. The girl's in a serious condition.'

'Right, Bas.'

'Phew!' Duncan gasped as he arrived at the ledge. 'It's not exactly the place for an extraordinary general meeting of the Faileadh Rescue Team!'

'Rough,' Chris agreed as he fielded his colleague. 'Here, clip on to this ...' He handed Duncan the end of a sling attached to a peg.

'Thanks. What's the score?'

'I think she's just passed away; have a look yourself. I can't get a pulse now, but we'll try resuscitation. It's a remote chance.'

'Here are the pegs.'

'Thanks. You try cardiac massage.'

'Okay.'

Chris took the bundle of pegs and, selecting one, cleared snow from a crack with his gloved hand and started to hammer it in. The ringing note of the driven steel was muted by snow and wind. Duncan, secured to the sling, bent over the girl and started work.

'Any luck?' asked Chris.

'I don't think so, I'll try the resuscitator.' Chris attached another sling to the new peg and tied it on to the casualty bag with which he had covered Joyce.

They attempted to revive her for 20 minutes, without saying a word. Then they finally decided to give up.

'It's no use, Ken. I just can't get a flicker from her.' He shook the snow off his helmet and looked at the girl's eyes, pulling up the lids. 'We did our damndest!'

'Well, that means no evacuation problem. We can collect the body when the weather clears. No point in endangering further life on a night like this.'

'I suppose not,' Chris agreed, straightening up, holding on to his belay sling. 'I'll tell the others. They'll be wondering what the hell's going on.'

After informing the top party and base about the death of the girl, Chris started up the rope with jumar clamps. However, the rope was now so badly iced that the clamps didn't grip properly and he slid back down, landing on top of Duncan, his crampons ripping the other's anorak.

'Sorry! These bloody things are clogged up with ice. It's cold as charity.'

'Let me know next time you're visiting like that, Chris; I'll move aside to avoid getting a puncture!'

Half an hour later they were both back at the top of the Wall. Most of the team were inside the large bivvy tent.

'Come on, you creutars!' Chris shouted. 'We're going back. We'll come up and get her off with the chopper as soon as it clears.'

Douglas Stewart led, picking his way down the ridge like a diligent fox.

'Look out for loose rocks here,' he warned. 'It's only the snow that's holding them in position.'

'Aye, I remember this bit from last summer,' Watty reminisced from above. 'When we took that couple down who were benighted – the man was as clumsy as a pregnant cow!'

'Below!' The call climbers fear rang out through the night as clear as any curfew bell, then the heavy crunch of falling boulders. Lights scattered. The Inspector, who was at the rear, swore later that he actually saw sparks from the falling rocks, despite the snow cover.

The boulders leapt down the ridge, disintegrating like shrapnel. There was a cry, then ominous silence. Lights rearranged themselves, returning more or less to the same zigzag line as before.

'Is anyone hurt?' It was the deep voice of Duncan.

'Watty!' Douglas shouted. 'He's been hit.' He moved up a few paces to where the keeper lay in a widening mess of bloody snow below his left leg. The others joined him moments later. Duncan was already bending over the keeper, examining him by the light of his torch.

'It's his leg,' he muttered quietly. 'Compound fracture ... Give me the first-aid pack, will you, Donald.' The Constable handed him the rucksack. Chris was also now kneeling beside Watty, feeling for his pulse.

'How do you feel, fella?' the team leader asked.

'I'll get by, Chris, but I doubt if I'll be after hinds tomorrow.'

'Have the stretcher unfolded, Archie,' Chris called, 'and get the cas bag and splints.'

'Right.'

'Who the hell knocked those rocks down?' the Inspector demanded aggressively. Nobody answered. 'They came from behind me,' he added.

'And me,' Archie echoed.

'Of course they did, Archie Campbell,' the Inspector expostulated. 'You were below me!'

'So I was, Angus.'

'Well, the boulders came from below where I was, and

to my left,' Douglas said. 'And I was above you, Inspector, so it must have been from between us.'

'Who was there then?' Angus demanded. He shone his light round the group which had now closed up but were still more or less as they were with the exception of Chris and Duncan.

'Well, it must have been either – let me see …' Duncan shone his lamp again. 'Clem, Basil, Willie or Ken …'

'No, by Chesus not me, Angus!' The publican expostulated indignantly. 'I was right below yersel', Angus.'

'Yes, so you were.'

'Was it you then, Mr Fular?' asked Duncan. 'I saw the unstable powder moving; it could have taken the rocks with it.'

'Well, it's no use worrying about it,' Chris butted in abruptly. 'We've got to bloody well think how we're to get Watty down.'

'Who's got the nitrous oxide,' Ken asked, his voice raised. 'He's in a lot of pain.'

'I guess that's the cylinder in my pack,' Clem said. 'Here.' He took off the rucksack and passed it to Ken. Ken placed the mask over the keeper's face and within a couple of minutes the splint was in place, then both legs were tied together. The stretcher was brought alongside. Duncan shone his headlamp on the face of the keeper, now partly covered by the mask.

'I hope putting the splint on didn't hurt him too much,' Ken said.

'Okay.' Chris' voice cut the cold air. 'Let's get him aboard.'

Several of the team gathered alongside the keeper and at a word from Chris lifted him smoothly on to the stretcher.

'That gas sure works well,' Basil observed. 'He's out like a light.'

'I'll have to get some for the missus,' Archie laughed. 'I could sneak out to the pub whilst she took 40 winks.'

'That's probably why it's called laughing gas,' Duncan interjected. 'You could laugh all the way to the boozer.'

They had been carrying Watty down the steep shoulder for about 10 minutes when the Inspector called a halt.

'Feeling your age?' the Sergeant asked, amused and wiping fresh snow off his anorak hood.

'I'm just thinking that it's been an age since Watty was conscious,' Angus said in worried tones. His lamp was shining on the flushed face of the keeper, whose eyes were still closed. 'I think we had better have a wee look at him.'

'Yes, it is odd,' Chris rejoined. 'We should have been paying more attention.'

'I'll slacken off the top straps and try his pulse. I don't like his colouring,' Duncan cut in with alarmed tones.

A silence fell over the small group; only the rustling of nylon and the throb of the wind in a nearby gully could be heard. Duncan eased back the patient straps to try to find a pulse. No-one spoke and small ice crystals were flying in the air due to the extreme cold. There was a sense of foreboding. It was as if they had each been touched by a cold clammy hand. Duncan's rugged face was etched with concern as his companions looked on. Slowly, he straightened up, then raising one of Watty's eyelids, tried again for a response from his carotid artery.

'Try oxygen and CPR,' Chris said tensely. 'Who's carrying the oxygen?'

'Here.' Basil dropped his rucksack in the snow beside the stretcher. Duncan grabbed it and in seconds had the mask out and the cylinder at full flow, but there was no response despite their frantic efforts. Watty had departed. There was a stunned silence which seemed to last ages.

Then everybody tried to speak at once.

'How the hell,' Chris spat out.

'I bet it was that nitrous oxide; it's cold enough to freeze the balls off a toad tonight,' Duncan intervened. 'Was that cylinder covered up, Ken?'

'Clem had it, but the cylinder was just loose in the rucksack when he gave it to me.'

'You had it, Clem; was the cylinder wrapped up?'

'I guess not,' the American replied, his voice raised. 'I had my duvet in the pack when I set off, but put it on at the start of the difficulties. How the hell was I to know it had to be nursed?' he asked.

'Didn't you check to see if the cylinder was insulated, Ken?' The Inspector's voice was raised.

'No, I never thought,' replied the young laird so quietly that he was almost inaudible. 'I never thought.'

'It's no use deliberating over what cannot be changed in a situation like this,' Duncan returned tersely. 'Let's get him down. A PM will determine if his death was caused by the nitrous oxide separating in the low temperature.'

Chris told base what had happened and once more they took up their burden with the rear ropes angling up the slope behind in a wide v demarked by their headlamps.

Four hours later, the ice-covered figures staggered into Queenshouse and the ambulance departed with the body. They threw their equipment in a pile inside the front door. There was hardly a word spoken.

Chapter 14

'Come away in, lads,' Annie Fyffe said. 'I've got hot soup for everybody ... My,' she added with concern, 'you do look pale, Douglas.' (Peelywally was the expression she was about to use.)

The atmosphere was humid with steaming clothes and there was a feeling of despondency. The usual bonhomie which follows a rescue was conspicuously absent. Each member of the team knew that it could have been himself who was being removed in that ambulance. It was not a pleasant thought. Ken seemed the worst affected, thought the Inspector, as he spoke to him.

'Will you break it to Kirsty, Ken?'

'Yes. My God,' he said bitterly. 'This is a bit much, Angus. How the hell could it happen? I swear I didn't dislodge those rocks.'

'It's only a wonder it doesn't happen more often,' the Inspector replied. 'Think back on past rescues; on every one, some bugger knocks a rock down. We've both seen and heard boulders the size of fridges whistle past our heads in the dark.'

'Aye,' Duncan agreed. He was fondling one of Watery's

massive drams. 'I've encountered narrow squeaks half a dozen times now. These things happen at night, especially on the edge of the Red Wall; hell of a place, altogether,' he added vehemently.

'Bad luck seemed to dog Watty,' Basil interjected. 'It could just as easily have been Douglas here who got clobbered: he was alongside.'

Annie leant over the pinewood bar and spoke to Ken.

'Your sister telephoned a wee while ago, asking when you'd be back. I gave her a ring when I saw your lights near the road, so she'll be up shortly,'

'Thanks, Annie,' he replied as he drank soup from a large plain white mug.

Bookam entered. He joined them clustered round the large table by the bar and sat down with an air of resignation.

'The chopper will be here at first light, sir,' PC Munro addressed his Inspector. 'Is anyone going up with it?'

'Somebody from the team must … or they'll never find the body. What do you think?' The Inspector addressed Chris.

'Perhaps you would go, Douglas?' he asked the Glaswegian who had just accepted one of Annie's beef sandwiches.

'Sure. If I go on a rescue I get paid for the morning shift anyway, by Highland Smelters.'

'You can have a couple of hours shut-eye here,' the publican suggested. 'It'll save you going all the way back home. We'll get your things dried for you.'

'That would be great, Willie.' The young man accepted thankfully.

'What are you working at just now?' Duncan asked him.

'I'm on the conduit just below Freshwater Dam, cementing one of the top culverts. With this snow we couldn't do anything just now, anyway.'

'What's a conduit?' Clem asked. Like the rest, he had taken off his anorak and revealed a purple pullover with the monogram 'C.F.' on its front. His off white trousers looked rather sad, having been chastised by the rigours of the rescue even beneath his windproofs.

'It's the covered water channel from the Freshwater Reservoir down to the Highland Smelters factory in Kinlochsanda, Clem. It supplies the turbines for the power supply for the furnaces.'

'Oh, I see. A hydro-electric plant, like Loch Gorm?'

'That's what it is, but an outdated version, Clem,' Douglas smiled. 'The conduits – or concrete tunnels – are about 10 feet square.'

'It's a gae big dam, the Freshwater,' Duncan put in.

'We could do with its catchment,' Basil grumbled. 'But pumping stations like ours weren't thought of at the turn of the century when Highland Smelters moved in.'

'Aloominum?' Clem queried.

'Yes,' Douglas affirmed. 'The firm has its own rolling mills, too, down at Risechapel, near Glasgow.'

'Is the road clear?' Basil turned to the Constable.

'Aye, just aboot,' the policeman replied. 'The Council lads have been out all night wi' the ploughs and salt.'

'Well, I think I'll be going,' the engineer said. 'Goodnight, everyone.'

'Guidnight, or guid mornin',' Archie replied. 'Whatever way ye want it!'

Just as he was opening the door, Deirdre entered, dressed in her sheepskin jacket; only now she wore brown tweed trousers and green Wellington boots. She looked quickly round the company and, seeing her brother, went over to the table.

'Hello, Bas.'

'Morning, Deirdre.' He went out and along the hall, not wanting to be present when she was told about Watty.

Deirdre asked after the girl.

'We couldn't do anything for her,' Chris answered gently. 'We did our damndest.'

'She's dead, then?' the girl asked.

'Yes,' her brother now replied tersely. 'And there was another accident – on the way down. Watty was hit by rocks ...'

Everything was still in the room; only the crackle of the log fire punctuated the silence.

'Oh, no!' Deirdre sat down abruptly on the seat just vacated by Basil.

'Yes, I'm afraid Watty's dead, Miss Dewar,' the Inspector replied quietly. 'We brought his body down. The dead girl's is still up there.'

'Poor Kirsty,' Deirdre murmured, tears welling in her eyes. 'We have known Watty for years, Inspector.' She looked up at her brother.

'I think we'd better go, sis, and break the news,' he said.

'All right.'

'You ready, Clem?' he asked the American.

'Sure, I'll just get my wind-cheater.'

After they had left, Angus asked the Constable when Dr Khan had returned home.

'As soon as we had confirmation that Watty was dead,' the Constable replied.

'And the survivor - what's his name?'

'Hunter – Barry Hunter. He's upstairs, sleeping ...' PC Munro turned to Archie and asked, 'How did the rocks fall, Sergeant?'

'We're not sure. We were descending, zigzag like, down from the Red Wall – you know how steep it is,' he added, looking at the Constable who was holding a large bowl of soup. 'Then some boulders were knocked off. It was difficult to tell if there was solid rock below or crap, with the depth of snow.'

'Aye,' Douglas cut in. 'We were lucky it didn't avalanche lower down; there might have been a further tragedy.'

'Was Watty killed outright, then?' Bookam persisted.

'No, it was his leg that got it – a massive rock it was; a nasty compound fracture, but we think it was the nitrous oxide that did the ultimate damage for he never regained consciousness after it was administered.'

'My God,' the constable spluttered. 'Watty seemed destined to snuff it. One thing after another – you'd think that Fate had been playing games wi' him and Isaac!' James Munro's normally fresh complexion had a blanched appearance.

Archie stood up. 'Well,' he said. 'I'm for home. Who's wanting a lift?'

'You'd better get down to Faileadh, James,' the Inspector addressed his Constable. 'I'll send one of the police team round from Kinlochsanda to be here when the helicopter arrives.'

'That would be appreciated,' the Constable replied, leaning back on his chair – a habit he had. 'I'll go with you, then, Sarge. Robert here can take the patrol car back.'

'Aye, I'll do that,' the big policeman replied.

'Thanks again, Willie,' the Inspector said.

'Not at all, not at all,' Willie Fyffe beamed. 'After all, we make our daily crust from climbers and skiers. It's the least we can do, the very least.'

'I'll tell Kirsty,' Ken said to his sister when they stopped in the yard close to the keeper's cottage. 'You go back to bed.'

'All right. I don't envy you the task. I'll have a cup of tea ready when you come over to the Lodge. What about you, Clem?'

'I'm not crazy about tea,' Clem answered, 'but I sure could do with some sleep. I'll see you later, Ken.'

'Fine, and thanks for your help.'

'No problem.'

Ken kept the lights of Deirdre's Citroën on until Clem and his sister reached the back door of the Lodge. He went over to the darkened doorway of the cottage which was close by, moving silently through the snow, then knocked. There were a few stars out now and the bitter frost made that pre-dawn brittle and still. The storm had blown itself out. He tried again, louder this time. A light came on, then another, the one in the porch. Kirsty peered out. She had a dressing gown on. She was taken aback, seeing Kenneth. 'Oh, it's you!' Her voice held a note of uncertainty; she didn't ask him in.

'Can I come in, Kirsty? It's important.' She opened the door wider and went back into the sitting room without saying a word. It felt chilly for it was bitterly cold even down here. She bent down to switch on the electric fire.

'Well, what brings you at this hour, Ken?' She sat down on the sofa.

'I've bad news, Kirsty ...' She looked at him sharply.

'Watty ...?'

'Yes.' Her lips compressed slightly and she brushed a wisp of hair off her forehead.

'What about him?'

'He's dead. He died on Eagal Mor.' Kirsty's face drained of colour. Ken continued quickly. 'It was an accident. Some boulders got knocked down and he was right in their path. His leg was broken. Doug only escaped by a miracle ...' Kirsty stood up again, a look of disbelief etched on her face.

'But,' Ken continued quietly. 'It wasn't the rock fall that killed him, Kirsty. We think it may have been the anaesthetic gas that separated in the cold – it does that sometimes. We won't really know until we get the result of the PM.'

The orange-coloured Sea King poised like an over-nourished kestrel above Queenshouse, then spiralled down to make a landing on the white crusted moor. The cacophony of its engines brought Douglas out of his slumbers with a start – and, for that matter, everyone else in the small hotel. When the rotors jerked to a halt, PC Callum Lafferty went over to meet the crew as they emerged. They took their helmets off and stood in a tight group looking up at the Eagal Mor which reared up in dazzling splendour across two miles of snow-covered bog. The overnight British Rail sleeper was just passing between Queenshouse and the main road. The line had been cleared during the night by the huge bogie-mounted snow plough based at Kinlochsanda Station.

'Morning,' the Constable greeted the crew. 'Thank goodness it's a good day.'

'Hi there,' the winch man, Rob Swift, raised a hand in response. 'Heard you've had a long night.'

'Not me,' the policeman replied. 'I was out after poachers earlier, but the team had a grim time on the Eagal.'

'Is it true that one of your lads was killed?' the pilot asked.

'Yes, one of the local keepers. The lines to the hotel have been jammed all night with the press trying to get through. Willie Fyffe, the owner, has taken the phone off the hook.'

'I suppose it'll cause a sensation,' the co-pilot – whom Callum Lafferty didn't know – spoke. 'That mountain's well named 'the Big Horror'.'

'Aye, that's what it means in the Gaelic, right enough,' Callum confirmed. 'And it's been living up to its name, lately.

One of the team is still here, Douglas Stewart; he's a climber and will go up with you.'

'Thank goodness.' The winch man sounded grateful. 'I had visions of complications!'

'Well Mrs Gilchrist,' the inspector addressed Kirsty as he stepped into the cottage. 'This is a trying time for you.'

'Come into the living room, Inspector,' she replied and led the way. Angus observed that her mourning dress would hardly have been approved by Hellfire or Isaac. She was dressed in trousers and a Shetland pullover which suited her and calf length boots. She seemed composed enough, though powder had been sparingly applied to her face.

'You wanted to see me, Kirsty?'

'Yes, Inspector, I have some things to say to you ... I spoke to Watty at the time. He should have told you, but he wouldn't hear of it. He was stubborn in some ways.' She was sitting on the same chair as earlier that morning, when Kenneth broke the news. Angus was perched on the edge of the sofa; it gave so much under his weight that he was scared to lean back – besides hardly being a suitable posture in which to conduct an interview. He made no reply now but let her continue in her own time. He had found by experience in questioning that this often proved more productive than continual prompting.

'It was about Mr Dewar's death, Inspector,' Kirsty carried on. 'Watty saw Kenneth come back out of that gully on the face. He was well up towards the ridge, but he recognized him all right. Watty has – had,' she corrected herself, 'eyes like a hawk.'

'Are you sure?' Angus was somewhat taken aback at this revelation.

'Of course I'm sure! We talked about it for ages, but

Watty decided that Ken was just taking pictures, like he said.'

'Did Watty say anything else – about the gun, for instance?'

'He knew it was missing because he went to the gun room as soon as he got back to the Lodge.'

'Did he now?' Angus pondered, annoyed by the late keeper's reticence. There were too many part time sleuths in the area for his liking. 'By the way, what prompted this disclosure, Kirsty?' he asked curiously, looking directly at her and admiring the fine bone structure of her face. At times she had an almost aristocratic look, even when distressed.

'I didn't say anything before because Watty didn't want to cause any trouble for the house – but I thought it was my duty now.'

'You're quite right, Kirsty.'

'What will happen?' she asked, raising her eyebrows and self-consciously patting her hair.

'It's a pity he didn't volunteer that evidence,' Angus commented as he got up. 'It's a bit second-hand now. I don't know what his motive was in not telling us about it at the time, other than loyalty, but it has caused us some trouble,' the inspector added grimly. 'What was Ken wearing that day?' he continued after a pause. She thought for an instant before replying.

'Green anorak and brown cords.'

'And those were the colours of the clothes that Watty saw?' This caught her momentarily off balance and she hesitated.

'He didn't mention clothes; he just recognized Ken.'

'It's a fair step from the strath to the top of that gully,' Angus commented. 'Unless Watty used his glass it would be difficult to recognize anyone, even with eyesight as good as his.'

'Watty didn't make mistakes like that,' she repeated evenly.

Chapter 15

Inspector Wilson laid the concrete cast down on his desk and leant back in his swivel chair, deliberating on the day's activities. He hadn't had time for lunch though that didn't bother him unduly; he had phoned his wife Mary to tell her he was up to his ears with work. They had no family which didn't worry Angus, but Mary sometimes fretted for she was a motherly sort of person. He thought fleetingly of her now and wondered if their planned holiday to visit relatives in Canada during the spring would come to anything.

Sadie's voice over the intercom startled him.

'Would you like a cuppa and a sandwich, Inspector?'

'You're a wonder, Sadie. You'll make some policeman a fine wife!'

'That's what I thought once, Angus.' She gave a brittle laugh. 'But it'll soon be my thirtieth.'

'Wheesht, lass. You shouldn't say these things out loud. Or was that a hint for a present? Oh, while I remember, Sadie, can you arrange a meeting for me with the late Mrs McWhirter's solicitor? I think it's MacAndrew and Weir.'

'Right, Inspector.'

A few minutes later she bustled in with a heaped Guinness tray and a steaming cup. 'Mum made a pile of ham sandwiches for me and she knows I sometimes don't eat lunch.'

'She probably knows I like them!' The Inspector laughed. Archie came in through the open door, followed by Duncan.

'Probably these two buggers like them as well, you just can't win,' Angus muttered in disgust.

'Thanks, Sadie,' Duncan seemed to fill the room. 'You must have known I was coming.'

'You would smell out a sandwich in a midden MacGillvery.'

'Now, Angus', Duncan grinned as he took a large bite. But it didn't prevent him replying. 'I wouldn't dare make such a disparaging remark about your office.'

'Thanks, Sadie.' Archie grabbed one of the substantial offerings.

'Anything further on the tests on the bullet, Sergeant?'

'Just a telex confirming that the bullet was fired from the Weatherby rifle. As we know, there were no fingerprints on it,' Archie continued. 'It had been wiped clean, but the blood on that bit of rope used to tie the dog is human all right. I asked PC Munro about it – he tidied up the body of the Pinnacle Buttress victim. Duncan here mentioned that it might have been used on that call-out and I had heard James say that the victim was wearing an identity tab. His blood group was the same as the blood on the rope and the lab boys thought it was about the right age, too. Of course it was silicon on the brake discs, as you know and also, confirmed – no prints other than Isaac's, yours and Duncan's on the handlebars or other parts.'

'Umm. Not a great deal of help,' Angus grumbled. 'But at least it tells us that the dog's sling in Watty's case was most likely picked up by a team member or someone who had access to the rescue gear. That now ...' He mused to himself and on impulse opened his desk drawer and took out the photograph Kenneth gave him.

'Both of you have a seat – we have things to mull over.'

'Have a look at this.' He put the enlargement on the desk in front of them and waited. 'What does that suggest to you, Duncan? You've seen it before, Archie.'

'It's Ken's?' Duncan asked.

'Yes. Does it suggest the particular day that the laird was killed?'

'Was this taken the day that the laird was shot?' Duncan spoke quietly.

'That is what Ken said,' the Inspector asserted. The poacher picked up the print and studied it with renewed interest. Archie took his pipe out and filled it deliberately whilst glancing across at the enlargement on Duncan's knee.

'Well?' the Inspector prompted.

'It wasn't taken on that day.' Duncan looked over at Angus. 'It was overcast. I recall it well; black clouds sort of pressing down. In this,' he pointed at the sky in the enlargement, 'it's brighter.'

'Well he told me it was taken that day. He said he went up the back, towards the ridge, to take it.'

'I think he's lying,' Archie agreed, abstractedly lighting up.

'But there's more to it than that.' Duncan continued. 'We need more than soggy cloud, something more conclusive. It would be difficult to use just that in evidence.'

'I guess that's why I'm a country Sergeant and you're a successful poacher, Duncan.' Archie returned. 'I probably can't see the wood for the trees.'

'That remark's more significant than you imagine, Archie.'

Duncan laid the enlargement down on the desk with a puzzled frown on his face.

'Here's the evidence, we couldn't see the tree for the wood.'

'What the hell do you mean MacGillvrey. Spit it out, don't talk in riddles.' The Inspector was annoyed and he showed it.

'Don't lose yer rag with me, Angus. Let me explain. Between the day that Ken took the photograph and the day old Horror died the scenery changed.'

Archie's almost dropped his pipe.

'You see this tree?' Duncan looked at the two policemen in turn and stabbed a large finger down on the photograph.

'What about it?' Angus barked. 'A tree's a tree!'

'It's no longer there,' Duncan said almost casually. 'it was blown down in a gale a couple of months ago. I thought of going over to get some firewood from it.'

'Well I'm buggered' Archie shook his head.

'That was a good bit o' observation Duncan,' Angus admitted.

The Inspector continued and outlined his activities, Archie now had his pipe fired up and Angus leant back to open the bottom of the window, he was obviously well practised.

'It has been a busy time,' he remarked.

'It looks gae bad for Ken,' Archie responded 'but, damn it all, Angus, I like the lad! He's a bit mixed up in his views though, mind you, I havena heard him spouting politics for some time – I wouldn't be surprised if he turned to Scottish Nationalism.

'We must accept the fact that he had opportunity – equal opportunity – with others in the various shenanigans, including the attempt on Watty in the mine.'

'Aye, that's true, Angus,' Duncan observed, picking up

a teaspoon from the tray and looking at it abstractedly. 'And from what I hear both Spielman and Clem Fular, have a finger in the pie.'

The Inspector picked up the phone and dialled a number. 'Mr Frew?' he asked at length, twiddling a blue biro. 'Inspector Wilson here. I'd like to see you whenever it's convenient.'

'All right, I'll be here,' the Fiscal replied and put the phone down.

The Inspector turned to his two friends. 'There's to be a post-mortem on Isaac; a pathologist from Edinburgh and Dr Grieve are doing it.'

'One to slice, one to scribe,' Archie murmured.

Next day Toń cleared fresh snow from the path to the road and stood surveying his handiwork. Already, there were signs of continuing thaw and he'd heard on the shipping forecast that a south-west air-stream was moving in. He knew that this might make conditions dangerous on the hills for the snowfall of the previous night had been considerable. His back was stiff, a legacy from the fall on Pinnacle Buttress, and he acknowledged ruefully that he wasn't getting any younger. It might be a good day for the hinds, he mused. I'll take a turn up over to the Freshwater – I could use the conduit to send them down. Going inside, he took his .270 rifle from inside an old grandfather clock, then dismantled it and put half a dozen rounds in his pocket. Thoughtfully, he made his way out to his van, the rifle hidden beneath his well-worn jacket.

Old Mrs Cameron was peering from her window and saw him getting into his van, with his left hand held beneath his left jacket pocket. She turned to her husband, an invalid for the past 15 years. 'Duncan's away for a beast.' She said it softly in the Gaelic and her husband nodded his head sagely and moved his wheel-chair towards the window. He saw Duncan slipping behind the wheel and admired the way the big man moved into the van so easily with the rifle completely hidden.

'I don't think it'll be Glen Liath he'll go to today.' He spoke liltingly. 'No, it'll be over on the other side somewhere … Well, I wish him luck.'

As Duncan drove along the road towards Queenshouse, he descended the hairpins and over the bridge which spanned the burn. The steep descent was already sanded. Then he turned off the main road and ploughed through the wet snow down a short track on to an old General Wade road which led underneath the new bridge, a favourite place for hiding the van. With all that snow he'd need to get a couple of hinds at least to keep the back end down and get the vehicle back on the main road, he thought with amusement. Leaving the rifle in his van, he returned to the turn off and used a broken tree branch as a brush to cover the tyre marks.

Then he followed the bed of the burn up the steep slope of Bheinn Bruhm, rapidly gaining height. It would be nice if there had been hinds here, he thought, to save him going over the top to the Freshwater Dam, but he knew from years of experience that they would be over the other ridge. The only weight he'd find for the back of the Ford this side of the hill would be a couple of boulders!

He was deep in thought as he climbed, automatically taking advantage of the cover of a cleft which deeply indented the hillside. The snow hadn't drifted within the gully which was wet under foot. As he climbed, he considered the various 'accidents' and the passing of Mrs McWhirter. Chris wouldn't be too bothered, he thought. He never did hit if off with her.

There was still not a sign of a beast, but he was high now with the watershed just above. He smiled at the thought of

Highland Smelters providing free transport for his deer. He would be poaching on their land, once over the ridge. Could the shooting of Dewar be divorced from the other incidents? He mulled over this new idea. If so, it shed a different light on everything. For a moment he considered Clem. He was quick thinking and, Duncan believed, absolutely ruthless under those loud clothes. Smart – wearing bright clothes – it took your attention off the man beneath and gave the American a distinct advantage. Women did the same thing with jewellery – it hid wrinkles!

The knot with which Gealeas was tied up in the mine bothered Duncan. He had seen someone using it before. It wasn't Watty, but who? It must be someone in the team, he deliberated, as he stopped to take the rifle from under his jacket and assembled it. He dropped four rounds into the magazine and one in the breech; then flicked on the safety catch. Now, approaching the ridge, he moved stealthily, conscious of the wind. It came from behind, on his left, stirring from the south-west. He knew he'd have to descend the other side of Bheinn Bruhm to get back into the corrie over to his right, otherwise any beasts in there would scent him. He peered over the edge, for here the crest was narrow, and saw below the familiar sight of the snow-covered moorland below the Freshwater Dam. The line of the conduit stood out like the trail left by an enormous snail. The snow was melting in the valley and had a reflective quality, and grey clouds were quietly gathering. Slanting down the hillside, he made for the corrie and spotted six stags, way over to his right. But it was hinds he was interested in today. The stags were tired after the rutting.

It wasn't often Duncan missed a deer, but he did by at least a foot. It had ricocheted of a stone. His next shot, however, following seconds later, brought the beast down as if it had been poleaxed and, swinging the rifle round through 20 degrees, he dropped another – a fine yeld hind. That'll do for the day, he muttered with satisfaction, no need to be greedy.

The dam was full and spilling over the edge. There'll be nobody paid off at the Smelters for a wee bit o' time to come yet, he thought, despite the predictions in the local rag. There's enough water to feed the generators for months. It was the Company policy to put workers on short time during prolonged droughts.

It took him an hour and a half to reach the ground immediately below the dam, where the water poured into the inlets of the conduits. He stopped here and wiped his brow gratefully. Placing his rifle against the railing surrounding the opening, he gazed into the frothy depths. Then, turning to the deer which he had dragged over the snow, he lifted the first carcass up over the rail in a single easy movement and dropped it into the water behind a heavy steel grill. In a trice it was sucked down the square tunnel, really a covered channel. The other hind followed a minute later. Then he took his rifle to pieces and, whistling a few bars of a pibroch, started down the track which was now almost clear of snow. He had the satisfaction of knowing that his meat requirements for the next few weeks were being transported three miles down the glen to the penstocks where they would be waiting for him at a similarly designed steel grill. Later he would be able to drive his van to within 300 yards of the spot, provided the thaw continued. It gave him a sense of fulfilment to use this means of transporting deer, by courtesy of Highland Smelters; both booty and transport – what more could a poacher ask for. He gave a satisfied smile.

It was almost dark when Duncan got back to his cottage.

He parked his old van alongside the fence and greeted his cat as she walked with stiff legs down the concrete path from the house.

'Good evening, Jezebel,' he greeted his pet. 'I suppose you know the routine and want your share?' The cat mewed in reply and soon the two 'jobs' were hanging from the rafters, each with short hazel sticks keeping the legs apart. He took off his old jacket and washed his hands in a bucket of water.

'Have a seat, Inspector. The post mortem has just been completed, a broken neck as expected.' The Fiscal indicated a chair to the side of his desk.

'Thanks, sir,' Angus answered gratefully. He was feeling tired. Things seemed to be happening all of a sudden.

'MacGillvery seems to be acting the Highland detective,' Frew smiled. 'Even down to the hat.' He stroked his chin in an abstracted way and lifted a paper knife. 'I hope he's not playing with fire.'

'It would be no use telling him that, sir. He's obstinate.'

'Umph,' the Fiscal grunted. 'It doesn't sound as if you've had the full co-operation you would expect, Inspector. What with Duncan MacGillvery rooting round for clues and the minister possibly concealing information before he was murdered and the keeper's wife coming up with belated evidence... Do you think there was some other reason why Watty Gilchrist didn't tell you he'd seen young Dewar on the hill that day?' He looked keenly at the Inspector.

'Having known Watty, it could easily have been concern for the family – not blackmail.'

'Quite so. From what I understood of the case, Inspector, things seemed quite damning for young Dewar. But there may not be enough solid evidence for me to take further action on the strength of the recovered bullet. No prints on the rifle that was found and Gilchrist's death. There's nothing definite, its like a spider's web, possibly the work of a homicidal genius.' He smiled briefly, revealing fine, even teeth. 'Nothing more has surfaced?'

'No, sir.'

The P.F. continued, 'Had any word from the LAPD on Clem Fulmar's background?'

'Yes, I got a telex a short while ago. He seems in the clear: big wheeler-dealer in the States, by all accounts. He's had some rather dubious transactions in the past, but they were in Brazil; there's not much information available about these.'

'Umph ... So it looks as if he likes getting what he wants?'

'Yes, but these types usually stop short of murder! Still, he's high on my list.'

'Who *is* on your list, Inspector?'

'All the size nines.' He gave another smile. 'Duncan, Ken, Chris, Clem, Basil and Douglas, though I reckon I can rule Douglas Stewart out – there just doesn't seem to be any motive for him, or for Basil Thorndike, for that matter, or any other members of the rescue team. Sergeant Campbell had them checked out.'

'How deeply is Chris Watkins involved in this old mine business?' The Fiscal glanced casually out of the window at a typical late afternoon Kinlochsanda street scene. Last minute shoppers were rushing about and a traffic warden was laboriously taking the number of a car as if she had only just learned to write in English.

'I don't know,' Angus ruminated uncertainly. 'Bookam ... Constable Munro's nipper saw Clem Fular coming out of Chris' one morning. But, of course, Chris had been stalking earlier at Grey Corries with the guests, so that may have been quite innocent.'

'It all seems an incredible chain of events, Inspector,' the Fiscal interrupted. 'Let's hope you can clear it up soon. Have you everything you require?'

'Yes, I think so, sir.'

The phone rang. Peter Frew picked it up.

'Fiscal here ... Hello, John, have you anything new?' He listened intently for a few minutes and eventually replied, 'I see. Well, many thanks. Ask Dr Grieve to send in the written report ASAP. That was the pathologist, Inspector,' the Fiscal said, putting the phone down. 'Isaac died from a broken neck, as we knew.'

'And,' Angus said, 'a little help from a "friend".'

Chapter 16

Angus drove slowly up the glen thinking of the three cases: Watty, Isaac and the late laird. It was incredible that this chain of tragedy could have happened in his back yard. They certainly had their share of sudden death, but that was on the hills in genuine climbing accidents; this wave of evil that had descended sent a cold shiver down his spine. The rescue team, of which he was so much a part, a dedicated bunch who went out of their way to help others, were themselves being picked off one by one. The Chief had yet again hinted that morning that outside assistance may have to be requested. That meant the Regional Crime Squad and ignominy for himself. He clenched his teeth savagely.

Beyond the village of Faileadh, the road descends steeply to the gorge where Isaac was killed, taking in several hair-pin bends before clawing its way back up to the moor where Queenshouse nestles in its peaty fastness. On the left was Bheinn Bruhm, that long northerly retaining wall of the glen. To the right, before exiting from the confines of Glen Faileadh, Eagal Mor hung over valley and moor, as if hurriedly executed by some crazy architect: a mass of rock

walls, gullies and towers slapped together and terminating in
a steely summit. But, as Angus glanced up at it, it looked
resplendent in its new white gown; he caught a glimpse of
two circling golden eagles.

A car came into view ahead, taking the corner in an
elegant slide. He flashed his lights to stop it. PC Callum
Lafferty swore.

'Just my luck, Douglas! I take the bend a wee bit too
fast and who should see it but the bloody Inspector. You
just can't win!'

'He's not exactly a Fangio himsel',' the climber replied.
'I've seen him take that roundabout in Kinlochsanda the
wrong way, when he thought nobody was looking! It saves
him a few seconds.'

But it wasn't about Callum's driving that Angus wanted
to speak. 'Good morning, Constable,' he said to Callum
when he came over.

'Morning, sir. We've completed the evacuation.'

'Yes, I heard over the radio. Good going – any complications, Douglas?' he asked the climber who had also
emerged from the vehicle.

'No, it went like clockwork, Angus. But we had to go
down almost 300 feet on the winch wire: quite airy.'

'You had better write it up for me, Douglas. It appears
that Joyce Kennedy's father is a High Court judge, so we'd
better dot all our i's on this one.'

'I'll get it done this morning.'

'Thanks.'

'A fair man, that,' the Constable remarked to Douglas
as he got behind the wheel. 'I wish there were more like him
at headquarters.'

The Inspector encountered two more cars when he turned
off into Glen Liath. The first, a small Citroën, belonging to

the Dewars and driven by Deirdre; he gave her a wave and turned into a layby to let her pass. The next car was probably owned by Penelope Almen; at least, she was driving it: a new Alfa. It seemed to suit her station in life, he thought. Angus assumed that she had vacated Grey Corries Lodge for good. It had not been a very pleasant holiday for her, he concluded.

As the Inspector drove slowly back up the glen he knew he had two more visits to make before seeing the Superintendent. His first stop was Queenshouse.

'Camera ha.' Willie Fyffe's Gaelic greeting reached him as he passed through the front door. Watery always did have one eye on the door handle to welcome customers.

'Hello, Willie. Are your new guests installed?'

'The reporters, Angus?' the publican countered.

'No, heaven forbid! Keep them out of my way, will you? No, Karl von Spielman and Clem Fular.'

'I think they're in their rooms. Wait and I'll ask Sadie Marquis, yes, I'll ask Sadie.' He went through a door leading to the kitchen. Watery didn't keep a receptionist during the winter months. 'Aye,' he confirmed, returning a minute later. 'I'll go up and get them for you. You can use my office, Angus, if you want to speak to them. You'd be wanting to see their gun licences, nae doot?' He peered interrogatively at the Inspector.

'We don't ask what time you close the bar on a Saturday night, Willie ...'

'No, no, you don't, Angus. I take the point.'

'Sorry to bother you, gentlemen,' Angus commenced once the two business men were seated in the tiny cubby hole which Watery called his office. 'There are a couple of matters I have to clear up, for the records.'

'Vat is this?' von Spielman asked. 'I believed we were finished with investigations.'

'Not quite,' the Inspector replied coolly. 'I'm curious to know if there is some affiliation between your two companies?'

Von Spielman flared. 'Goddamen, what has our business to do mit the politzei? You are not politzei, you are ...' he paused, searching in vain for a suitable English word. 'You are dootle-sacks – you pass vind and make much noise.'

The policeman, had, however, got his answer and hardly required the confirmation offered by Clem Fular.

'It's still confidential, Inspector,' Clem said. 'But a merger has been proposed between American Copper Incorporated and Deutsch Non-Ferrous Metals – Karl's company. It will be announced next month.'

'I see,' the Inspector said slowly. 'And what is your interest in the old Glen Liath mine?' Von Spielman cleared his throat and glanced at his colleague. Clem, on the other hand, didn't appear in the least perturbed by the question. He seemed almost to welcome it. He carefully brushed a piece of fluff off his two-tone jacket and replied.

'We sure are interested in the franchise of the Liath Mine, Inspector. It is once again a practicable proposition. But when our agents approached the late Horatio Dewar (he pronounced the name 'Doo-er') it was thumbs down. No way would the old boy come across – even though it's owned by the Grey Corries Company. He didn't know that I was asking about it though.'

'And Kenneth?'

'I have mentioned to young Herr Dewar our interest, Inspector.' Von Spielman waved his cigar expansively. 'But he don't wish to make any – vat do you say? – firm offer, until his father has longer been deceased.'

Clem cut in. 'That was the agreement which he made with the estate shareholders. There was to be no sale or development of the property in his lifetime.'

'Surely before the mine could be assessed as a viable business proposition a survey would have to be made?' The Inspector looked quizzically at the two men.

'We did get an independent report, Inspector,' Fular stated carefully. 'That is what interested us.' Von Spielman kept studiously silent, Angus observed.

'I would like to know how this was obtained, gentlemen, without the consent of the late Horatio Dewar.' He looked at each of them in turn, presenting an uncompromising figure.

'I understand your desire to get the low-down on that report, Inspector.' Fular spoke slowly and deliberately. There was a steely quality to his voice which Angus hadn't noticed before. 'But I assure you,' the American continued, 'the report and the acquisition of samples were not instigated by either of our companies. I will put your request to our Board. I haven't got authority to divulge that information to you.'

'And you, Herr von Spielman?'

'Like Herr Fular, Inspector, I cannot say anything at present.'

'I see.' The Inspector rose with finality and stated curtly, 'Many thanks for your time. You will appreciate that we have to consider all aspects of this case. And I want that information as soon as possible, Mr Fular. By the way,' the Inspector paused at the door as if just remembering something. 'Did you lose a green anorak, Mr Fular?'

'Green anorak?' Clem echoed. 'Not my colour, Inspector. I like things bright and beautiful,' he added unnecessarily. 'Why, have you found one?'

'No, I just thought that you wore one sometimes.'

Clem gave him a puzzled look, then, changing the subject, said, 'I heard Douglas did a good job with the chopper crew.'

'Yes, it went smoothly,' Angus acknowledged. 'They got the body.'

'You sure have your cleaning up to do, getting dudes off the hills. I've never seen anything like it!'

'You've arrived at a bad time, Mr Fular. It's not normally like this. By the way,' he added. 'Can you remember who asked you to take up the gas cylinder last night? There seems to be some confusion over that.'

'No-one, Inspector. It was with the stack of goodies to go up the hill and I took it. As a matter of fact, I guessed – wrongly – that it was oxygen.'

'You carried it down to where Watty was hit, then?'

'Sure, Angus. It was in my pack and I had no idea that it had to be coddled. '

'Well, good day, gentlemen. I'll await details of that report,' he added, unbending slightly. 'I hope you'll get some stalking after all.'

Karl seemed to brighten up at this prospect. 'Meester Fyffe tells us he has many hinds.'

'Yes, after this weather they should be down low,' Angus agreed.

'I've another question to ask you, Duncan.' Angus was back in the poacher's kitchen, where the owner was stacking peat beside the fire. The cat rubbed against the policeman's leg and he stooped to scratch her ears.

'Jezebel likes ye, Angus; she doesna usually care for the male sex.'

'I don't know whether to take that as a compliment or not,' Angus grinned. 'Now … Take your mind back, Duncan, to the time you said that you thought of returning to the birch wood in Glen Liath, after our visit to the old mine.'

'Aye, I went back,' Duncan agreed.

'You never told me.' Angus spoke huffily.

'You don't overburden me wi' blethering either,' Duncan retorted.

'Well, are you going to tell me or not?'

'It was like a quagmire.'

'So you didn't find anything?'

'Oh, yes, I did. There was one print at the bole o' an old alder which was among the silver birches, and it was made by a size 9 climbing sole.'

'Why the blazes didn't you tell me? We could have got a cast of it; my men didn't find a print.' Angus sounded exasperated. Retrospective information was not what he was after, especially when it was unusable, and this seemed the day for it.

'I didna think ye were co-operatin' wi' me all that much,' Duncan replied mildly. 'But I took a cast o' it mysel'.'

'What! How!'

'Wi' cement. I had a wee dollop left over from the founds o' ma hut. And I took Paddy McManus from the Gorm Tailrace owre tae the wood wi' me. I thought I micht require corroborative – or whatever you call it – evidence.'

'You're the bloody limit, Toń!' Angus laughed despite himself. 'Where's the cast?'

'On the mantelpiece over there,' Toń nodded his head. 'It was there when you were in last, but ye didna see it.' The Inspector went over and picked up a lump of concrete.

'I did see the back of it, Duncan. But I thought you'd gone in for making concrete blocks.' He studied the almost perfect mould of a cleated rubber climbing sole.

'Aye, weel,' Duncan rejoined. 'I did take an old tin box wi' no bottom in it, for the cast, so to speak.' The Inspector smiled as he noticed the side of the block bearing the signatures of Duncan MacGillvery and Patrick McManus, with the time and place of signing. 'Tae save ye time, Angus,' Duncan continued. 'There are five men in the team wi' size 9 soles like that: Chris, Kenneth, Douglas and Basil – and Clem Fular makes a sixth.'

'And the other?' Thumper asked.

'Me,' replied the poacher.

'I've already checked on people's feet, Duncan – they seem to feature prominently in this case. For the moment I'll rule you out as a homicidal maniac. You have, despite your wayward ways, certain standards and killing fellow humans is not your line o' country; you don't eat them – yet.' His eyes twinkled. 'But you can lend a hand in getting to the bottom of all this.' He shot a quick glance at the poacher who gave the impression of a philosophical block of granite, if not concrete.

'You can count on me, Angus,' Duncan replied quietly, picking up his cat and placing her on his lap. 'How are the investigations going?'

'We're making progress in a lumbering sort of way,' Angus confessed deliberately. 'I got a lead a short time ago from Kirsty.' He told the poacher of Watty spotting Kenneth in the gully.

'Well, now, that's interesting,' the poacher said. 'Well, well … I can't see Ken bumping off his old man, though, but it sounds gae damning.'

'It does,' the Inspector replied solemnly. 'I don't like it any more than you do, Duncan.' There was a pause, then Angus continued. His voice dropped a fraction and he looked at Duncan concern etched on his rugged face.

'I saw the preliminary report on Watty, Duncan.' He paused. 'It was nitrous oxide!'

'What,' Duncan barked out the word. 'Good God, it could be another murder. I had a think about it and came to the conclusion that he may have suffered from an air embolism or some such thing.'

'Such a possibility occurred to me as well, Angus.'

'It did seem to be stretching coincidence too far for those rocks to have come down under someone's clumsy boots,' Duncan looked studious. 'Especially with all that snow. You know, Angus, I think we're dealing with an opportunist with a devious and sinister mind, maybe even a psychopath. Doesn't Murphy's Law state that if something can go wrong, it does? And in my experience often happening to the one person – possibly an intended victim.'

'I suppose it will be officially classed as misadventure,' the policeman said with resignation.

'Will there be an inquiry then – there's bugger all evidence?'

'It's up to the Procurator Fiscal,' Angus returned. 'I have my doubts. If it had happened in England there would be.'

'We don't seem to have got far in our hypothesising, Angus.' Duncan forced a smile. 'I suspect we've been outsmarted 'How about Isaac? At least there's a shred of evidence.'

'One thing I'm sure about,' the big policeman said with vehemence, 'and that is that Isaac was murdered as if stabbed in the back.'

'I agree, Angus.' The poacher stood up, putting the cat gently down on a chair. He went over and stirred the smoored peat in the grate and presently blue smoke curled up. 'You know, Angus, one doesn't get this fragrance from central heating.'

Angus laughed. 'No, and the smell o' the Persian Gulf and the North Sea costs a lot more money. You stick to your peat.'

'Have you got any leads on Isaac's case?'

'Nothing tangible that's come to anything. We thought it was possibly a grudge by one of his congregation. Hellfire hated that motor cycle, but he'd never dare touch the machine, and Isaac was well liked. Have you any ideas?'

Chapter 17

The Inspector had gone home to collect some papers when the phone rang. He was feeling tired and cursed as he lifted the receiver.

'Inspector Wilson,' he barked.

'Aye, it's yersel', Angus. It's Willie Fyffe.'

'Who the hell were you expecting, Fingal?' Angus retorted.

'Now jest haud yer wheesht, Angus,' Watery soothed. 'Here I am, doing ye a good turn, and ye snap at me like a gin trap.'

'Well, what is it?' Angus answered, somewhat mollified. He realised that the case was getting him down – Mary had said at breakfast that he was becoming unbearable. Also, now he regretted being short with Duncan.

'Now it may be naething at all, Angus,' Watery warned, 'but you know the twa Hungarians that live doon Glen Liath.'

'Yes?'

'Well, it's jest that they were a bit fu' last night and Janet Smith – a new waitress o' mine – heard them speaking ootside the bar.'

'And?'

'Weel.' There was a pause. 'I'm no' yin tae tell tales, Angus, but one has a certain duty. It was jest that one o' them – the lad called Eugene – saw Kenneth on the hill above the glen the day his old man was shot. He – that's Eugene, I mean – was jest going owre the top o' that gully on the ridge when he saw young Ken below with a rifle in his hands.'

'What!' Angus returned. 'Are you sure?' His wife came through from the kitchen at his shout, a look of concern on her face.

'Of course I'm sure, or at least Janet is ... There's nae doot at a' that that's whit he said.'

'I'll be up, Willie. Keep Janet there.' He banged the phone down.

'Important?' Mary asked.

'It could be confirmation of an important aspect of the case,' her husband replied.

'Now, Janet,' Angus spoke quietly to put the maid at ease. 'The information Mr Fyffe has passed on to me could be important. What did you hear Eugene Banderoski saying?' He offered her a cigarette. Though he was a non-smoker, he sometimes carried a packet around to help people to relax.

'Thank you, Inspector.' She took one and Archie lit a Swan Vesta for her. 'Well,' she began, inhaling with obvious pleasure. 'I was working at the kitchen window when those two came out. As you know, Inspector, the window faces the back door of the public bar. They were a bit fu'.' She gave the Inspector a nervous smile. 'I can't mind the exact words, you know,' she warned. 'But the small one – Eugene he calls himself – his English isn't good, but he was boasting that he could ...' She hesitated for a moment. 'He used a bad word, Inspector,' she blushed. 'He said he could muck up the young laird's schemes if he wanted to, because he'd seen him in the gully the day the laird was killed and he'd a rifle wi' him.'

Archie had been busy taking this down; now he looked up at the girl and a thought occurred to him.

'You're a friend o' Ian Cuthbert, the gillie, aren't you, Janet?' She blushed again.

'Yes, that's right, Sergeant. We're thinking about getting engaged, but that's still a secret.'

'Congratulations,' the Inspector said. 'You must know the Gilchrists, too? At least, Kirsty, now Watty is no more.'

'I've met her.' Her tone suggested that there wasn't any great love lost in her short relationship with the late keeper's wife. Angus was quick to pursue the point.

'Of course, Kirsty is a very attractive woman, Janet?' He gave a knowing smile.

'I suppose she may be to some men,' she grudgingly admitted.

'I understand she was fond of Kenneth?'

'Och, yes, Inspector. There were ructions a while back, when old Dewar found oot aboot it, or so Ian told me.'

'Janet, we'll have to go,' the Inspector said, when it was obvious that nothing more of value was forthcoming. 'Don't mention our conversation to anyone. I've told Mr Fyffe to keep it under his bonnet as well!'

'Nobody'll get anything oot o' me, Inspector, mark my words. I'm no one for tittle-tattle.'

'Archie,' Angus began as they negotiated the Glen Liath road. 'That was not an unproductive interview?'

'No, indeed. Maybe we're getting the breaks at last. But damn it, man, I've a feeling aboot the thing. I just canna see Ken killing his father.'

'Stranger things have happened, Archie. We've got to consider evidence impartially.'

Eugene was a thick, dark man with an inborn distrust of police. He had stayed on in Scotland after the war. Though Hungarian by birth, he had been brought up in Warsaw and had, at the age of 17, joined the Polish Army and later fought in the Italian campaign. He didn't invite the police into the forestry cottage which he shared with his friend, also a bachelor.

'We are here on a matter concerning the death of Horatio Dewar, the late laird of Grey Corries Lodge.' The Inspector was at his most official.

'I had nothing to do with it,' Eugene quickly protested, slurring his words.

'I'm not saying you had, Eugene, so don't get worried.' Angus became more human. 'But we were told that you saw someone that day in the gully above the strath.'

Eugene licked his lips nervously and said, 'You had better come in.'

'Sergeant Campbell will take a few notes, if you don't mind, Eugene,' Angus said, giving the room a quick look over as he sat down on a threadbare sofa. It was a typical bachelor's pad. A pile of logs on the carpet, empty bottles and the remains of a meal on an old table by the window. A pungent smell of cooking and garlic emanated from the open door of the adjoining kitchen. Mr Banderoski was fond of 'fries', he observed.

'You stay with a friend here, don't you, Eugene?'

'Ja, Ivor, but he works late tonight.'

'Well, if you'd just tell us in your own time what you saw from the gully, then we'll be getting on our way.'

Eugene had little more to add to what Janet had already outlined to them, except that he was quite emphatic that it was

Kenneth he'd seen – he knew him well enough and his eyesight was good.

'What clothes was he wearing?' asked Angus. The forester rubbed his dark chin and thought a moment.

'I zeenk eet vas a jacket – how you call it? – anorak ... green. Ja, green and brown trousers. The rifle I remember had a glass – a teelescrope.'

'Umph,' Thumper grunted in acknowledgement. 'And what time would this be?'

'About 2.30. I vas back here again at 3.45 and I walked down the glen.'

'What was it that took you over there on a weekday, Eugene? The Inspector looked up casually from an examination of his nails.

'I like to walk on the hills on my day off; it ees so – so peaceful.'

'Well, usually it is, or perhaps I should say, it used to be! Did you hear a shot, or several shots?'

'No, I went down the other side to the road; I was going quickly.'

'Well, Eugene, the Sergeant will have your statement typed and you'll have to sign it. What time do you finish work?'

'Five p.m.'

'We'll arrange that tomorrow, then,' the Inspector informed him. 'Oh, by the way, did you see anyone else?'

'No, just ze young Dewar and that big man, MacGillvery; he was further along the – how you call it – ridge.'

When they were back in the car the Inspector said, 'Check up on the time it takes to walk from the top o' the ridge above the gully through the glen to here at a good pace, will you, Archie.'

'I've made a note to have that done, Angus.'

'Good. Just as well Duncan dug up the evidence of the bullet or it would look gae black for Kenneth now,' the Inspector said, more to himself than to the Sergeant. He drew into a layby to let a car and caravan past. 'Bloody caravans!' he muttered. 'Look at that one, Sergeant – the driver hasn't even got rear view mirrors!'

'Are you bringing him in – Ken, I mean?'

'I'll have a word with the Superintendent and the Fiscal first, but it looks as if we may have to. Can't risk any more "accidents". The press are swarming round Faileadh like blue-arsed flies. I can just see the headline … "Highland Laird's son arrested!"'

The Chief Constable was on the telephone to the Procurator Fiscal. 'Things seem to be moving at last, Peter.'

'Thank goodness, John. I was getting worried. Isn't it strange that witnesses have been so reluctant to come forward? Firstly, the Gilchrist woman and her husband before her, then this forest worker.'

'I suppose it's better late than never, but I can understand it in the case of Banderoski; he had a hard time of it during the war. I think we should have young Dewar in for questioning.'

'Yes, though I've still qualms about it, but tread warily.'

'I can appreciate that. I've also known the family a long time. By the way, we must have that round of golf tomorrow, if the course is clear of snow.'

'That's a provisional date, John.'

Peter Frew, the PF, looked up at Angus as he came in. 'Hello, Inspector, I was just speaking with the Chief. You're taking Kenneth in? I hope you get it tied up.'

'I'll let you know, sir. Things are moving.'

Sadie Marquis had stayed on after normal working hours and Eugene Banderoski's statement was already typed. She was enjoying a cup of tea with Archie Campbell whilst waiting for Angus.

'You're a great girl, Sadie. You'll be making a wee fortune wi' overtime, just now!'

'I'd be working for one of the oil companies if I was wanting to make my fortune, Sarge,' she smiled at him.

'Aye, lassie,' he replied running his finger up his large nose. 'But you know where you're appreciated, don't you?' The Inspector came in tossing his cap on top of a filing cabinet. He glanced at his Sergeant who had his pipe stoked and looked contented.

'Make yourself at home, officer. I see you're relaxed.'

'You should relax yourself a bit, Angus, get a pipe and put your feet up.'

'Well let me extract you from your meditation.' He picked up the concrete cast as he sat down and handed it to his colleague. 'Duncan got this print.'

'I noticed the concrete block when I came in.' Archie observed 'and thought that you might be considering being a bricky when you retire. What's the score?'

'It matches your graveyard print, Serg.'

'Well, well now.' Archie spoke in a slightly raised voice, which was the closest he ever got to excitement. 'Duncan uses his loaf!'

'So did Isaac, if you ask me, and lost it. I was worried about our ecclesiastical pal before he departed.' Angus swivelled round in his chair and looked out of the window. 'It's all connected I'm sure.'

The Inspector stood up, then said, 'We'll have a bite to eat, and I'll fill you in on details then go down to the Lodge, Archie.'

'Whatever you say, sir,' the Sergeant agreed placidly.
'I feel peckish, I must admit. Oh, before I forget, Duncan
was wanting to get hold of you. He gave me a call a wee
while ago.'

'Anything important?'

'Too important, obviously, to tell a Heather Mixture
Sergeant,' Archie muttered, packing the tobacco more firmly
into his pipe.

'Umph,' Angus grunted. 'I wonder if he's dug anything up.'

'The only thing of importance, as far as I'm concerned,
that's been dug up recently was the Reverend Isaac
McMillan,' Archie mused thoughtfully. 'Only to be put
back again – or will be shortly.'

'It gives me the willies!' Sadie voiced her opinion. 'Like
something from … from *Dracula*! That reminds me,' she
gave a smile. 'I was once told that the *Dracula* book was
written in the north of Scotland.'

'Goodness woman you'll be having nightmares!'

Later, Archie Campbell was surprised when Angus suggested
that they call in and see Duncan on the way to Grey Corries
Lodge.

'You should enrol him as a Special Constable, Angus,'
Archie suggested. 'He seems to be doing a pickle o' work
for us – or getting in the way, depending which way you
want to take it.'

'Duncan's a help, Archie,' the Inspector pointed out as
he turned into the entrance to the poacher's cottage. 'He uses
his loaf.'

'Aye, I don't suppose I can deny that,' the Sergeant
acknowledged. They slammed the car doors and walked up
the footpath.

'Come in,' a voice boomed from within.

'Good day, Duncan,' Angus remarked, almost hitting his head on the door lintel. Duncan merely nodded, his mouth full, and pointed to two chairs.

'Eugene Banderoski has given us a statement concerning the shooting, Duncan.'

'Oh?' The big Highlander looked up with interest. He was pouring tea into old china cups with a floral design. 'That would be about seeing Ken with the rifle?'

'How the hell did you know that, Duncan?' Angus retorted tersely, his usually equable temper rising.

'Oh now, haud yer wheesht, Angus,' the poacher replied soothingly. 'I havena been holding back anything vital. It's just a logical bit o' thinking: today I found oot something mysel', concerning that nasty business. But first, tell me aboot Eugene's bleating.'

In a few brief sentences Angus informed the poacher how the forester had seen Ken in the gully with a rifle. Duncan handed them their tea before continuing. He took a sip. 'Is it too strong, Archie?' he inquired. 'I know the Inspector takes it like tar!'

'No, fine, thanks.'

'Well,' the poacher leant back in the chair and absently stroked the cat which had emerged, stretching, from her basket in the corner. She observed the visitors. 'The reason I didn't find that bit o' news unexpected is that I had a look roon' the Grey Corries mysel'. I was at the Glen Liath gully, then over by the bealach where old Horrible got his lot ...'

'And?' Angus asked expectantly. 'We know that now.'

'I couldna quite understand the laird's death,' Duncan continued. 'Of course, there was the business o' the auld copper mine and a' that, but I didn't think Spielman or Clem Fular would have gone to those sort of lengths to get haud o' it. But, against that, there was no real reason why Ken should want to bump off his old man either. Ken couldn't sell the mine even if he wanted to; he's not exactly hard up, as far as I know, and he didn't dislike the auld man that much, despite their bickering. No,' he reflected. 'It just didna make sense ...' Angus absent-mindedly prodded the peat with a poker and it flared up suddenly, lighting the snug little room. 'I could see him trying to give his dad a scare, just to bring home the point he was making about shooting a' those years ... giving Horror a bit of his own medicine, so to speak.'

Archie had a puzzled look on his face. 'You mean his dislike of stalking?'

'Exactly that, Archie. I'm sure Ken did fire the fatal shot that day, but he didn't mean to kill his father; just to give him one hell of a scare. It's quite frightening to have a bullet whistling about your arse. It can be disconcerting as I know mysel'! There used to be a bastard of a keeper over on the Kinlochsanda Estates ... but I won't bore you with that just now.'

'But the laird was more than scared,' the Inspector remarked dryly. 'He was almost minus his neck ...'

'That's so, Angus, but it was a mistake. You know that I found the rock off which the bullet ricocheted, and that was at least 60 feet from where the laird was lying. The old man was killed by the deflected bullet off the rock I found – the rock is clearly marked and your eggheads wi' their magnifying glasses have confirmed it. I telt you aboot a ricochet at the time, and some o' the stalkers heard it as well.'

The Inspector was silent for a full minute. His eyes had a far away look as they gazed at the glowing peat.

'It was negligent of me not to take the statement about

the ricochet more seriously, but I was diverted by the third shot idea.'

'I was a bit slow myself,' Duncan admitted.

The Inspector and Sergeant had much food for thought as they drove on to the Lodge. It was Deirdre who answered the door.

'Oh!' she exclaimed, seeing the two policemen. 'Come in.' She led the way into the hall.

'Sorry to trouble you, Miss Dewar,' Angus said. 'But we'd like to have a word with Kenneth.'

'I'll get him. We've just finished dinner, he's gone upstairs. Come into the drawing room.' She opened the door for them.

A large fire was burning in the hearth. They declined Deirdre's offer of chairs and she went out. They both had their police caps on. A few minutes later Ken entered, looking nonchalant.

'Hi there,' he greeted them. 'What brings such an exalted deputation to my humble doss?' He saw, however, by the expression on the Inspector's face that this wasn't a social call.

'We've come down to run through a few things with you, Ken,' the Inspector spoke heavily. Ken sat down on the sofa and crossed his legs. 'First of all, about your statement made to us concerning your movements on the day your father died.' Ken didn't say anything. 'You said that you went up the hill behind the house that day, ostensibly to take some photographs. You gave me a copy of one of them ...'

Angus produced the photograph and placed it on a small table with an intricate top of Florentine mosaic work.

'There seemed to be something not quite right about this photo when I first looked at it. In fact it was Duncan that spotted the anomaly.'

'And?'

'It wasn't taken the day your father died. On that day there was complete cloud cover. You may remember later it developed into quite a storm ... But that was a small mistake, Kenneth. You made a much bigger one.'

'Go on.'

'Between the day you took this photograph and the day your father died the scenery changed. You see this tree?' The Inspector placed a large finger on a tree in the foreground of the photo.'

'What about it?'

'It's no longer there. Look now at your photograph. It was blown down in a gale. You may have been down south at the time, or maybe you just forgot. Duncan didn't!'

He adjusted his bulk in the chair and continued. Ken wasn't being exactly voluble, he thought. 'Now, about your statement. You said you didn't go near the gully on the day in question, but we have a witness who actually saw you at the gully – with a rifle,' he added emphatically, studying the young man for a reaction but, other than a slight tightening of his lips, there was none. 'What have you to say?'

Ken went over to the mantelpiece and stood looking into the flames. 'I suppose it was silly of me, Angus, but everything was so unexpected ... Yes, I shot my father, but it was an accident. How was I to know that the bullet would ricochet off a rock?' He whipped round suddenly. 'You'll never bloody well believe me, will you?' he shouted angrily. 'But it's the truth. I wanted to scare him – he was so fucking indifferent to the suffering of animals; they're all the same – this mania to kill – and then I ended up killing my own father! It's ironical, isn't it ... "and all men kill the thing they love."' His eyes welled with tears and his voice cracked. The policemen were quiet. 'I panicked, of course,' he continued more quietly, running his fingers through his hair. Then he seemed to get a grip of himself. His voice now held some of its old clarity. 'I hid the rifle and made my way back here. Yes,' he confessed, glancing at the photograph, 'it was silly of me to print that enlargement for you. It was taken at the same time of year, with about the same covering of snow on the tops, but I might have known someone would spot the mistake. Not to lie, should be my motto, Angus, and never elaborate on a lie.'

'So you were out to scare the daylights out of your old man?' Angus commented.

'And succeeded,' Archie put in.

'Yes, I succeeded, Sergeant,' Ken confessed and, pausing for an instant, then carried on. 'I know you think it's all lies, Angus, but honestly it's the truth.'

'Well,' the Inspector said at length, 'we'll have to arrest you, Kenneth, and I'll submit a full report to the Fiscal in the morning. You may contact your solicitor if you wish.'

The following morning Angus was speaking with the PF. He had already given a report to the Chief.

'What I find strange, Inspector, is that there doesn't seem to be a logical link between the various incidents, but surely they're related?' He looked questioningly at the policeman.

'The rescue team seems to be the common denominator, sir, with the exception of the Dewar fatality and even there at least one rescue team member is involved, two if you count the keeper and, of course, Duncan MacGillvery who witnessed the incident.'

'MacGillvery, the Robin Hood! Robin – Robbing – Hood. However, to get back to the nitty-gritty.' He twiddled his pencil. 'Now you've taken young Dewar in.'

'Yes. The further piece of evidence which Duncan found – that rock with the bullet gouge on it – and the bullet; cunning bit of work that, Angus, it appears to absolve Kenneth of murder, at least.'

'Yes, it would seem so,' the Fiscal agreed. 'We know definitely where the laird was lying when he was shot?'

'MacGillvery does – and so did Watty Gilchrist – and they've shown us; they have now agreed on the place and that was before the damaged rock was found,' he added. 'Either Kenneth's an incredibly bad shot, or he's telling the truth, sir.'

'Telling the truth now,' Peter Frew corrected.

'Quite so. But any trace of rock particles in the neck should clear that point."

'The statement from the forest worker? There's no doubt about that?'

'No, I think it's straightforward enough. He was just apprehensive about coming forward and volunteering the evidence. The time has been checked from the top of the gully back to his house; he seems to have got his timings right.'

'About this phone call – the one to the manse.' The Fiscal changed the subject again. 'There's no way of tracing it, I know, but Mrs Watt ... that's the housekeeper's name, isn't it ...?'

'Correct.'

'... Mrs Watt must have known if it was one of the usual team members, surely?'

'She knew it wasn't anybody she recognised, but emergency calls are often made directly to team members if we can't be contacted.'

'So she thought it quite normal?'

'Well, let's say she didn't question it. One doesn't with

call-outs. It's not like people calling out fire brigades on false alarms. I don't think I've ever heard of a deliberate false alarm for a rescue here.'

'Has young Dewar asked for his solicitor?'

'No, he didn't bother. I advised him of his rights, but I also suggested to Archie – Sergeant Campbell – that he should give Hector MacAndrew, the family lawyer, a ring. He'll probably see Ken this morning, even if the laird doesn't want him!'

'Could he have been responsible for the bogus call?'

'I suppose so. He was at home at the time and the call was made about 7.10 p.m. Nobody saw him using the phone, but he has an extension in his room. He told us he was studying a chess problem from Tattersall's *End Games*. The movements of all other team members have been checked. Chris Watkins was in Glasgow until the following morning.'

'No reason why a call couldn't have been made from there,' the Fiscal observed thoughtfully.

'No,' Angus agreed. 'Murder by proxy. Chris's alibi appears sound enough – he was attending a lecture. He would have had difficulty making that call, but not impossible'

'I suppose you've seen the press this morning, Inspector?' Peter Frew asked, dropping his pencil into a tray in front of him.

'I had a word with them when I arrived, sir. I haven't yet told them that we arrested young Dewar.'

'Well,' the Fiscal's tone indicated that the interview was drawing to a close. 'Let's meet again later.'

'Right, sir,' Angus said, standing up. 'I've to see the chief in half an hour, then I'll deal with the other matters before I call back.'

'Thank you, Inspector.'

Duncan was at his front gate collecting his mail from Donnie the post when Chris passed in his car. He gave a toot on his horn and a wave.

'I suppose Chris will be involved wi' his aunt's affairs now she's departed,' Donnie observed; he knew everybody's business in the village.

'Aye, but he wasn't very close to her,' Duncan remarked, taking a letter from Donnie. 'He will be a wealthy man now that both Isaac and Mrs MacWhirter have snuffed it.'

'I heard aboot Ken being arrested,' Donnie commiserated. 'A terrible thing. I canna think he'd harm onybody, least of all his father!'

'So they've taken him in,' the poacher said. 'Well, it was to be expected, I suppose.'

'It's a sad day for the glen,' Donnie replied. The postman had at one time been an ardent poacher himself and had more than once used the official post van for transporting the beasts, a practice he had terminated when he was stopped by PC Munro's predecessor. Luckily, the constable hadn't questioned the sanctity of a sealed mail bag inside of which Donnie had fortuitously lodged his venison.

'Well, I'd better be on my way, Duncan. Thanks for that bit o' meat you left the other night – it had a grand flavour …' He started up his van, but then switched it off. Duncan, who had turned away, wheeled round.

'Something the matter, Donnie?'

'Just a thought, Duncan. Remember that night poor Isaac was buried?'

'Yes.'

'Well, I was just putting the dog out for a couple o' minutes, aboot one o'clock it was and Watty was just getting into his van. He'd been at the cards with the Blacks and had a bit more o' Jack's home brew than was good for him. Anyhow, the point o' it is that he called to me, asking, did I spy the one o'clock jogger getting some sly practice in?'

Duncan was thoughtful as he went up the footpath to his cottage. The cat met him with a rabbit in her mouth.

'Aye, Jes,' the big man remarked affectionately. 'You're as bad as your master ... and your master decided just a minute ago to go back to the hill again. I think I need to do a bit more hunting!'

Chapter 18

'Well, Sarge., we've just got to keep at it. What about the rock? Has the analysis been completed?' It was the Inspector that asked.

'The forensic boys have identified Duncan's bullet. Minute fragments of nickel match the metal on the recovered high velocity bullet, and the round was fired by the Weatherby magnum – .270 wby – the weapon held in evidence.' He glanced down at his pad, before continuing. 'Scoring by a granite type rock evident on bullet case: oh they were impressed with Duncan's deductions. It also appears that rock particles are below blood traces found on the casing. That,' Archie looked up from his note book, 'could be good news for young Ken.'

'You know,' Angus mused, 'I remember reading about the possibility of rock particles on the bullet in the first ballistic report, but assumed that the bullet could have been in contact with rock after passing through Dewar – not before. You've got to be psychic as well as scientific in this trade! At the risk of sounding like Willie Fyffe, I was a bit negligent, I should have taken more heed of those ricochet reports by witnesses.' The phone rang. Archie answered.

'Sergeant Campbell.'

'Duncan MacGillvery here, Sergeant. Is the Inspector there?'

'Hold on a minute. For you, Angus – MacGillvery.'

'Yes, Duncan?'

'Angus, I want you to position yourself by the input to the conduit at the Freshwater this afternoon – with a pair of binoculars, a camera and a witness!'

'What's this, Duncan?' the Inspector demanded tersely. 'You could be playing dangerous games.'

'I may be, Angus, but you just do that for me, will you. Go to the conduit input and keep yourself well hidden. It may be a short-cut for us.'

'It may be a short-cut for you, Duncan. If I do it I may have to wear my black tie – tell me more.'

'I can't at the moment, Angus … Have faith, as Isaac would have said, and keep your eyes skinned.'

'Well,' the Inspector reluctantly acquiesced. 'I'll be holed up there from 3 p.m. onwards, much against my better judgement!'

'Thanks. I knew I could depend on you.'

'What the hell is he up to now?' Archie asked as Angus hung up.

'That man thinks he's Sherlock, or perhaps Moriaty.' The Inspector told him of the poacher's request.

'Och, well,' the Sergeant replied with resignation. 'At least I'll get some fresh air! I've been attached to this bloody telephone for the last three hours; it feels like a manacle. It could be dodgy, Inspector. Our local exterminator isn't playing tag!'

'Well, I warned him. If we don't go up there he could

get hurt. I've no idea what he's up to but I've a feeling he's toying with fire!'

'We could stop him going.'

'Yes, we could, but, as he said, it could be a short-cut.'

'There are few genuine short-cuts in life, Inspector.'

'True, Archie. However, we'll go up early and, as Clem Fular would possibly say, case the area.'

'By the way,' Archie spoke. 'Isn't this the night of the ceilidh at Queenshouse?'

'It is,' Angus confirmed. 'These fatalities will put a damper on things.'

'Oh, I don't know. The Rev was certainly never the life and soul of a party and I'm sure Watty wouldn't want to spoil the evening – dead or alive.'

'That's true,' Angus agreed. 'It's supposed to be for rescue team funds, though, and here we are, with two of them dead.'

'It'll maybe pay for funeral expenses,' the Sergeant suggested.

The Inspector looked at his watch, then stood up slowly as if he was tired.

'I've got to see Ken, so I'll leave you to it, Archie. You seem to manage all right without me ... Did the boys have any luck asking if anyone was seen prowling round Isaac's lab? I asked Hellfire myself at the time, but he's as close as a fish's arsehole.'

'No one's seen anything as far as I can gather, Angus. Perhaps Bookam will get a lead from one of the calliachs; those old wives have eyes like midden hens!'

'Have you seen your solicitor yet, Kenneth?' the Inspector asked.

They were in his office. A constable sat quietly in a corner, taking notes.

'Yes, I saw MacAndrew. He may be okay for drawing up deeds, but he's not exactly on the ball when it comes to murder or accidental death or whatever it's going to be called.'

'A pity,' said the Inspector. 'I suppose you realise the evidence against you is very damning.'

'So I hear. But I assure you it was an accident. Even I am not such a bad shot, and I did hit a rock wide away from my father. He was a conspicuous target from where I was lying.'

'The Inspector was silent for a moment. He didn't say anything about the ballistic report. 'Was Watty Gilchrist trying to blackmail you?' he asked suddenly.

Ken looked up, startled, at the Inspector who was watching a mechanical digger at work outside.

'Watty! Never! He was as dedicated to the family as our dog ... Whatever made you think that?'

'He saw you in the gully.'

'Well, he certainly kept it to himself,' Ken said, evenly enough.

'Kirsty knows about it, too. And you were seen by one of the forestry workers, as I told you.'

Ken gave a short laugh. 'As I said, I'm not cut out for a life of crime.'

'You had a powerful motive for wanting your father out of the way.'

'Because I might have inherited something? No such luck. A lot of people have that motive, but most of them draw the line at patricide. Anyhow, I've enough money of my own.'

'What about the old mine?' the Inspector asked quietly.

'You heard about that? I should have guessed, I suppose. Spielman and Fular are both interested in it. Dad was against it, of course.'

'How interested are they in getting hold of the rights?'

Ken considered for a moment. 'They're pretty keen. Especially Spielman ... That's probably why Fular came over.'

'Did you know that a survey was done recently?' The Inspector watched. There was now a wariness in the younger man's face.

'No, I didn't ... Look!' Ken sounded exasperated. 'There's no mystery! The shooting was an accident. I'm genuinely sorry about it. I'll accept the punishment of the court, or whatever. But there's no other subterfuge, I assure you ...'

'You were in Faileadh the night Isaac was buried?' Angus said quietly.

'Yes. Along with the rest of the population. You know very well that I visited Chris about 10 o'clock that night and left about 11. I've already told the Sergeant.'

'So you did, Ken, so you did,' the Inspector murmured. 'Tell me, did you know that the brakes on the minister's motor cycle were tampered with?'

'I heard a rumour. In fact, it got into one of the papers.'

'Aye, there's been a leak somewhere ... Have you ever used a silicon spray?'

'No. But Dad did once, for re-proofing a jacket. I don't think it did any good, though ... Why?'

The Inspector ignored the question. 'Is the spray still at the Lodge?' he asked.

Ken shrugged. 'It might be. Kirsty would know. Or Deirdre. Or better still, Jean MacBain. She knows everything she's not supposed to know.'

Some time later Duncan MacGillvery gazed down from the easterly flank of Bheinn Bruhm. There were not many hinds about; he only saw four in the back corrie.

'Do you see them?' he asked his companion.

'Yes, down at the wee stream near those snow patches.'

'Right,' the poacher agreed. 'We'll skirt round that bit o' blind ground in their lee and see how we go.'

Archie was feeling mortally tired. He just couldn't do without his sleep – though it was even worse on night shift, he recalled, when he'd been based down in Dunoon. How he hated the long, still hours of night! He marvelled at Angus; the man was an automaton, he thought, but then, the big bugger kept himself fit. Archie had seen him on more than one occasion going off for a morning run, at a time when local alcoholics were weaving an erratic course homewards.

They had reached the rough ground a short way beneath the dam when Angus finally stopped.

'How about over yonder, amongst the silver birks, Archie?' The Inspector pointed to where an isolated clump of stunted trees occupied an otherwise featureless section of heathery desert.

'Suits me, Angus,' the Sergeant replied. 'It gives an uninterrupted view o' the conduit.'

'Aye,' agreed his superior. 'It'll do fine – we'll take turns having a snooze.'

'Now you're talking, man.' Archie cheered up. 'That sounds better than taking turns keeping watch. If this case goes on much longer, I'll have to indent in triplicate for sleep!' Angus laughed.

'Aye, Archie; it's age that's telling on you!'

'Age yer arse, Inspector!' the Sergeant replied heatedly. 'Just because buggers like you have a conscience and can't sleep doesn't mean that honest men – like me – can't.'

Both men were dressed in ex-army camouflaged anoraks and had taken plenty of warm clothing. The

Inspector's rucksack also contained a ground sheet, two flasks of coffee, a stalker's telescope, binoculars, a camera and a walkie-talkie.

'What do you think teuchter MacGillvery is up to?' Archie gasped. They had reached the copse and he looked round approvingly.

'Blowed if I know, Archie, but he's playing with his life. If I'm any good at guessing, he's taking the murderer over the hill to meet us!'

'Queer way o' doing things when there's a perfectly good road round the bottom! But then, Duncan's a queer chap. He's been creeping about ever since old Horror was bumped off, poking his big nose into things – he'd do better to stick to poaching!'

The Sergeant had been asleep for almost two hours. The Inspector hadn't the heart to wake him, but took a photograph as evidence. It would give them a laugh back at the station. Then he replaced the telephoto on the camera. He was about to wake Archie when he saw a movement high up the hillside. He raised his binoculars and spotted two figures, dressed in clothing which merged perfectly with their surroundings – like a couple o' stags, he thought, giving Archie a nudge. The Sergeant yawned and sat up, momentarily blinking uncomprehendingly.

'Just for a moment, I thought I was in hell, Angus! And I see that in fact I am … What gives?'

Angus pointed silently up the hillside.

'Bugger that knot,' Duncan muttered as the line he had tied round one of the hinds came adrift.

'I'll retie it,' his companion volunteered.

'Good man,' the poacher accepted thankfully. 'Once the

snow goes, it's hell, dragging the beasts.' He glanced casually over the ground below and thought to himself that the police would probably be in the clump of trees overlooking the conduit input. Best cover around, he mused. He turned his attention once more to his companion.

'Okay – that should do,' the other man spoke, slinging the poacher's rifle on to his shoulder. Duncan looked approvingly at the way the nylon line was secured round the lower jaw of the beast.

'Aye,' he remarked. 'That won't come undone in a hurry. It's a good knot! The same as the one Gealeas was tied up with in the old mine.'

'It's two hinds they have, Angus,' Archie observed, adjusting the telescope.

'Aye, a couple o' nice beasties,' the Inspector said approvingly.

'I wonder what Duncan's thinking aboot?' the Sergeant continued. 'Perhaps he's a bit senile!'

'Don't you believe it,' said Angus, looking thoughtful. 'It's all very logical.'

'Well, to risk mixing my metaphors, if Duncan is offering us a bum steer on this latest escapade, we can always clobber him for poaching; it's no' every day we photograph a poacher on the job!'

The two figures moved easily and fast, considering that they were dragging heavy hinds. Soon they had arrived at the top of the conduit. The dam was still overflowing with melt water which spilled over into sluices leading into the conduit. The two poachers stared down into the seething water and the policemen could see Duncan pointing. Angus was now observing the scene through the telephoto lens of the camera, whilst Archie had the binoculars glued to his eyes. Silently, they watched the two men drop both beasts into the water ... What happened next followed so quickly that both policemen could hardly believe their eyes. One moment Duncan was beside the low rail which ran round the perimeter of the entrance to the conduits, the next he was toppled over by his assailant who had used the top of the rail as a fulcrum for throwing the larger man. He would never otherwise have had a chance of overpowering Duncan.

Angus had taken shots in rapid succession with the Nikon. Archie said urgently, 'Quick, get him!'

'Let's get Duncan, you mean, Archie! We'll run down to the penstock – that's where the conduits feed into the main tunnels to the turbines. There a big grid there to prevent debris going down – and poached deer, let's hope it'll stop him.'

'What about him?' Archie pointed to the fast retreating, valley-bound figure.

'We've got him here,' Angus replied, patting the camera. 'He's in the bag, Archie. Anyhow, I'll alert HQ by radio – he won't get out of the area. First things first!'

The two policemen ran down the slope to the conduit; once there they could move faster on the concrete. A narrow gauge railway used for maintenance ran to the side of the concrete-covered channel.

'Archie,' the Inspector shouted as he took the lead. 'The wee bogie here – the one the maintenance squad uses – we could go down on that!'

'But is there any way of stopping the bloody thing?' the Sergeant gasped, valiantly attempting to keep up.

'Aye, I think it has brakes – those two handles are for propelling it, at least ...' The Inspector skidded to a halt close to the point where the poacher had been thrown in and quickly observed that there was actually a primitive brake operated by a screw handle which activated it. They pushed it to the start of the decline.

'Quick, Angus man, you'll be late for your funeral!'

'That's just what I'm contemplating,' the Inspector retorted as he clambered aboard. 'Late for my bloody funeral!'

The bogie quickly gained speed. Though its maximum velocity could only have been about 40 mph, to the two policemen it felt like the ton at least. Sparks gyrated from the wheels and the rusty contraption shuddered and bounced alarmingly.

There was no springing – just four small flanged wheels, a wooden platform and the two pump handles. These were now oscillating like a tuning fork.

The policemen caught a glimpse of the other man on the dam track far below, but he didn't see them as they hurtled down on their precarious steed. Ahead, the penstock loomed larger every second. Angus applied another turn of the brake wheel and a smell of burning wood reached their nostrils. They realised that the brake shoes were in fact made of wood.

'Christ!' Archie said to himself, since the Inspector would never hear him above the noise. 'Why the hell did I ever join the force.'

Almost imperceptibly the speed of the bogie diminished, due more, Angus thought, to the lessening of the gradient than to the effect of burning brakes. By the time they neared the penstock he had reduced the speed to about 20 mph; slower it would not go. He thought of grabbing one of the pump handles, but decided against it – it would probably pull his arms out of their sockets. He saw Archie's look of alarm and yelled.

'We'll have to jump for it, Archie, before it hits the buffers!' The buffers were in fact heavy steel channels. The Sergeant nodded in dumb agreement; he had already reluctantly reached that conclusion. Twenty feet from the point where the rails abruptly ended they jumped – one either side – landing heavily and rolling with a complete absence of dignity on to a flat concrete area only partly snow-covered. Simultaneously came the crash of the bogie. Archie observed the scene with a jaundiced eye and a sore posterior, thankful that he had baled out in time. All that remained of the machine were fragments of cast iron, buckled steel and splintered wood which had caught alight. Angus was already up and sprinting for the exit of the conduit, shouting, 'Duncan!' But the poacher had not yet arrived.

Chapter 19

'He's not here yet,' the Inspector gasped as Archie stopped at the railing surrounding the penstock, a duplicate of the one at the top. 'But a hind has just come down.' The Sergeant had no breath left with which to pass further observations; he gulped air greedily as he clung to the safety rail. 'There's the other one,' Angus pointed. 'Let's get down, Archie. We'll fish them out before they jam in the grating.'

The last 40 feet of the conduit top was open, forming a channel with the steel grill angled down into the current at the bottom end. On top of the grill ran a narrow steel catwalk, no doubt often frequented by Duncan and other poachers, thought Angus. The water was a mass of white foam. As he reached down to grab a hind, he thought he heard a noise above the din of jumping water.

'By Jove, Archie!' he shouted. 'What do you know?'

'Very little, I'm thinking, but what's on your mind?'

'Listen, you idiot!' It came again – faint and distorted, but a distant call. Archie's face exploded in a wide grin.

'Angus, man,' he remarked. 'I'm thinking that Duncan MacGillvery is very much alive!'

'It must be his ghost.' The Inspector spoke without conviction.

From out of the gloomy depths of the tunnel a body came swirling towards them. It was Duncan – travelling fast, head first, floating face upwards …

'Field him, Archie, or he'll hit the grating!' Angus shouted as the Sergeant was closer to the end of the catwalk.

'Dinna fret, Angus. I used to be a dab hand at the rugby. Duncan has a muckle big heid and it's the only chance I'll get o' kicking it, so I'd better make the most o' it!' The Sergeant slid his feet down the grating and held the deck of the catwalk firmly as he waited with both boots poised to save the poacher.

'Look out, Duncan!' Angus yelled warningly. 'The grating!' The poacher turned round with a swift arm movement and they saw him blinking just as Archie's foot caught him on the shoulder. The sheer momentum of the big man doubled up the Sergeant's outstretched legs and, though managing to absorb some of the shock, he was projected upwards and over the catwalk through the tubular rails behind, to fall into the penstock reservoir on the far side. Luckily, he was a powerful swimmer and, despite the current, he managed to reach the rungs of a ladder built into the concrete. He dragged himself up on to the plinth, emerging at the same time as the Inspector was unceremoniously dragging Duncan out, his plus-fours bulging with water. Angus loosened off the buckles at the bottom of the tweeds and a deluge descended, down through the steel mesh of the catwalk.

'My,' Duncan grinned weakly. 'That's like relieving myself!' It was several minutes before he could say anything more; he lay slumped on the catwalk, gulping like a landed fish.

'I've come to the conclusion,' the dripping Archie

remarked bitterly, 'it's no' a day for buffers – animate or inanimate!'

'You did well, Archie,' the Inspector consoled him. 'The mistake you made was that MacGillvery is just a shade heavier than a rugby ball!'

It started to snow; lightly at first, then with steady determination. They moved off down the track to Kinlochsanda which was the closest habitation. When descending the steep zigzag, Angus saw that his two friends were recovering rapidly. The afternoon was once again developing into a full scale blizzard and he wondered where the police Land Rover was; he had radioed for one to come up the track to meet them. He had also asked for road blocks to be set up on the three roads leading out of the district. He knew that the murderer was unaware that he had been caught red-handed and therefore wouldn't make a dash for it, but it was always better to make sure. He couldn't afford to lose him at this stage of the proceedings.

Just when the Inspector was thinking of recalling HQ, the lights of a police vehicle loomed out of the white maelstrom. It shuddered to a halt and they bundled inside. The heater was going full blast; both the Sergeant and Duncan reacted by shivering violently.

'When your teeth stop clattering like the diesel, perhaps you can tell me of your excursion – the one over the hill,' the Inspector laughed.

'Well, it worked, you must admit, Angus,' Duncan said, coughing. 'And Archie had his second shower that day.'

'If I had more sense, Duncan, I never would have attempted to save that hard head of yours from hitting the grating.'

'Now, children,' the Inspector intervened. 'Back to business ...'

'I know you thought it was damned silly, Angus, and upon reflection, it was! However, I also knew how damned cunning Chris is; he's a really intelligent man, but a man with a screw loose.' The poacher adjusted his position on the seat where a pool of water was forming. He continued. 'He was pestering me to take him out poaching sometime, but I always put him off; it's a sort of personal occupation. You know as well as I do that the downfall of all poachers is bragging in a bar ... Not that I think he'd do that.

'Anyhow, to get back to the day's outing, Chris knew that I was suspecting him. I could tell that by his manner, little subtle things. I knew it wouldn't take much to make him have a go at me, but I wasn't as stupid as he thought. I assumed that he would try to shoot me; as a matter of fact I arranged that he carried my rifle, after I had shot the two hinds. He had seen me putting five rounds in the magazine and he knew that I took two rounds to shoot the two beasts. What he didn't know was that the bottom three rounds were blanks – I took the cordite out.'

'At least you showed some common sense,' Archie acknowledged, trying to check his shivering.

'I didn't show enough, Sergeant,' Duncan confessed. 'I was expecting him to use the rifle and wasn't enough on guard for that cross-buttock over the rail into the conduit. He was mighty slick.'

'He certainly was,' the Inspector agreed. 'We saw the whole thing and it was photographed.'

'Well, we've got him,' the poacher said. There was just a trace of weariness in his voice.

'He won't get away, that's for sure,' the Inspector agreed. 'There are only the three roads out of this neck of the woods, and these are sewn up. Anyhow, he thinks all's well.'

Later, when the Inspector and two constables went round to arrest Chris at his house, he was not to be found. The Inspector was not unduly perturbed; they would be able to pick him up later.

After Duncan had a bite to eat and a bath he felt better, though deep inside he was still chilled to the marrow. When he parted from Angus, the policeman had suggested that they should meet at Queenshouse later. The poacher had felt reluctant then, but now contemplating the trials of the day, he came to the conclusion that a few glasses of Watery's whisky wouldn't do him much harm. In fact, he concluded, brightening at the prospect, they would do him a power of good. It had been half expected that Chris would have cancelled the ceilidh, but this was easier said than done in such a scattered community, so it was still on. Half an hour later Angus called.

'Are you ready, Duncan?'

'Aye, but I shan't be doing any jigging tonight, Angus!'

'A quiet "sensation" in the corner by the fire will do you fine, man,' the Inspector assured him as they walked down the path. 'And, anyhow, there's unfinished business to attend to. We haven't yet got Chris.'

'You think he'll turn up at the ceilidh?' Duncan inquired.

'Of course, he couldn't afford not to ... He's no idea that Archie and I saw him today, or that you haven't departed to your land of plenty to be stalked by the souls of Watty and Isaac.'

'I'm quite happy on these grounds, Angus – the other, or at least the passage to it, was a wee bit damp. I felt like that bloke Charon! I'll be glad when everything's back to normal.'

'Won't we all,' Angus echoed.

There were two constables sitting in the back seat of the car. They drove in silence up the glen, now under a heavy blanket of snow, until they had passed the place where Isaac had been killed. Then the Inspector broke the silence by telling Duncan he had been right about Ken trying to scare his father with a shot that went awry.

'I take no pleasure in being right about that, Angus,' the poacher admitted with a sigh, feeling apprehensive at Angus's driving. 'The lad must feel bad about it.' He paused for a moment and added, 'The scarred boulder will stand him in good stead.'

As they approached Queenshouse, the conditions deteriorated yet again. Despite a frenzy of activity by the snow ploughs, there was heavy drifting into the road – a mere cutting through the white uniformity. They bumped over the level crossing, then eased along the final 50 yards to the hotel.

'You boys keep out o' the way in Watery's office,' Angus instructed his two constables as they entered. 'He's had instructions.'

'Right, sir,' the taller of the two replied.

The ceilidh was being held in the lounge, a long low room with the small bar at one end. Inevitably, a cluster of team members held council there, but the Inspector noted there wasn't the usual carefree laughter. Clem Fular had just bought a round and von Spielman, perched on a bar stool, wore a satisfied smirk. Chris sat alongside him, his back to the door. Two fiddlers were hard at it elbowing an eightsome reel with more diligence than ability, whilst Watery, acting as MC, tried to persuade the menfolk to dance, with little success. As usual, wives and girlfriends had been abandoned to cluster round the fire or occupy the various tables round the edge of the dance floor.

The publican, seeing the Inspector, raised a fat arm in a Mussolini-like salute of welcome.

'Come in, lads, come in. But,' he continued, a frown on his face, 'you're in uniform, with a night's relaxation ahead. Aye, I suppose some of us must work. Police and publicans have a hard time o' it,' he commiserated. The Chief Constable and his wife were in a corner sharing a table with the Superintendent. Angus gave them a nod in greeting. Clem was recounting an episode with a bear on the Wind River.

'Hello, Angus,' Basil greeted the Inspector. 'I see you're on duty tonight. I suppose it's all work these days; you'll be glad to have that holiday in Canada.'

'I certainly will, Bas.'

Ian Cuthbert, looking smart in Highland dress, now took the place of the fiddlers who had gone over to the bar to refuel, and shouldered his pipes. With the minimum of tuning he erupted into a brisk, foot-thumping strathspey.

Duncan had moved in unnoticed through the side door. In a brief lull, when Ian dextrously changed to a lament, he moved up to the bar and said, 'Good evening, Chris.'

He spoke almost into the ear of the team leader. The result was electrifying. Chris dropped his glass with a crash and for a split second seemed mesmerised, evading Duncan's grasp then moved like a flash of light. Before Angus could grab him he was halfway across the dance floor. He knocked over a woman and side-stepped past Archie who had sprung into action, then shot through the door and away. It was unfortunate that his three pursuers all tried to pass through the doorway together. The result was that Archie was almost knocked out when his head hit the door frame. Duncan was the first to disentangle himself and rushed down the passageway to the hotel foyer. The two constables were standing outside Watery's office, speaking to a keeper and his wife who had just arrived.

'Where's he gone?' Duncan gasped, breathless. Angus appeared behind him; he had lost several buttons from his tunic and his tie was streaming over his right shoulder.

'He didn't come along here, sir,' Constable MacKay shouted.

'Well, he can't get out the back,' the Inspector panted. 'I asked the Sergeant to secure all windows and doors.'

'The toilet,' Duncan barked. 'I bet he got out the top o' the window ...' The poacher made straight for the front door, like a charging bull. The other followed.

Outside the snow was deep and their feet made no sound. In the car park ahead a vehicle barked into life. Headlights swung round and focussed on the narrow white gap of the road. They saw the silhouette of the police Land Rover, its four wheels spinning its way in the direction of the main road.

'Striker' Bowie had been driving railway engines since steam locomotives plied from Kinlochsanda to Glasgow; later he continued his career in the 1500 hp diesels. In winter he was given the task of keeping the line open. His snow plough was a prodigious affair, 12 feet high and almost as wide. It took the shape of a classical ploughshare mounted on an old steam bogie. At that particular moment he was reminiscing to his co-driver.

'In winters when winters were real winters, Leo, we used to charge drifts at 40 mph. Even the bloody engine would shudder to a halt.' He gazed at the whiteness through the cab window with pale nostalgic eyes.

That night there was no such trouble and the great machine scoured its way in a deep channel across the Moor of Bannock with the ease of a seamstress cutting a bolt of cloth. Striker had no way of telling that the automatic gates at the Queenshouse were frozen up and Chris never gave the crossing a thought. Besides, he knew trains didn't run at night on the line, though he was aware that British Rail kept it clear in winter ...

His crossing of the line coincided precisely with the great shear of the steel plough. It ripped through the side of the Land Rover on the passenger side like the bows of a corvette. The locomotive eventually shuddered to a halt with the rending of metal. Fifty yards further on two horrified men jumped down from the cab.

The police and Duncan arrived on the scene minutes later. It was illuminated by the large single detached head-lamp of the Land Rover now hanging from its wires. Chris was a crumpled heap, both spine and neck snapped.

Chapter 20

The following morning a few sleepy-eyed members of the rescue team were assembled in Inspector Wilson's office. Each suffered a common complaint – a hangover. The party at Queenshouse, despite the sombre background of events, had been a great success despite the distraction. Most of the team directly involved in the case had arrived for this present informal gathering, eager to have the gaps in the murder jigsaw explained by the Inspector and Sergeant Archie Campbell.

The Inspector was leaning back in his chair behind the large desk. There were several bundles of papers stacked at random and an abandoned cup was perched precariously on the old intercom.

Sergeant Archie Campbell, who was occupying a white canteen chair, cleared his throat and looked around. 'Is everyone present who's going to be present?'

'Oh, I'm sure we have a full house,' his boss cut in. 'I see you've all made yourself at home; and why not.' About 10 team members were scattered around the room, most

with their backs to the wall and Basil was poised, Oor
Wullie-like on an upturned waste paper basket.

'I had a word with my superiors,' the Inspector continued,
'and they agreed to my suggestion to explain – unofficially
that is – the sequence of events over the last few weeks. But
it's for your ears only.' He looked over the tight knit group;
individuals who put their lives in each other's hands without question and often in extreme situations. He carried on
and with a nervous gesture, ran his fingers through his hair,
his low, well modulated voice filling the room. 'You all know
that Kenneth Dewar has been charged with the death of his
father and claims that the incident was an unfortunate
accident. That will all legally unfold in due course. The
incident was complicated and the late laird was killed by a
ricochet from a bullet from a high velocity rifle. Duncan
MacGillvery was instrumental in finding both the bullet
and the rock in question. Even if I say it myself, a remarkable bit of observation and DIY detective work.' Duncan,
who was leaning back on the old cast iron radiator gave a
mock bow and touched his fore and aft.

'I suppose the best way to kick off is to tell you what
you also already know, that Chris Watkins, had he survived
would have been charged with the murder of the Reverend
Isaac McMillan and the attempted murder of Duncan
MacGillvery.' He nodded at the big poacher. 'One such
incident in this normally peaceable place is bad enough, but
the epidemic of serious crimes strained our resources. The
trouble was that the breaks only came at an advanced stage
of the investigations, in addition to which, the possible motive
for the murder and attempted murders was only apparent
about 30 hours ago. Now, on another slant, the late Mrs
McWhirter left her estate, which was a considerable one,'
he paused again and looked round the attentive faces, 'to

Isaac and this would have passed on to Chris on Isaac's demise. But to go back for a minute; the death of Horatio Dewar started off the unfortunate chain of events and then there was the Glen Liath mine. Two international companies are interested in it; not in copper which was originally extracted, but beryllium. Chris, who was a geologist, realised the potential and, without authority, presented samples with a report to the American company of which Clem Fular is the boss. Beryllium is used for a super-light metal. Chris would have got a percentage out of the deal had it came off. This too was done in secret.'

'Was that why he made an attempt on Gilchrist's life in the old mine?' It was Willie Fyffe who asked the question.

'No, that wasn't the reason. We'll come to that in a minute,' Angus replied. 'Duncan was also responsible for finding out how Isaac was eventually murdered. He discovered that the motor cycle had been tampered with; silicon was sprayed on the front discs and the rear brake adjuster was taken back which ensured that the Reverend would never make it round the bridge corner in his usual ton-up manner!

'But there I'm a bit ahead of myself; the first attempt to bump off Isaac was unsuccessful. It would have been unique to have the minister sharing the same grave as a deceased alcoholic! Who would think of looking in an open grave for a missing buried preacher? We checked everybody's alibi – most of the prime suspects were team members, with the exception of Clem Fular. The phone call which sent Isaac on his final fateful ride was a difficult one. Chris was attending a geological seminar in Glasgow, called incidentally "Scots on the Rocks," and must have been very quick at making the call from a telephone in the foyer during the interval. The time of the phone call to the Manse coincided with the lecture break. No-one at the seminar, as far as we could ascertain, recalls him doing so, but it is the logical assumption – it's easy enough to disappear for a few minutes when everyone's debating a favourite subject at full volume or scrambling for a Scotch. We knew we would have trouble cracking his alibi. On the other hand, we did suspect Kenneth even then of being implicated somehow or other, especially in view of his father's death.'

'So the stories about the old copper mine had no direct bearing on the case?' Basil queried from his bucket.

'We thought that initially, Basil,' Angus admitted. 'I got the details of Chris's geological report last night. When one looks back on a case,' he continued with a tired look in his eye, 'there is always something significant which, at the time, didn't seem to be of vital importance. We did a check on Chris – as we did on every other suspect connected with the case. To begin with, none of our prime suspects seemed to have a motive.'

'Yes,' Duncan now cut in, running his tongue over his lips as if he was in need of some hair from last evening's dog. 'The copper mine was Chris's first attempt on Watty. But Chris made a serious mistake when he tried to fool us by using Constable Munro's size 14 Wellingtons for faking footprints – he pinched them from James's van. And,' he continued looking over towards Angus, who now relocated the teacup to a safer stance on his desk, 'inadvertently left his own foot prints amongst the trees by the Glen Liath road, where he had caught Watty's terrier. He knows Gealeas well enough, so that wouldn't have been too difficult. But Chris used a special knot to tie the dog up inside the mine. No doubt he'd used it for years and did so without thinking. He tethered it with an old climbing sling.' The poacher now gave a longer pause as if dwelling on an unpleasant memory.

'Yes, he used that same knot on the back o' Bheinn Bruhm with me yesterday when he attached a cord to a hind. That clinched the matter for me.'

'It almost clinched you full stop!' the Inspector remarked dryly.

'Yes, Angus, it did.' Duncan returned quietly. 'But only the good die young ...'

'Duncan had a remarkable escape yesterday,' the Inspector explained. 'And, as I hinted a moment ago, he almost got killed for his efforts.' He then outlined the vigil of the Sergeant and himself at the conduit and the subsequent events and wound up by saying, 'If it wasn't for Duncan this case could have dragged on till Doomsday, but he precipitated things at great personal risk and much against my better judgement.'

'What I can't understand is how Chris knew that Mrs McWhirter's will was in favour of Isaac?' It was Watery Fyffe who spoke and the present group were amazed that for once he didn't repeat himself.

'It was Constable Munro who found that out, Willie,' the Inspector replied. Bookam gave a start and swivelled inadvertently on a spare office stool. 'He discovered only yesterday from her housekeeper that Chris and his aunt had words about a year ago when she told him of the contents of her will. Isaac knew this, so he must have been aware of a possible motive for being buried alive, but he didn't say a word to anyone, not even Duncan. But the legacy would allow him to him build his orphanage.'

'Mind you,' the Sergeant now had his say. 'It was quite on the cards that the Rev didn't suspect Chris. Why should he? He was his cousin and highly respected locally.'

'Talking about cards,' Duncan said, with a smile. 'It was cards that caused Watty much anguish. He'd been playing cards with his sister and brother-in-law the night Isaac was buried. By pure chance he was getting into his vehicle when Chris shot past on his flight from the graveyard. He must have realised that Watty saw him, but didn't know that Watty had mentioned it to Donnie the post who was out just after that with his dog. Chris must have had some consolation in the fact that Watty usually had a more than a generous helping of Jack Black's silver birch wine.'

'Evidence was almost non-existent,' Angus took up the tale. 'But of course the photographs which Sergeant Campbell and I took yesterday are 100 per cent damning. It's not every day you get photographic evidence of attempted murder. Incidentally, there's a fine portrait of you on duty in the shrubbery at Freshwater Dam, Sergeant.' The Inspector gave a broad grin, whilst Archie merely looked puzzled, removing his pipe for an instant. 'Also,' he continued, 'the police received a telex from forensics saying that they had found traces of silicon on a bushman saw blade in Chris's woodshed, also on his overalls, identical with the silicon on the disc brakes of the Laverdo.'

'How did Chris come to be with you yesterday, Duncan?' Basil looked curiously at the poacher.

'I asked him if he'd like to go out for a beast. He'd wanted to do so for some time,' the poacher replied. 'He knew that the conduit was used for transporting deer – Highland Smelters did that themselves before they let out the stalking.'

'Yes,' the Inspector cut in again. 'Archie and I watched the whole drama. We saw Chris throw Duncan into the intake of the tunnel, obviously convinced nobody could survive the journey to the penstock. We've also found out that Chris had been a fine light-heavyweight wrestler in his youth, otherwise he wouldn't have succeeded in budging Duncan even unawares. We were both surprised to see him alive at the bottom end of the conduit, almost as surprised as Chris was, seeing him later in Queenshouse.'

There was now an uncanny silence in the room and everyday town traffic could be heard outside. It was as if they were all digesting the information which had been divulged – straight from the horses' mouths, so to speak.

It was Duncan who broke this emotional impasse.

'But there's still more to these revelations that we haven't discussed.' He pushed his fore and aft back further on his broad forehead and adjusted the position of his back on the radiator. 'There's the missing evidence, or was it just malicious fate playing games? The latter I don't buy. As far as I'm concerned there were three other murder attempts. The first on the Red Wall rescue when Watty got clobbered by that big rock – an accident? Well it could be or the work of a psychopath, a homicidal opportunist with a razor sharp brain, who with complete disregard to danger seized a possibility seen in the individual beam of his own head-lamp. He gave a precariously balanced rock a push directly down on Watty. We were all descending zigzag pattern as you know on that dangerous snow slope. I have now come to the conclusion that Chris did this. I recalled later that he was just above me to my right straight above Watty. All of you in this room know that on a call-out in the dark each rescuer will have recollection of what happened within the beam of his own headlight and remember a different sequence of events from his colleagues. It is as if you are individually witnessing a private view of the scene, like selective camera shots. All the rocks and boulders on that steep face are loose and there's a pretty good chance that if you give one a push with your boot that it will crash down, fresh snow or not. Watty was about 40 feet below where I now think that rock came from, and,' he added, 'it didn't

have the usual sound effects, being muffled by all the snow
and an arctic gale whistling just round the corner; but that
rock still had the same fatal mass! Watty was lucky just
then for only his leg was smashed.'

No one spoke a word as Duncan continued. 'Then we
have the anomaly of the nitrous oxygen separating on one
of coldest nights we've had here in 20 years, resulting in the
death of our friend Watty. Who was to blame? We all knew
of the remote risk of this happening. Unfortunately, Clem
Fular volunteered to carry the cylinders, not aware of the
necessity of keeping them insulated in sub-zero conditions.
We are all to blame for not informing him, but the fact was
that night was just too bloody cold! Now the earlier business at the old mine with Watty has all the hallmarks of
attempted murder and there is damning evidence against
Chris. However he did succeed in the end in killing Watty,
even if it was indirect.'

'What about the drama in the tunnel?' It was Basil who
spoke. 'Have you any theories, Duncan?'

'I know it wasn't through any fault of yours that our
Land Rover was swept away and I'm sure that Chris, who
was at the top at the time, took on the spot advantage by
dashing into the upper control room as soon as the light of
the kids in the hill party caused a distraction. In my opinion
that was the only way it could have been done. Everyone
else is accounted for. Chris knew the layout well. In fact he
had been consulted by your company on a geological problem
about three years ago and was quite familiar with operations.
I timed it and found I could dash to the control room, press
that red button and be back at where the Land Rover was
parked in two and a half minutes. Remember, this was all in
the dark, with the vehicle's engine still running so nothing
would have been heard.'

Duncan looked down at his boots and seemed intro-
spective, as if contemplating the recent deaths and perhaps
his own narrow escapes.

Angus's voice was grave and had a slight tremor.
'You've heard from Duncan what we in the police can't
dwell upon. Our business is facts and evidence, though in
our investigations we have also to evaluate leads and possibilities. In the end, we got our man. Unfortunately that man
got two of our team members. That's the bottom line. We
may never know for certain the true facts of that falling rock
on Eagal Mor, or the nitrous oxide, or who turned on the taps
on Ben Gorm, but in the end we did get the murderer.'

There was movement in the room now, a rustle of
restless bodies and a feeling of finality pervaded, of moving
on. It was as if it was the end of an unfortunate episode.
Their two friends had gone, but the snow was still on Eagal
Mor and the beasts on the hill. Across from the police headquarters the school opposite was having the morning break
and 100 of so young voices squealed in excitement.

Angus stood up. 'Well,' he concluded, 'that's about it.' He
looked round the room for the last time. 'My final words are
to Duncan who, for once in his life, directed his unlawful
talents as a poacher to that of a successful investigator.'

Willie Fyffe's voice boomed across the room. 'Before
you all go,' he raised his right arm. 'Lads,' he addressed
them, 'this is a sad occasion, but our forefathers dealt with
such sorrows by having a wake, a proper wake, there will
be free drams at Queenshouse tonight. There was a momen-
tary pause followed by cheers then Duncan's deep voice was
raised above the din.

'Can you say that again Willie Fyffe?'